Dragon Falls

Dragon Falls

Standing Up to Beijing's Shadow War

Bob Gourley

For speaking engagements and media inquiries:
www.oodaloop.com

ISBN: 979-8-9930996-0-6

Printed in the United States of America

First Edition: 2025

Chapter 1: Cyber Immortals

August | Tianfu Cup Conference, Chengdu, China

They called it a conference, but General Qiao Liang knew better. The Tianfu Cup was a recruitment fair for the invisible war being fought in servers and smartphones across the globe. Forty thousand hackers sat in carefully orchestrated rows, each one vetted, each one catalogued, each one a potential asset in world changing operations. The red banners overhead weren't decorations, they were reminders. Loyalty. Obedience. The willingness to serve without question. And today, three individuals would be elevated above the rest, granted access to secrets that could bring governments to their knees or economies to collapse with nothing more than elegant lines of code.

In the third row of the VIP section, General Qiao Liang studied the arena with the same calculated precision that had made him the architect of China's cyber warfare doctrine. General Qiao's hands rested on his knees. Twenty years since he'd written the doctrine that redefined warfare. Today, he would see it implemented. General Qiao's gaze swept the arena methodically. Third row, left: CEO of Baidu Robin Li and a group of other CEOs that want to be him. To his right, members of the Party's Central Cyberspace Affairs Commission milling about trying to get attention. Over in section seven: Ministry of State Security Deputy Director Chen's people clustered together, pointedly ignoring the

Ministry of Public Security contingent in front of them. The general's fingers drummed once against his knee. Everything as expected.

"The Americans are watching this broadcast," he murmured to the MSS deputy director seated beside him. "Let them watch. Let them worry."

The lights dimmed suddenly, plunging the arena into momentary darkness. When they reactivated, they focused on the central stage where a Party official stood before a podium emblazoned with the national emblem. His voice boomed through precision-engineered acoustics.

"As we open the seventh year of the Tianfu Cup, it gives me great honor to represent the people and the party in bestowing a special honor upon three great champions of the digital battlefield. All three unyielding in the face of adversity, resolute in their loyalty to the Party, and unwavering in devotion to the people."

"The People's Republic of China proudly presents the champions of the digital battlefield!"

The crowd erupted as three figures emerged from below the stage on a rising platform, spotlights converging on them from multiple angles. The applause erupted on cue. In the balcony, a Party official lowered his hand after three sustained minutes.

Ming Liu, known in classified Pentagon threat assessments as IronPanda, stepped forward first. His powerful frame and military bearing betrayed his PLA Unit 61398 background. The medals adorning his chest commemorated victories the public would never know: the exfiltration of F-35 schematics, the penetration of the Office of Personnel Management that compromised millions of American security clearances, the silent mapping of critical infrastructure across three continents.

Beside him stood Lao Xun, slender and composed, his eyes constantly scanning the crowd with the habitual vigilance of an MSS operative. Where Ming projected strength, Lao emanated precision. His exploits were legend in the corridors of the Ministry, the aerospace industry penetrations that accelerated China's hypersonic weapons program by a decade, the patient compromise of European diplomatic communications that had given Beijing unprecedented negotiating advantages.

Wu Yifan completed the trio, his stance casual yet alert, a half-smile playing at the corners of his mouth. His connections to APT41 were carefully obscured in public settings like this, his dual role as state asset and entrepreneurial criminal known only to handlers with the highest clearances. The ransomware campaigns that had crippled Western healthcare systems and manufacturing plants had filled both state coffers and his personal accounts.

"Dear Comrades, I give you Ming Liu! Lao Xun! Wu Yifan! Together now known as The Three Immortals!"

The giant screens above the stage displayed their greatest publicly acknowledged achievements, sanitized versions of operations that had advanced China's position in the perpetual shadow war of the digital age. Behind these carefully curated images lay darker successes: exfiltrated weapons designs, compromised intelligence networks, and the quiet reshaping of global information flows to Beijing's advantage.

3

As the crowd chanted their new collective title, General Liang noted the subtle tensions between the three men. Ming stood slightly apart, his military rigidity a contrast to Wu's relaxed posture. Lao's eyes never rested, constantly assessing, analyzing. Ming leaned further away from the others as cameras flashed. Wu's smile never reached his eyes when he looked at Lao. Even in triumph, they maintained careful distance, three magnets of identical polarity.

Perfect, Qiao Liang thought. The most effective weapons are those with competing internal forces, each striving to outperform the others.

His secure phone vibrated in his pocket. The message displayed briefly before automatically erasing itself: "MALAYSIA OPERATION REQUIRES IMMEDIATE ACTIVATION. ACTIVATION AUTHORIZED."

Liang slipped the phone back into his pocket and allowed himself a moment of satisfaction. On stage, the three hackers raised their fists in unison as thousands of red flags waved throughout the arena. The spectacle was impressive, but merely prologue.

The real operation was about to begin.

* * *

Room 17B did not exist on any official blueprint of the conference center. It is reserved exclusively for MPS and MSS use.

The cramped chamber was bathed in the cold blue glow of surveillance monitors, its air heavy with unspoken rivalries and institutional paranoia.

Director General He Jing of the Personnel and Training Department at the Ministry of State Security, did not acknowledge the presence of Liu Qiang, Director of the Personnel Training Bureau at the Ministry of Public Security, though they sat less than a meter apart. Six junior analysts, three from each ministry, occupied workstations along the perimeter, documenting and categorizing talent with the methodical precision of diamond appraisers.

Forty-two monitors displayed real-time feeds from the competition floor. Facial recognition software continuously cross-referenced competitors against national databases, generating scrolling profiles beside each feed: university affiliations, political reliability scores, psychological evaluations, and, most crucially, exploitable weaknesses.

"Terminal seven," Qiang murmured, breaking twenty minutes of calculated silence. He tapped his stylus against a screen showing a young woman with close-cropped hair and military posture. "Three household penetrations in under four minutes. Full extraction of credentials, complete mobile device compromise. No digital fingerprints."

Jing's eyes flicked to the screen. The candidate's dossier appeared instantly on his secure tablet: LiPei Wei, 22, Shandong Province, rejected from three universities before being recruited by a front company linked to Qiang's department. A deliberate provocation.

"Skilled," Jing conceded with practiced indifference. "Though our priority is terminal twelve. The Siemens train scheduling system breach." He didn't elaborate on why the MSS would be interested in European railway infrastructure. He didn't need to.

The game continued for another hour, each man flagging candidates, each pretending their selections were arbitrary rather than calculated moves in a decades-long institutional chess match. Their junior officers traded glances, sensing the subtext beneath the cordial exchange.

"The defender in booth eighteen shows promise," Jing noted. "Seventeen intrusion attempts neutralized while maintaining system integrity."

"Perhaps we should share this one," Qiang replied through a smile. "Both our ministries require network defense specialists."

Jing nodded, though both men understood sharing was theoretical at best. Since Xi's consolidation of power, the ministries had become locked in a zero-sum competition for resources, influence, and talent.

The air in the room shifted imperceptibly when Qiang's tablet pinged. Jing noticed his counterpart's fingers tighten around the device.

"Terminal twenty-three," Jing said suddenly, having tracked Qiang's gaze. "The one who breached the digital twin of the U.S. Department of Energy systems." His tone was casual, but his eyes narrowed. "Your people have flagged him."

Qiang set his tablet down with deliberate care. "Yes. His particular talents align with our current requirements."

"Energy infrastructure penetration is traditionally MSS territory," Jing said, allowing a hint of challenge to enter his voice. "Why would the Public Security Ministry need such specialized offensive capabilities?"

The question hung in the air like a trip wire. Qiang's junior officers suddenly found reasons to study their screens with renewed intensity.

"The ministry's mandate has... evolved," Qiang replied, each word precisely measured. "Our overseas service centers require enhanced capabilities to protect Chinese nationals abroad."

"Service centers," Jing repeated, the euphemism for the MPS's rapidly expanding global network of surveillance outposts tasting bitter on his tongue. "And these enhanced capabilities, they would operate independently of existing MSS targeting infrastructure in these countries?"

"Coordination remains a priority," Qiang said, his practiced diplomatic smile never wavering. "Our ministries have never been closer."

The lie was so perfectly delivered that Jing almost admired its craftsmanship. He returned his attention to the monitor showing candidate twenty-three, a slender man whose unremarkable appearance belied his extraordinary abilities. The candidate had just compromised a system designed to mimic critical infrastructure controls.

Jing's mind raced through the implications. The MPS had traditionally focused on domestic control, monitoring dissidents, suppressing unrest, ensuring Party loyalty. Their overseas operations had been limited to tracking Chinese nationals abroad and occasional extrajudicial repatriations.

But this, targeting critical infrastructure, developing offensive cyber capabilities, this was something else entirely.

"I see," Jing said quietly.

He did see, with sudden, crystalline clarity. Wang Xiaohong, the ambitious new Minister of Public Security, wasn't content with his agency's traditional role. He was building a parallel intelligence service, one that could operate globally without the constraints and oversight that sometimes-hampered MSS operations.

The MSS had competition. And in the zero-sum world of Chinese intelligence, competition was indistinguishable from threat.

As the recruitment session concluded, both men exchanged pleasantries with the hollow precision of diplomats on the brink of war. Their subordinates gathered their equipment in silence, each side careful not to leave any data behind.

In the arena above them, the celebration of China's cyber dominance continued unabated. But in Room 17B, the first shots of a new conflict had already been fired.

* * *

The VIP lounge at the Tianfu Cup operated like a microcosm of Chinese power dynamics, opulent yet functional, welcoming yet surveilled. Behind the veneer of celebration, beneath the surface pleasantries exchanged by keynote speakers and corporate and government leaders, calculations of advantage and leverage continued unabated.

In the corner farthest from the surveillance cameras, the Three Immortals maintained a careful distance from each other. Even when forced to position next to each other for the press and their cameras, within minutes they would drift apart.

Lao Xun slouched in his leather chair with practiced nonchalance; one leg crossed over the other in deliberate contrast to the military rigidity of his companions. His MSS training had taught him that true power never needed to announce itself. He watched the monitors displaying the competition with half-lidded eyes that missed nothing.

"Primitive," he muttered, just loud enough for Ming to hear. "That network defense could be bypassed by a first-year student at Tsinghua."

Ming Liu, Major Liu to his PLA Unit 61398 subordinates, didn't take the bait immediately. He sat with crisp military precision, spine erect, eyes forward, jaw set. The ceremonial medal still hung around his neck; unlike the others, he hadn't removed it the moment the cameras stopped rolling.

"Not everyone has the luxury of infinite time to craft the perfect attack," Ming finally replied, his voice measured. "In actual operations, you execute with the tools at hand. Something your theoretical models don't account for."

The barb found its mark. Lao's casual posture stiffened imperceptibly. "Theoretical? The Taiwanese Defense Ministry might disagree. Or perhaps the German aerospace executives who still don't know why their prototype designs suddenly appeared in Beijing."

Wu Yifan watched the exchange with the detached amusement of a man accustomed to playing both sides. He tapped his fingers against the arm of his chair, a rhythmic pattern that might have been mistaken for impatience but was an old habit, counting exits, cataloging threats, measuring response times.

"While you two compare trophy cases," Wu interjected, "the actual innovation happens elsewhere." He gestured toward one of the monitors. "That team from Hangzhou just implemented a zero-knowledge proof verification system I've never seen before. Perhaps if either of you spent less time serving your respective bureaucracies, you might actually learn something new."

Ming's eyes narrowed. "Easy to innovate when you answer to no one. Some of us serve China, not just ourselves."

"Is that what you call it? Service?" Wu's smile didn't reach his eyes. "Interesting definition."

"At least I don't sell my talents to the highest bidder," Ming shot back. "Loyalty still means something in the PLA."

Lao gave a short, derisive laugh. "Loyalty? Is that why Unit 61398 takes credit for breaches that contractors executed? Or why your commanders claim my Quantum Dawn infiltration as their own work?"

Ming's hand tightened around his ceremonial medal. "You're questioning my loyalty? That's rich coming from someone who operates through six cutouts to maintain deniability. How many of your operations were for the Ministry, and how many for your private collection of leverage?"

"Careful, Major," Lao said softly, the honorific sounding like an insult. "Some accusations can't be taken back."

Wu leaned forward, enjoying the escalation. "The irony is exquisite. Two servants of the state questioning each other's dedication while both your agencies build competing empires that serve themselves first and China second."

Ming rose halfway from his seat, fury flashing across his face. "You opportunistic parasite..."

The double doors swung open with synchronized precision. Four MSS officers in immaculate uniforms entered, their faces expressionless. The room immediately fell silent, conversations throughout the lounge dying mid-sentence.

"All personnel clear the room," the lead officer announced, his voice calibrated to carry without seeming to raise it. "Except for Ming Liu, Lao Xun, and Wu Yifan."

The exodus was immediate and wordless. Corporate executives, mid-level party officials, and support staff filed out with the practiced efficiency of people accustomed to unquestioned authority. Within thirty seconds, only the Three Immortals remained, their previous animosity suspended in the face of official intervention.

The officers positioned themselves at the corners of the room. One checked his watch, nodded, and opened a side door.

General Qiao Liang entered with the quiet confidence of a man who had never needed to raise his voice to end a conversation. At seventy-two, his face carried the weathered lines of someone who had witnessed China's transformation from impoverished revolutionary state to global superpower. His eyes, however, remained sharp as obsidian, missing nothing as he surveyed the three hackers.

"Gentlemen," Liang said, taking a seat that positioned him slightly above eye level with the seated men. "I trust you're enjoying your new status."

None of the three responded. They recognized a rhetorical opening when they heard one.

"The title 'Immortal' carries significant weight in our culture," Liang continued. "Immortality isn't merely about endless life, it's about transcending ordinary limitations. About operating on a higher plane." He paused, studying each man in turn. "The Party has bestowed this honor upon you not just for past achievements, but for what you will accomplish."

Wu shifted slightly in his chair. "And what exactly will we accomplish, General?"

Qiao Liang smiled thinly. "Something worthy of your talents. Something that requires the unique capabilities of all three of you, working in concert."

"The three of us don't work in concert," Lao said flatly. "Our methods are incompatible."

"That assessment is precisely why I'm here instead of a junior handler," Liang replied. "This operation transcends your individual preferences. It serves interests beyond your respective histories."

Ming straightened. "What operation?"

Instead of answering directly, Liang removed a small device from his pocket and activated it. A faint electronic hum filled the room, signal jamming. The general's voice dropped lower, forcing the three men to lean forward.

"Malaysia has become a problem," he said simply. "Specifically, certain elements within Malaysia who do not understand their destiny and would resist the inevitability of our influence."

Lao's expression didn't change, but a muscle in his jaw tightened. Wu's eyes narrowed fractionally. Ming remained perfectly still.

"We are well positioned in Malaysia for coming operations, and you will be fully briefed on our cyberspace operations there. We see a need for your talents to ensure orchestration across all fronts in cyberspace. You will form a coordination cell that reports to me directly. You will earn your title of Three Immortals."

The implication hung in the air. This was not a request to be refused.

"Your mission is threefold," Liang said, his tone shifting to one of clinical precision. "You will review the status of our positioning in Malaysian government infrastructure and their financial and transportation systems. And you will produce plans for plausible deniability for eventual operations, and you will oversee execution of plans on my behalf."

Wu was the first to break the silence that followed. "That's remarkably vague, General."

"Necessarily so, for now" Liang replied. "You will see it all in Beijing."

"So, we're supposed to trust you?" Lao asked, skepticism evident in his voice.

"No. You're to operate with faith in the Party's vision," Liang corrected. "And with the understanding that success will cement your positions as the preeminent cyber operators in China. Failure..." He let the word hang in the air. "Failure would suggest the title of 'Immortal' was prematurely bestowed."

Ming nodded almost imperceptibly. "When do we begin?"

"You already have," Liang said, standing. "You are to return to your hotels, tell no one of your change in plans, and travel with me tonight for your first briefing."

The general moved toward the door, then paused. "One final point. While you may not trust each other, and perhaps you're wise not to, remember that you now share a common fate. The Three Immortals will succeed together, or they will fall together."

After Liang departed, the three hackers sat in silence, each calculating the angles, the risks, the potential betrayals. None spoke the obvious aloud: that they were being used as pawns in a larger game between competing power centers within China's security apparatus. That their new title was both honor and leash.

Wu was the first to stand. "Well, gentlemen, it seems we've been volunteered for an impossible task with inadequate information and mutual suspicion. Just another day serving the motherland."

Lao rose next, straightening his jacket. "Try not to compromise the operation with your entrepreneurial side ventures, Wu."

"And you try not to disappear halfway through when the MSS decides to change priorities," Wu countered smoothly.

Ming remained seated, his expression unreadable. "Malaysia," he said quietly, as if testing the word. "There's something they're not telling us."

"There always is," Lao replied. "That's the game."

As they exited separately, each man made mental calculations, revised contingency plans, and prepared for betrayal. The title of "Immortal" might have been bestowed upon them collectively, but each knew that immortality, like power in China, was never guaranteed.

It had to be seized and defended, every single day.

Chapter 2: Digital Footprints

The sixty-fifth floor of The Seraya Residences existed in a different atmosphere than the streets below. Up here, the air was thinner, the silence absolute, the view commanding.

Li Jianhong set down his tea, tilting his head to bring attention to a book.

"You've read his book?" Li asked without turning from the window, his voice soft yet somehow filling the room.

"Yes, sir," his subordinate agent replied from where he stood near the door. "Twice."

"And?"

"It's dangerous. Cleverly written. He hides real disclosures behind polite theory. But his pattern is clear, he exposes our long game."

Li's reflection in the glass remained impassive. He picked up the book from the side table, running his thumb across its cover. No markings. Just *The Dragon's Digital Claws* printed in clean serif.

"He is not just a critic. He is a mapmaker. He is showing others how to resist us."

Li turned the book over in his hands, his movements deliberate, unhurried.

"The Americans sent him here, with purpose. Very likely CIA non-official cover."

The agent shifted his weight. "Should we cancel his appearances?"

Li set the book down and finally turned. His face was lean, aristocratic, with eyes that assessed rather than observed.

"No. That would confirm his importance." Li stood, straightening his immaculate suit jacket. "Tanner believes he understands our methods. Let him continue thinking so."

Li walked to a cabinet, poured a single glass of baijiu, and left it untouched on the counter.

"Monitor him closely. Record everything. But do not interfere with his schedule. Attend his presentation at the bookstore and at the university."

"And if there's an opportunity...?"

Li's mouth formed what might have been a smile on another man. "Take no action. I want patterns. Behavior. Fear response. Note who he interacts with."

He gestured dismissively. "That will be all."

The agent bowed slightly and turned to leave.

Li remained motionless, watching the city below, a chessboard where pieces were already in motion.

***

1200 Hours | Kuala Lumpur International Airport

The pilot's voice crackled over the intercom. "Beginning descent into Kuala Lumpur." Jack checked his watch and straightened his tie. "This is the life," he thought to himself. Last leg of a book tour and a lead for a consulting engagement to boot. Civilian life can be really cushy.

Upon touchdown, he unbuckled his seatbelt and glanced at his watch, determined to start the day on schedule. As he stepped off the jet bridge into the terminal, Jack passed beneath a mounted placard:

Kuala Lumpur Airport is under continuous CCTV surveillance. Video and audio may be recorded for safety and security purposes in accordance with Malaysian law."

"Ha," he muttered under his breath. The airport authorities didn't seem to realize, or didn't care, that nearly all their surveillance infrastructure was manufactured in China. Most of it could be remotely accessed. Anyone walking these corridors should assume it is not just airport security watching them.

He didn't break stride, but his eyes began quietly tracking every dome camera, every wireless repeater, every mirrored glass panel that might double as an optical sensor.

Clearing customs was efficient but not quite routine. A uniformed officer held his passport a beat too long, glancing between the page and a monitor just out of Jack's line of sight.

Then came a clipped nod, a practiced thump of the final stamp, and a polite but impassive: "Welcome to Malaysia, sir."

Jack nodded his thanks but caught the second agent watching him from the far end of the booth, too casually to be casual.

The arrivals hall opened ahead in a gleam of polished tile and soaring glass. The air was cooler than expected, recycled and dry, but still carried the tang of jet fuel and something faintly tropical. Jack adjusted the strap on his carry-on and slipped into the moving current of travelers headed toward the main terminal.

His iPhone buzzed in his pocket.

Verizon: Welcome to Malaysia. You're now connected. $10/day with TravelPass. Local Carrier: CelcomDigi. Enjoy your stay.

He smiled wryly as he dismissed it. Verizon would sting him for roaming fees, but it beat the hassle of swapping SIMs mid-transit, and he would not need the extra security on this trip. Sure, Verizon and the local carrier would know where he was always, but he wasn't here to run ops, this was just a book tour.

He slid the phone back into his blazer and scanned the signs. Arrival Hall – Main Terminal – Food Court.

The journalist had asked to meet at a café just past the escalators. "A place with decent espresso," she'd promised, "not the chain stuff." Jetlagged Jack appreciated the sentiment.

As he moved past the foreign exchange counters and SIM card kiosks, his instincts stirred, not out of fear, just routine. The café came into view: warm lighting, teakwood bar, and the gentle steam of frothing milk. And there, at a corner table was a woman who looked exactly like a *New Straits Times* reporter would- dark blazer, tablet open, eyes sharp behind thin frames.

Jack approached, nodded once, and asked, "Ms. Suri?"

"Commander Tanner." She stood just enough to shake his hand. Firm grip. Measured eyes. "Appreciate you making time so soon after landing."

He settled across from her, scanning the café's perimeter. Nothing overt, but that didn't mean much. A server arrived; he ordered an Americano.

The background noise of transit filtered in, luggage wheels, boarding calls, the hiss and knock of the espresso machine.

Ms. Suri tapped her phone to record. "First let me mention," she said, raising the phone slightly. "Your book stirred things up across Asia. Especially your chapter on Chinese digital infrastructure."

Jack raised an eyebrow. "Stirred things up is usually code for pissed people off."

She smiled. "Some officials in Malaysian government aren't thrilled about the implications. Others call it a blueprint for raising defenses."

A silence passed between them as he thought and sipped his coffee, then he leaned slightly forward and pretended this was not a rehearsed line:

"There's a human nature that transcends all cultures. We all seem to be coded to resist change. People will tend to believe all is best if nothing changes, especially when we are dealing with the invisible world of cyberspace. The whole point of my book is to help people understand the cyber threat in a way that motivates change."

Jack's gaze flicked toward the corner of the café. A camera dome.

"You see the lenses," he said quietly. "They are everywhere now. So ubiquitous they are ignored, invisible."

"But you feel watched" she replied.

"I feel mapped and realize that it is not just the good guys who are watching."

She paused. "Your book made a lot of claims about Chinese tech. Backdoors. Surveillance. Control."

"They're not claims if they're already happening."

"Then why do countries keep buying it?"

"Because it works. It's cheap. And because most leaders don't think it'll bite them, until it does."

"Are you saying Malaysia is compromised? she questioned.

"I'm saying if I were running operations for the MSS, I'd start with the infrastructure no one questions. Cameras. Traffic systems. Smart grids. The Cellular network. The places where access is disguised as convenience."

Ms. Suri lowered her phone. She wasn't smiling anymore. "And is that what you're here to talk about?"

"I'm here to talk about what happens when the wrong people control the information domain. Surveillance is just the warm-up act."

"We've found surveillance curtails crime and helps find criminals, I'm sure it is the same in your country?" She asked

"We all expect it in public places these days," Tanner started, "But it is right to expect that the data collected in public areas is handled appropriately and not provided to any who would harm us, criminal groups, hostile governments, even those in our own governments who would misuse it."

Jack decided long ago that privacy was worth fighting for, for all of us today and for future generations.

They chatted for another ten minutes, with Jack providing example after example of how the PRC has exploited the infrastructure of democratic nations to their advantage.

He checked his watch.

"Sorry to be so brief, but I'm about to lose control of my schedule..."

They exchanged cards. She stood with him.

"One last thing," she asked. "Don't you think it is hyperbolic when your book calls PRC surveillance cyber warfare? Do you really think it's that bad?"

Jack hesitated.

"I think most people still believe occupation has to come with tanks. It doesn't. Digital occupation comes with terms of service. And the result can be total loss of sovereignty."

Jack stepped out of the café and into the airport's broad concourse. He opened the Grab app on his phone and confirmed his ride, a black sedan, two minutes away.

He moved through the terminal at an easy pace, scanning the tide of arriving passengers. A couple in matching backpacks argued over a QR code. A group of Chinese businessmen spoke rapid Mandarin near a coffee kiosk. A woman in a bright yellow hijab took a selfie under a Visit Malaysia banner.

The airport was clean, well-policed, and humming with normalcy. Still, Jack found himself noting camera positions, exit points, and the lag between security patrols. Old habits. Not paranoia, just muscle memory. He exited to the Gab pickup point.

A sleek black car rolled up to the curb. Jack checked the plate and approached.

"Mr. Tanner?" the driver asked through the window.

"That's me." Jack climbed in and set his carry-on beside him.

As they pulled into traffic, the driver glanced at him in the mirror. "First time in KL?"

"No, but it has been a while," Jack replied.

"Ah, then you'll be surprised. A lot has changed. Still, Ritz is the best. Very central."

Jack offered a polite nod and turned to the window. Kuala Lumpur unfurled around him, glass towers rising from jungle green, elevated trains gliding overhead, construction cranes marking the edges of ambition.

His phone buzzed. It was his old shipmate Mike Murphy.

"Mike," Jack said, smiling. "Right on cue."

"Tanner, you dinosaur. You land in one piece?"

"Soft touchdown. En route to the Ritz now."

"Perfect. Admiral Harrison says your book's making the rounds. He wants a signed copy, and to grill you over scotch on the Blue Ridge tomorrow night."

Jack chuckled. "Happy to oblige. I owe him."

"Just be aware," Mike added, tone softening. "Malaysia's not quite the same. Bit more tense. Lot more eyes in the wrong places."

Jack raised an eyebrow. "Anything I should be worried about?"

"No, just... don't assume it's all business as usual."

"I never do," Jack said, but without concern. "Thanks for the ping. See you tomorrow night."

He ended the call and pocketed the phone. The city moved around him, confident, fast, full of texture. He didn't feel unsafe, just watchful, like always.

The Ritz-Carlton appeared ahead, elegant against the skyline. As the car slowed, Jack scanned the entrance: bellhops, taxis, a group of businessmen clustered near the revolving doors. Nothing out of place.

He stepped out and thanked the driver.

A man stood near the edge of the hotel forecourt, hands in pockets, gazing vaguely at traffic. Not doing anything. Not looking at Jack. Just… there.

Jack gave him a passing glance. Probably another guest waiting on someone. Probably.

Inside the lobby, the air shifted to cool marble and low classical music. Jack rolled his shoulders once and let the jet lag settle.

He was here to speak, to sign books, to spark conversation.

That's all this was.

* * *

1400 Hours | Ritz-Carlton Malaysia

Jack stepped into the Ritz-Carlton's lobby, where the scent of lemongrass mingled with polished marble and piped-in piano music. The chandeliers glowed like inverted searchlights. Around him, tourists checked in with shopping bags and designer sneakers, the air thick with comfort.

He smiled without meaning to. Not because of the luxury, he'd slept in worse and better, but because he was walking into the Ritz as a published author, not an operator.

Check-in was quick. The receptionist handed over his key card with a practiced smile.

"Enjoy your stay, Mr. Tanner."

He nodded. "Looking forward to it."

The elevator ride to the top floors was quiet. Jack stepped out into a carpeted hallway, found his suite, and entered with the kind of instinctive sweep that had nothing to do with habit and everything to do with training.

The room was generous, tasteful lighting, modern fixtures, and an expansive view of the city skyline. Petronas Towers gleamed in the distance, framed by the early afternoon haze. Jack took it in, letting his body absorb the stillness.

Then he got to work.

He set his carry-on bag on the bed and unzipped it fully, pulling out two suits, casual clothes, travel meds, and his exercise shoes. He placed each item methodically into drawers or onto the room's luggage rack.

He sat at the desk and pulled his Chromebook out of his carrier bag. It had been freshly wiped, locked into Google's Advanced Protection Program, and configured to run all browsing through the TOR privacy network and the Snowstorm tool to mitigate any attempts to analyze his browsing patterns. His locked down tech would make it hard for anyone to observe what sites he visits or who he is communicating with or even what city he was communicating from. Not that he was planning to do anything sensitive on this trip but has to practice what he preaches. All of us should work to protect our piece of cyberspace.

The television played quietly in the background, a muted news segment on South China Sea tensions, maps glowing behind serious anchors.

Malaysia would be the final stop of this Asian-focused book tour, added after an invitation by the government's head of cybersecurity who set him up to speak at the University tomorrow who also wants to talk about a consulting relationship.

Malaysia reminded Jack why intelligence work never got easier. On paper, it was everything America hoped for in a regional partner: democratic, people-focused institutions, economic growth, religious tolerance. In practice, decades of Chinese investment had created dependencies that ran deeper than most Malaysians realized.

He opened his notes for the BookXcess bookstore event. Talking points, regional considerations, a few key excerpts flagged to read.

Jack closed the Chromebook, slid it into the slim shoulder bag, and stood by the window for a final glance at the skyline. The city shimmered with life, equal parts steel and humidity.

Jack's instincts stirred. Mike's words echoed: "Malaysia's not quite the same. Bit more tense." The man at the hotel entrance, hands in pockets, not looking at anything in particular. The confrontational tone some reviewers had taken toward his book's chapter on Chinese digital infrastructure.

Through decades of intelligence work, he'd learned to trust those feelings.

Chapter 3: Eyes in the Shadows

1630 Hours | BookXcess Event

Jack entered BookXcess. Main entrance, fire exit behind poetry, staff door near the café. Long lines at the checkout counter. The place smelled of coffee and old paper, the scent of every good bookstore. His eyes looked for movement beyond the literary browsers.

The event space held maybe two hundred people. Journalists with press badges, university students clutching worn paperbacks, a few obvious government types in the back rows. Standard book tour crowd, except for the woman near the rear exit.

Redhead. Western. Expensive suit that didn't quite hide the way she carried herself. Jack had seen that posture before, in briefing rooms and embassy corridors. Professional, dangerous, and undeniably attractive. Redheads had always been his weakness, even when they came with complications. Especially when they came with complications.

She wasn't here for the book talk.

After a brief and overly generous introduction from the organizer Jack took to the podium. "Thank you all for being here today," Jack began, forcing his attention back to the microphone. "We've entered an era where our enemies don't need armies to attack us. They need keyboards."

His presentation flowed automatically while part of his mind processed the room. The redhead hadn't moved. Hadn't looked at him directly. Professional surveillance? In his line of work, the most dangerous people often came in the most appealing packages.

* * *

The sun dipped below the horizon as Jack left the bookstore and stepped onto the bustling streets of Kuala Lumpur. The city pulsed with energy, a sharp contrast to the turmoil simmering within him. Darkness cloaked the buildings, shadows stretching like fingers across the pavement. Each footfall echoed in his mind, a reminder to stay alert.

His instincts kicked in, honed over years of service where complacency spelled disaster. Beirut, 2019 - he'd relaxed for thirty seconds watching a street performer. A sniper's bullet missed by two inches. Was Mike's comment a warning after all?

He navigated through the throng of evening strollers and street vendors hawking local delicacies. Bright neon signs lit up storefronts, but he kept thinking of his training: user your peripheral vision, don't use obvious counter surveillance tricks, scan faces.

A car rolled slowly by... a sleek black sedan with tinted windows. Jack's heart raced as he caught sight of its driver staring directly at him through the glass, expression unreadable yet heavy with intent. It felt like being back undercover in Hong Kong again, just as vulnerable yet instinctively ready for whatever might come next.

The door to the Ritz-Carlton loomed ahead, promising safety amid uncertainty, but he hesitated before stepping inside. The ambiance shifted from chaos to calm, an illusion against what waited beyond its polished facade.

Stepping into the hotel lobby, Jack found himself enveloped by the vibrant ambiance of the cocktail hour crowd. Laughter and clinking glasses mingled with the soft strains of live music, creating a stark juxtaposition to the paranoia brewing within him. Tourists moved through the space like butterflies, their animated chatter filling the air, blissfully unaware of the invisible webs of intrigue weaving around them.

Jack's gaze swept over the scene. A group of businessmen in sharp suits clustered near a bar, their laughter booming as they toasted to deals closed and opportunities seized. Nearby, a couple sipped cocktails, leaning in close to exchange secrets and smiles. The opulence of the Ritz-Carlton, gleaming marble floors and extravagant floral arrangements.

He moved further inside, scanning faces while trying to appear relaxed. Every smile he encountered seemed genuine, yet his gut twisted with suspicion. Someone watched him; he could feel it in his bones. Perhaps it was a remnant of past experiences where trust became a luxury he could not afford.

This is not a time to drink. But it is a time to quickly assess the crowd, so best play the part of the thirsty tourist. Jack approached the bar and ordered a Kettle One on the rocks. The bartender flashed a welcoming smile but quickly shifted his attention to another patron when they called for service. Jack took a moment to gather himself before turning back toward the crowd.

As he raised his glass to take a sip, he caught sight of someone across the room, a man in Japanese salaryman clothes seemed too far out of place. To his left near the coffee shop two stone cold silent bodybuilder types sat silently. Were they there on business or someone's muscle? A neuron fired when he saw a petite woman with bright red hair and sharp features enter the bar and stand alone near an ornate pillar. Now that is not a coincidence.

He set down his drink and stepped away from the bar, weaving through clusters of guests who continued their jovial exchanges. Jack's pulse quickened as he maneuvered through the crowd to the elevator.

The solid hum of the elevator's motors accompanied Jack as he rode alone to his floor. The rhythmic thrum became a stark reminder of his isolation. He leaned against the cool metal wall, fingers tapping lightly against his leg, each ding of the elevator increasing the tension building within him.

"Focus," he muttered under his breath, breaking the silence that enveloped him.

As the elevator slowed and came to a halt, he inhaled sharply. The doors slid open and Jack stepped out moving quickly to his room.

Jack checked the door frame out of habit. Should have set a container trap, he thought to himself. Upon entering he moved methodically, scanning the entire room, his instincts honed by years of intelligence work sharpening every detail into focus. The Samsung TV's red standby light blinked steadily - always listening. He unplugged it.

Time to focus on what matters. Who is the redhead? And what was the meaning of Mike's comment? The feeling of being watched, is it paranoia or the fact that his subconscious knows something?

Chapter 4: The Network Unveiled

Zhang Wei pulled through the gates of the Hibiscus Pavilion. The brass plaque read "Malaysia-China Friendship Association." He nodded to the gardener pruning roses - Senior Sergeant Huang, Guangdong Provincial Security. Always watching and in comms with the entire security team.

This entire compound was an MPS operation. An overseas police station, part of a massive network of outposts enabling the enforcement of PRC laws wherever the diaspora are.

Zhang stood at the window of his second-floor office, hands clasped behind his back, watching Senior Sergeant Huang watch others.

"Director Zhang," a young woman called from the doorway. "The morning briefing is ready."

Zhang turned, his expression betraying nothing. "Thank you, Liu."

He followed her down a hallway adorned with calligraphy scrolls and into what appeared to be a conference room. Once the door sealed shut, the room's true purpose revealed itself. One wall displayed six large monitors showing live feeds from across Kuala Lumpur, airport terminals, university campuses, tourist sites, and Chinese cultural events. Three technicians sat at workstations, their fingers dancing across keyboards as facial recognition software tracked individuals of interest.

"Report." Zhang commanded, taking his seat at the head of the table.

A middle-aged man with rimless glasses stood. "In the past twenty-four hours, we've flagged seventeen of our diasporas for concerning behaviors." He tapped a tablet, and images appeared on the main screen. "Of particular note, three students attended a Taiwan cultural festival, two businessmen met with known democracy advocates, and a visiting professor accepted an invitation to speak at a forum on South China Sea territorial disputes."

Zhang nodded. "Standard protocol. Record everything, notify homebase."

"There's something else," the analyst continued, swiping to a new image. "This arrived from our student group at the airport."

The screen showed smartphone video of a westerner shaking hands with a well-dressed Malaysian woman then sitting for a conversation. The man's face was instantly familiar to Zhang, square-jawed, alert eyes that missed nothing, the bearing of someone who had spent years in uniform.

"Jack Tanner," Zhang said, the name leaving a bitter taste. "The Navy man who thinks he understands China."

"He met a reporter from the *New Straits Times*. They're covering his book tour. Final stop here in KL before returning to the States."

Zhang studied the image, his mind calculating. Tanner's book, *The Dragon's Digital Claws*, had caused significant irritation in Beijing with its detailed exposure of Chinese cyber operations. The Ministry of State Security had already issued alerts about his presence in the region and expected arrival.

"Did MSS contact you about this?" asked Liu from the doorway.

"No," Zhang replied, a small smile forming. "And we won't be contacting them either."

The room fell silent. Everyone understood the implications. The rivalry between the Ministry of Public Security and the Ministry of State Security was legendary, two powerful dragons competing for the favor of Beijing.

"Flag the American for passive surveillance only," Zhang ordered. "I want to know everywhere he goes, everyone he meets. But maintain distance, no direct contact, no obvious tails."

"Should we inform Beijing?" the analyst asked carefully.

Zhang's smile widened slightly. "In due time. First, let's see what Commander Tanner is really doing in Malaysia. A book tour sounds like non-official cover for the CIA."

He walked to the wall of monitors and studied Tanner's face. "The MSS would love to claim this prize. But they're too focused on their precious influence project to notice what's walking right through our front door."

As his staff dispersed to their tasks, Zhang returned to the window, gazing out at the deceptively peaceful gardens. The hibiscus flowers swayed in the afternoon breeze, blood-red and delicate, much like the web of surveillance and control he had woven throughout Malaysia.

* * *

0900 Hours | Beijing MSS HQ

Minister Chen Yixin entered the MSS conference room. Twelve bureau chiefs stood in unison. No one sat until Chen took his chair.

Behind the head of the table, dominating the far wall, hung an enormous, framed oil painting in baroque gold leaf, the only color allowed to intrude. It depicted the Battle of Luding Bridge, rendered in meticulous historical detail and relentless ideological intensity.

In the scene, iron chains stretched over a churning, murderous river. Red Army soldiers, thin, filthy, determined, crawled forward under a hail of gunfire. One clung to the chains with bloodied hands, planks strapped to his back. Another had just been struck, his body falling in mid-arc toward the water below, but his outstretched arm still pointed forward. In the background, flames rose from the far bank where defenders burned what remained of the wooden deck, while a red banner snapped in defiance from the near bank. There was motion, sacrifice, and fire in every stroke.

It was not just a painting. It was doctrine.

MSS officials called it *the sacred moment of commitment*, a reminder that the survival of the Party depended not on diplomacy or negotiation, but on will, risk, and total control of the narrative. Here, beneath that battle scene, men plotted modern campaigns of data intrusion, psychological subversion, and strategic disinformation. The river had changed. The chains had not.

At the far end of the table, Minister Chen studied the painting as if measuring his own resolve against the ghosts of the Long March. When he finally spoke, his voice carried the precision of a scalpel.

"The Americans believe they can stop our rise." Chen's eyes moved to each bureau chief in turn. "They cannot but their influence introduces friction, it is our job to proactively shut that down at every turn."

The Chief of the 13th Bureau shifted slightly. Chen's gaze found him like a laser designator.

"Tell me about Guam."

"The infrastructure penetrations proceeded as planned, Minister. American analysts detected exactly what we intended them to detect. While they focused on those obvious intrusions..."

Chen raised a hand. The room fell silent.

"You speak like a man who believes his own deception," Chen said quietly. "Dangerous thinking. The moment we believe our own lies; we become vulnerable to those who see clearly."

The bureau chief's face drained of color.

"Show me Guam," Chen commanded. The screen displayed network intrusions. "The Americans detected exactly what we wanted them to detect. While they patched those systems..." He clicked to a second screen. "We accessed these."

He began to pace, each step measured and deliberate.

"Our networks across Southeast Asia collect information. They report on meetings, monitor communications, track financial flows. But intelligence without influence is merely expensive journalism."

The silence stretched taut as a bowstring.

Chen stopped directly behind the First Bureau chief, his voice dropping to a whisper that somehow filled the entire room.

"Are you the right leader to move our assets beyond observation to influence to complete control?"

The man's breathing became audible. "Minister, we are cultivating deeper access..."

"Cultivation is preparation. Control is results." Chen's hand settled on the man's shoulder with deceptive gentleness. "The Party does not reward preparation. It rewards outcomes. Assets that cannot shape events are not assets, they are expenses."

"Now tell me about Malaysia" Chen asked the First Bureau Chief "How is Li in his influence operation?"

Chen asked, knowing full well that no one in the room knows as much about Li and what he is up to than he does.

"Li reports we are nearly ready to execute, with total deniability of responsibility for what is to come. We have promised him additional cyber assets for final preparation and the entire First Bureau considers him our primary thrust."

"Keep it that way." Chen angrily responded. Chen trusted no-one, not even Li. But Li had been personally groomed for his current position by Chen. Few had mastery over the state's tools of surveillance and power like Li. A real protector of the party and the people.

Chen returned to his seat, providing a final message:

"We have established the foundation across the territories to our south. Now we must build the structure that will reshape the region according to our interests." His smile was winter cold. "Observation gives us knowledge. Influence gives us power."

The painting seemed to flicker in the recessed lighting, the Red Army soldiers forever frozen in their moment of supreme commitment. Chen gestured toward it.

"They crossed that river because retreat meant death and advance meant victory. We face the same choice now. The Americans believe they can contain China's rise through superior technology and alliance networks. They are mistaken."

He stood again, this time with finality.

"We will cross our river. And when we do, the world will understand that the century of humiliation is over. Forever."

* * *

2100 Hours | To the Damansara Warehouse, KL

The rain poured relentlessly over Kuala Lumpur, drenching the streets in a slick sheen that reflected the dim glow of streetlights. In the heart of the city, the PRC Embassy loomed, a fortress of diplomacy surrounded by meticulously manicured hedges and uninteresting walls. The Executive Secretary to the Cultural Minister of the PRC stepped out of the towering edifice, his tailored suit instantly soaked by the downpour, but exuding an air of calculated composure. He descended the steps, a large briefcase in hand, his expression momentarily contemplative as he stared up at the stormy sky, contemplating the forces swirling beneath the surface of his assignments.

He was immediately picked up by a black sedan driven by another MSS operative. The engine hummed a low growl as they sped into traffic, blending seamlessly into the chaos of the city. "You have the other package?" He asked. "huhm" the driver grunted with assertiveness.

He instinctually knew before looking. They had an MPS tail. The MSS had requested their MPS counterparts to stay away from their operations, but they had decided to follow him. "Lose them" he commanded the driver.

They darted left into a series of narrower roads. Each turn increased the gap between the vehicles. Rain hammered against the windshield, the wipers struggling to keep up as he accelerated away from the watchful eyes of his supposed allies.

Back at the MPS car, the driver gripped the steering wheel with a tense posture, his eyes narrowing as he exchanged glances with his partner. They were trained to observe, to analyze, and yet it seemed the MSS always found a way to slip through their fingers, shrouded in mystery with an aura of superiority. His teeth clenched, maintaining a façade of calm as frustration surged beneath the surface.

"Where is he headed?" his partner barked, fingers tapping anxiously on the dashboard.

But it was like they were chasing a ghost.

The MSS car turned sharply into an abandoned warehouse, the tires squealing against the slick pavement, just moments ahead of the MPS agents' attempts to follow. Inhaling deeply, the undercover agent observed the scene and exited the car.

Waiting for him were four heavily armed insurgents from Harapan Baru, their faces obscured by rain-soaked masks that shielded their identities and intent. They leaned against the battered vehicles, stone-faced and deferential, eyes scanning the surrounding area with acute suspicion for any signs of unwanted attention.

Without a word, the MSS officer approached, his movements smooth and assured.

From the trunk of his sedan, he revealed a bound and gagged Malaysian, barely conscious; his face painted with bruises and humiliation. With efficient precision, the insurgents hoisted the man out, their cold expressions betraying no emotion as he collapsed onto the muddy ground. The rain rolled off the rooftop, splattering onto the earth with a dull thud as the MSS agent pulled out the briefcase and handed it to the insurgents.

They nodded, their understanding apparent, but their loyalty nebulous in the murky interplay of power.

Caught between the MSS's grand designs and MPS's meddling and Harapan Baru's insurgent ambitions, the agent felt the heaviness of the moment settle. Trust wasn't a currency traded among friends or enemies; it was an illusion, a façade worn carefully on the stage of political theatre.

He stole one final glance at the grim scene, where the reins of power shifted between muted threats and hushed dealings. An uneasy alliance thrummed through the air, paranoia hanging heavily like the relentless rain. In the distance, the MPS agent must still be searching, still surveilling the darkness he inhabited.

With a nod to the insurgents, the MSS officer stepped back into the shadows, ready to slip again into the night.

* * *

2300 Hours | MSS HQ Beijing

MPS Minister Wang Xiaohong entered precisely two minutes late, enough to assert independence, not enough to show disrespect. Chen didn't acknowledge him. Both men understood the calculation.

The MSS conference room felt smaller than usual. Wang settled into his chair without removing his jacket. Chen's tea sat untouched, steam rising between them like incense at a funeral.

"Your overseas operations are progressing well," Chen observed, tapping his stylus once against his tablet. "The Chairman speaks favorably of MPS initiatives in Southeast Asia."

Wang's smile could have cut glass. "The rule of law knows no boundaries when it comes to protecting Chinese citizens abroad."

Protecting. Chen noted the word choice. Wang's people weren't providing consular services; they were enforcing Beijing's will on foreign soil.

"Of course," Chen replied, his voice dropping a degree. "Though I trust coordination remains paramount. Overlapping authorities can create... complications."

Wang leaned back in his chair; hands folded with deliberate precision. "The MSS maintains primacy in intelligence matters. However, when Chinese nationals require guidance, the MPS has both obligation and authority to act."

The qualifier hung in the air like cordite after gunfire. Chen understood perfectly, Wang was building parallel networks under the cover of citizen protection.

"The Chairman values efficiency." Chen's stylus stopped tapping. "Redundant capabilities waste resources."

"Which is why our operations complement rather than compete." Wang's voice remained steady, but his knuckles whitened slightly. "We handle enforcement. You handle the shadows. Both serve the Party."

Chen studied his counterpart's face. Behind the diplomatic mask lay ambition sharp enough to cut. The dance was over. Time for business.

"Malaysia," Chen said, activating the wall display. "Our networks require protection."

Wang straightened slightly. Chen rarely shared MSS operational details.

"Thirty-seven of our assets hold government positions," Chen reported, surveillance photos populating the screen. "Twelve in critical infrastructure. The Deputy Minister of Energy alone has provided access to the national grid for eighteen months."

Wang studied the faces on display; officials he'd assumed were clean. "Your penetration is deep, much deeper than I would have imagined."

"That's why coordination matters." Chen highlighted financial transfer records. "These assets represent decades of cultivation. Your enforcement actions cannot compromise their positions."

"Understood."

Chen's stylus resumed its rhythmic tapping. "With that out of the way, shall I describe what is to come next? Malaysia is about to get very interesting."

Chapter 5: Convergence Protocol

Day 3, 0830 Hours | U.S. Embassy, KL

Sam Blake entered the embassy conference room at precisely 0830 hours. Six analysts sat around the oak veneer table, laptops open, coffee cooling in Styrofoam cups. Malaysian intelligence maps covered one wall, red pins marking known MSS locations, blue for suspected MPS sites.

She didn't sit.

"The MSS is accelerating," Sam announced, clicking her remote. The wall screen filled with surveillance photos, Chinese nationals entering government buildings, meeting with local officials, disappearing into nondescript office complexes.

Her senior analyst, Rodriguez, leaned forward. "Pattern suggests coordination between MSS and MPS operations. They're not competing anymore, they're dividing territory."

Sam nodded. "Show me the network."

The screen shifted to a web diagram connecting faces, locations, what could be found on money transfers. Red lines indicated confirmed relationships, dotted yellow showed suspected links.

"My sources indicate at least four assets controlled by the MSS are embedded in government agencies, very likely more."

Rodriguez continued, highlighting nodes. "Banking sector, telecommunications, energy infrastructure."

"And Harapan Baru?" Sam asked.

"We have not found any evidence of direct financial support but would not expect to. But Harapan Baru has accelerated in growth, is dramatically growing in social media influence like they have been mentored by the best, and their propaganda is as agile as the PRCs." Rodriguez pontificated, "Same tradecraft, same operational security. This isn't coincidence."

Sam studied the connections. The insurgency wasn't homegrown, it was manufactured. Beijing was playing both sides, infiltrating the government while simultaneously funding its opposition.

"Assessment?" she asked.

"They're preparing for something big," Rodriguez replied. "The question is timing."

Sam's secure phone buzzed. Priority message from Langley: INDICATIONS SUGGEST IMMINENT CHINESE ACTION MALAYSIA. EXPEDITE COLLECTION.

She looked up at her team. Young faces, good analysts, but none had seen what she'd seen in Iraq, Afghanistan, the Balkans. None understood how quickly stability could collapse.

"New priority," Sam said, her voice cutting through the room's tension. "Find me proof of Chinese operational control. Something we can take to the Malaysians."

Rodriguez exchanged glances with his colleagues. "Ma'am, if we're wrong..."

"If we're right and do nothing, Malaysia falls." Sam gathered her files. "I need actionable intelligence in forty-eight hours."

The room fell silent.

Sam paused at the door. "And people, assume the worse. The worst case is not the least likely case. We may already be at war."

* * *

1300 Hours | Ritz-Carlton KL Hotel Room

Jack spread his lecture notes across the hotel desk like a tactical assessment. Outside his door, elevator chimes marked the passage of time. Footsteps in the corridor. Muffled conversations in languages he couldn't identify.

Twenty years ago, background noise was just noise. Now every sound mapped a potential threat vector.

He tapped his pen against the desk, reviewing contingencies. The University of Kuala Lumpur, multiple exits, mixed crowd, impossible to secure. Perfect venue for anyone wanting to make a statement about American interference.

His phone buzzed. Recorded Future alert: Bershi Movement scheduling protest rally downtown KL, three days.

Jack studied the notification. Another variable in an increasingly complex equation. Malaysia was heating up, and he was about to discuss Chinese cyber capabilities in front of God knew who.

He gathered his notes, slipped them into his satchel. Through the window, Kuala Lumpur's lights twinkled like a circuit board. Somewhere in that maze of glass and steel, people were watching, planning, waiting.

Jack checked his watch. Time to see who would be listening tonight.

* * *

1500 Hours | University of Kuala Lumpur

The green room at University of Kuala Lumpur lecture hall was standard academic fare, neutral walls, university photos, the smell of coffee and nervous energy. Jack adjusted his tie when footsteps approached.

"Commander Tanner?"

A lean man in wire-rimmed glasses extended his hand. "Dr. Farid Rahman, Malaysia's Chief Cybersecurity Officer."

Jack stood, measuring the handshake. Firm grip, direct eye contact. "Dr. Rahman. Honor to meet you."

"The honor is all mine! Thank you for accepting my invitation. I really look forward to your talk. Your book has generated considerable discussion." Farid's accent carried British education over Malaysian roots. "My entire team read it. Matches exactly what we face daily."

Jack settled into his chair. Behind the compliment lay something deeper. "What kind of threats are you seeing?"

"The usual progression. We strengthen defenses, they adapt. Social engineering, phishing, find another way in." Farid's expression darkened. "Our greatest threat happens to be our largest trading partner."

The unspoken hung between them. China.

"Are we still on for a visit tomorrow? Would love to show you our operations," Farid continued.

"Absolutely, excited to see what you are up to," Jack knew to say that, even though he has seen so many SOCs they all start to look the same.

A student volunteer appeared. "Mr. Tanner? We're ready."

Jack followed her toward the conference hall. Through the doorway, he glimpsed the audience, students, probably a handful of tech enthusiasts, policymakers, journalists. What he couldn't see were the hostile faces preparing to turn his academic presentation into a battlefield.

Jack stepped onto the stage as the auditorium lights dimmed. Four hundred faces stared back.

"Good evening," Jack began. "Tonight, we discuss something that affects us all, the global implications of cyber warfare."

He launched into the Volt Typhoon case, watching reactions. The students leaned forward. The suits took notes. In the back corner, a man with a diplomatic badge whispered into his phone.

"Imagine an adversary moving through your systems undetected," Jack continued. "Not using malware, just living off the land."

Murmurs rippled through the crowd. Concerned nods from the tech sector. Hostile stares from a Chinese contingent.

Jack shifted gears. "This is not only the famous MSS. The PRC Ministry of Public Security has evolved beyond domestic enforcement. They now operate globally, conducting unsanctioned law enforcement in sovereign nations…"

He was cut off by a man who shot to his feet. "Are you advocating digital colonialism?" His accent was local, but his talking points weren't. "This is Western imperialism disguised as cooperation!"

The crowd stirred. More voices joined the protest. Signs appeared, "Stop Western Surveillance!" Someone had come prepared.

Through the chaos, Lin Qiang emerged. Chinese Embassy, Public Affairs. His tailored suit cut through the crowd like a blade.

"Commander Tanner," Lin's voice silenced the room. "Your assertions reflect a colonial mindset that seeks dominance, not partnership."

Jack met his gaze. "Partnership doesn't require surrendering sovereignty."

"You mischaracterize our intentions," Lin shot back. "What you call espionage is simply China helping friends protect their interests against Western imperialism."

The room polarized instantly. Half the crowd nodded approval. The other half shifted uncomfortably.

Jack caught movement in his peripheral vision. Red hair, purposeful stride, heading for the exit. The woman from the bookstore. She wasn't random, she was operational.

Fire alarms shrieked. Red lights flashed. The crowd surged toward exits.

Lin's face contorted with rage. "You see? This is how you provoke chaos!"

Jack ignored him, tracking the redhead's movement. She reappeared near the emergency exit, flanked by the two men he recognized from the Ritz lobby. Not students. Security.

The crowd pushed past him in panic. Jack slipped through a side door, emerging into the night air. Behind him, Lin's protests faded into alarm bells and shouting.

Time to disappear.

He moved quickly toward the shopping center three blocks away. Neon signs cast colored shadows across the sidewalk. Perfect cover, crowds, multiple exits, security cameras that worked both ways.

Inside the mall, Jack ducked into a restroom. The mirror showed tousled hair, flushed face. He splashed cold water on his cheeks, controlled his breathing. Through the door, footsteps echoed past. None paused.

Back in the corridor, he opened the Grab app. Port Klang. The car would meet him two blocks away, outside the electronics market.

Jack moved through the crowd with practiced anonymity. Brown hair and Western features made him stand out, but Malaysia's multicultural flow provided decent camouflage. He kept his head down, eyes scanning reflections in shop windows.

The silver sedan arrived precisely on time. Jack checked the license plate against his app before sliding into the back seat.

"Port Klang," he told the driver.

As they merged into traffic, Jack's mind dwelled on the redhead. The bookstore. The hotel bar. This coordinated disruption. The two men who'd shadowed her exit.

The city blurred past through tinted windows. Somewhere ahead, the USS *Blue Ridge* waited with answers. Or more questions.

Either way, Jack was about to find out what Mike had been trying to tell him.

* * *

1900 Hours | The Seraya

Li Jianhong didn't glance up when the agent entered. He merely extended a hand, palm up.

The thumb drive was placed there with reverence.

"Timestamped?" Li asked.

"Yes, sir. Recovered from our internal observer at the university."

Li inserted the drive into a secure laptop. He read the transcript of Tanner's remarks first, then the summary of the successful confrontation by the diplomat and useful idiots doing what they do. He opened the video and fast-forwarded to images of the redhead.

"His message isn't just academic, and not just about his book" he said flatly. "It's provocation wrapped in policy critique."

The agent shifted uneasily. "He deviated from his own book content."

"Of course he did. Commanded to do so I'm sure. He's testing boundaries. Gauging response."

Li rose and stepped to the window. Below, the city's chaos hummed. "Do we know the woman who pulled the fire alarm?"

"Our facial match indicates she's Shelia O'Neil, CIA officer under official cover in the U.S. Embassy who operates here undercover as Fiona Kincaid."

Li's eyes narrowed.

"I want everything on her. Likely his handler and contact while he is in country."

The agent nodded, hesitating at the door.

"There's something else," he said. "Zhang Wei has requested a coordination meeting. He mentioned a growing MPS stake in the Tanner issue."

Li's voice was calm. Too calm.

"Of course he did."

He turned back to his desk.

"Schedule it."

As the agent left, Li reached for a second phone lying face down on the desk. It was air-gapped, hardware-modified. He tapped out a six-digit unlock and opened a secure thread.

One new message awaited:

Rafid Latif neutralized. Suicide in his apartment.

He stared at it a beat longer than usual.

Latif had been useful in helping plant a senior MSS agent inside the Ministry of Energy. As the only other Malaysian who knew of this high-level placement the risks were too high to have him around, especially when he revealed he was being tasked to be a double agent for Special Branch. Li already has enough of those, and not a one approached him first, an obvious double agent trick.

Li deleted the message like he deleted Latif.

Chapter 6: Fleet Intelligence

The USS Blue Ridge floated at Port Klang like a steel cathedral; her superstructure draped in diplomatic bunting for the evening reception. Jack stepped aboard and was escorted to the main deck for the event. Jack stepped onto the deck, awash in nostalgic feelings and a longing for his past life where this was part of his official duties. "That is enough time for nostalgia", he reminded himself, there is business to do.

A navy band played a lively tune, its notes weaving through the air and mingling with laughter and conversation.

The foreign diplomatic corps was out in full force, their attire reflecting a blend of local culture and Western influence. Among them were military attaches from every embassy, including the PRC.

"Jack! Over here!" Admiral Harrison's voice cut through the diplomatic chatter.

Jack approached, cataloging faces as he moved. PLA Navy officers in summer whites.

"Glad you could make it," Harrison said, clapping Jack's shoulder. "Loved the book. Really helps us make the case with partners that we need to elevate our game."

"Thanks, Admiral. That was the goal."

Harrison lowered his voice. "That demo you gave at Langley last year, your virtual intelligence center. Still has the old guard clutching their pearls."

Jack chuckled. "Some folks think if it wasn't collected by a spy or satellite, it can't be worth much."

"Their loss." Harrison's gaze drifted across the deck. "By the way, Mike's looking for you. Has some things to discuss."

The admiral moved off to glad-hand other guests. Jack studied the crowd, noting how the Chinese attachés positioned themselves with clear sight lines to every conversation.

"Jack! You old sea dog!"

Mike Murphy materialized with a genuine grin and a firm handshake. Twenty years of friendship compressed into that grip.

"Didn't think you'd have time for socializing," Jack said. "Don't you have a job to do?"

"When else can a sailor get a drink on a warship?" Mike gestured at the festive scene.

Mike leaned closer. "Remember Sam Blake? CIA liaison to INDOPACOM? She's Chief of Station here now."

Before Jack could respond, a woman approached. Samantha Blake, sharp features, confident stride, eyes that missed nothing.

"Jack Tanner," she said, extending her hand. "A sight for sore eyes."

Her grip was firm, professional. Jack remembered late nights in Pearl Harbor, planning operations that never made the news.

"Was the redhead yours?" Jack asked quietly.

Sam's smile was almost predatory. "That's Fiona. Her idea to go red, thought it would help you identify friendly forces. Seems like she was useful after all."

"I was holding my own."

"Besides," Jack continued, "I spotted the two muscle guys you sent for my protection."

"Oh, they weren't protecting you," Sam replied. "Fiona's a national treasure. I like keeping eyes on her."

Mike shifted closer, his expression darkening. "We need to talk about Harapan Baru."

The casual atmosphere evaporated instantly.

"What's happening?" Jack asked.

"PRC-backed insurgency," Mike said, scanning for eavesdroppers. "They're not just agitating anymore; they're preparing for destabilization operations."

Sam's eyes flashed with irritation. "You mean you *assume* they're PRC-backed. There's a difference between assessment and fact."

"My job is making calls for decision-makers," Mike shot back. "This isn't academic analysis, Sam."

"Better get facts before shooting off half-baked assessments." The two squabbled like a married couple, the product of years of working closely together.

Mike ignored the jab. "Harapan Baru is blending traditional insurgency with AI-driven propaganda. Social media mastery that doesn't emerge from jungle camps."

Jack felt the familiar chill of operational intelligence. "So, they're manipulating narratives while preparing kinetic operations?"

"Exactly. Coordinated, sophisticated, well-funded."

Sam crossed her arms. "If this spreads beyond Malaysia..."

"It destabilizes the entire region," Jack finished. "Beijing's been perfecting this for years. Look at how they destabilized the Philippines' maritime security while backing separatist groups in Mindanao."

The three stood in silence, each processing implications. Around them, diplomatic small talk continued, oblivious to the shadow war being discussed.

"I'm glad I'm on a book tour and not an intelligence mission," Jack said finally. "You all have the watch."

"Stay in the loop?" Mike asked. "Your insights could be valuable."

"Always, shipmate."

Sam's gaze drifted toward the Chinese delegation. "Jack, my hope is you get back to CONUS soon. It's getting dangerous out here."

Jack followed her stare to the PLA naval attaché, who watched their conversation with undisguised interest. Professional curiosity or something more?

"When do you head out?" Sam asked.

"Day after tomorrow. The Malaysian cyber team wants to talk about some consulting work tomorrow, then I take a direct to SFO." Jack paused. "This place does feel different, for sure. If I do engage, consulting from long distance is probably the right play."

The band struck up another tune, masking their conversation in patriotic melody. But Jack's instincts screamed that the real music hadn't started yet.

* * *

Jack moved toward the gangway, fatigue settling in his bones. The evening's conversations echoed in his mind, trade agreements, cybersecurity measures, regional stability. All diplomatic theater masking deeper currents.

He paused at the rail, scanning the crowd one final time. The PLA naval attaché was still watching, still calculating. Did Beijing's navy know what the MSS was doing in-country? Probably not. The left hand rarely knew what the right was planning.

"Safe travels," he murmured to himself, then headed for the exit.

Twenty meters away, Sam and Mike remained at the rail, watching Jack's departure.

"You ever get the real story on why Jack left the Navy?" Sam asked.

Mike's expression darkened. "He was the best fleet intel officer I'd seen. Came to the staff with a vision: intelligence would drive operations, not just support them. Every move the Admiral made would be based on our assessments."

"Sounds familiar. In Hawaii, he made the J2 look like an amateur."

"Exactly. He didn't just do the job; he outshined everyone above him. That's why the knives came out." Mike's voice carried old anger. "Too much jealousy. Too many people who thought he made them look bad."

"So, they sandbagged his promotion?"

"Quietly. No formal reprimand. Just made sure his number never came up." Mike watched Jack disappear into the night. "He put in his retirement papers like it was another mission wrap-up. Said he didn't want to spend five years polishing apples in D.C. while China rewired Southeast Asia."

Sam nodded slowly. "He's still serving. Just without the bureaucracy."

"Yeah," Mike said, his voice carrying certainty. "And I think that makes him more dangerous to the bad guys than ever."

The string lights reflected off the water as the USS *Blue Ridge* continued its diplomatic mission. But for Jack Tanner, the real war was just beginning.

Chapter 7: Digital Sovereignty

Day 4, 1000 Hours | NACSA

Jack's car approached the gleaming glass facade of the National Cybersecurity Agency headquarters. The building stood as a testament to Malaysia's commitment to digital sovereignty, twelve stories of mirrored windows reflecting Kuala Lumpur's skyline, with subtle but unmistakable security measures integrated into its modern design.

Dr. Farid Rahman waited at the entrance, his tailored suit and confident posture marking him as the senior government official he was. He extended his hand with a warm smile that didn't quite reach his calculating eyes.

"Commander Tanner, welcome to NACSA. Your timing couldn't be better; your book has sparked quite the conversation in our corridors."

Jack matched the firm handshake. "The honor's mine, Datuk Dr. Rahman. Your efforts are renowned in the community, a real exemplar."

They passed through the security checkpoint, Rahman's credentials bypassing the usual protocols. As they entered the elevator, Rahman pressed his thumb against a biometric scanner.

"Your analysis of attribution challenges in state-sponsored attacks was particularly insightful," Rahman said as they ascended.

"Few Westerners understand the nuances of operating in our regional context."

Jack nodded appreciatively. "And fewer still appreciate how Malaysia has navigated between superpowers while building indigenous capabilities."

Rahman's expression revealed a momentary gleam of satisfaction. "Perhaps we might discuss that further after the tour. I believe there could be valuable perspectives to exchange."

The elevator doors opened to reveal the SOC, a cavernous room with curved walls of monitors displaying threat maps, attack vectors, and defensive postures. Analysts hunched over workstations, their faces illuminated by multiple screens.

"Our crown jewel," Rahman announced proudly. "State-of-the-art intrusion detection, AI-powered threat hunting, and integration with seventeen government agencies. We've invested heavily in keeping our digital borders secure."

Jack surveyed the room, noting the familiar configurations of SIEM dashboards and threat intelligence feeds. He'd seen dozens like it, from Pentagon cyber war rooms to the NSA's famous Technical Operations Center to corporate security centers in the greatest international corporations. Overall, quite boring after a while. Every SOC begins to look the same. They all use Splunk and some commodity endpoint management tools and common network visualization systems.

What interested him more were the analysts themselves, their body language, their interaction patterns, their level of engagement. Technology could be purchased; the human element determined whether a SOC succeeded or failed.

"This is so impressive," Jack said diplomatically. "Not sure I've ever seen anything like it before."

A woman in her mid-thirties appeared at Rahman's side as if she'd been there all along. Malaysian, with smooth café-au-lait skin and black hair drawn into a no-nonsense knot, she carried herself with parade-ground precision. Her eyes took Tanner in with the quick, tactical sweep of someone trained to notice weaknesses, and exploit them.

"Commander Tanner, welcome. I'm Lila Tan, SOC Manager and Deputy Director." Her handshake was brief but firm. "We've implemented your attribution methodology from chapter seven. We totally believe you are right, you can never do attribution with cyber information alone. The results we got in doing that were... unexpected."

Jack caught something in her tone, caution, perhaps, or a warning. "Unexpected how?"

"Perhaps that's a conversation for a more private setting," Rahman interjected, gesturing toward a hallway. "Ms. Tan has prepared a detailed briefing."

As they moved towards the hallway, Jack noticed SOC analysts hunched over terminals displaying the same visualizations he had seen in 100 other SOCs.

Rahman guided them to a conference room with frosted glass walls. Once inside, he activated electronic countermeasures with a tap on his phone. The room hummed faintly.

"Commander Tanner, I didn't invite you here merely to showcase our capabilities." Rahman leaned forward. "I need someone who can assess our operations without institutional blindness or career concerns of others."

Jack studied the man. "You know, when I left the Navy and started consulting, I asked a friend for advice, he told me a consultant is a person who knows less than anyone in the organization they advise but their opinions are listened to because they traveled from far away."

"Ha! There is some truth to that," Rahman replied, his expression unreadable. "And in my experience, most consultants just repeat back to me what my staff told them and over charge me for that!"

Lila placed a folder on the table and spoke as if she had never heard a joke in her life. "That is not what we are looking for here. We need external evaluation from a non-biased actor with experience and credibility. We're prepared to offer a month-long consulting contract. The compensation would be... substantial."

Jack hesitated. His flight was scheduled for tomorrow. He had no intention of extending his stay in a country increasingly feeling like a chessboard for competing intelligence services.

"I'm interested, but not available now, and would have to work remotely" he said, "I leave tomorrow..."

Cutting him off, Rahman interjected, "Jack, I know you want this, I read your book!" continuing "You went on and on about how countries and individuals can stand up to the MSS and make a difference. This is your chance to prove to the world that it can be done."

No doubt about that, Jack thought to himself.

Meanwhile, Rahman continued, "We have reason to believe that their infiltration runs deeper than previously thought, our analysts have detected anomalies within critical sectors, financial institutions, telecommunications, and even government networks."

Jack leaned back slightly, arms crossing over his chest as he absorbed the implications. "And how are you certain these aren't just the usual noise? Cyber threats are a dime a dozen these days."

"Because we've assessed the tactics of several of these activities," Rahman insisted, passion igniting in his tone. "These aren't random intrusions; they follow a pattern aligned with our strategic vulnerabilities. And most are the "living off the land" tactics you briefed yesterday. If we don't act now, Malaysia could find itself in a precarious position, ripe for destabilization. This is the MSS."

Jack felt a chill run down his spine at the mention of the MSS. The implications rippled through him; it wasn't just about espionage anymore but about destabilizing critical infrastructure and sowing discord within Malaysia, a democratic nation the PRC would love to dominate for due to its positioning at the crossroads of critical maritime trade routes.

Rahman leaned closer, his voice dropping even lower as he revealed details Jack had only suspected before, the ongoing campaigns against Malaysian businesses and government networks aimed at exploiting their weaknesses.

"We must collaborate," Rahman urged firmly but quietly. "Your experience could help us build a more resilient framework against these cyber threats."

The chill down Jack's spine was replaced with an intoxicating thrill, a reconnection to purpose that had eluded him since retirement. This was more than just consulting; it felt like stepping back onto familiar battlegrounds where every line of code held significance and each breach represented a potential crisis.

He realized that this opportunity might not only test his skills but also reaffirm his commitment to safeguarding what mattered most, freedom, privacy and security in an increasingly volatile world. Not a bad payday either.

"Yes to working with you, yes to standing up against the MSS with you, but I'm taking a huge risk here. If you guys can't move fast you might as well just surrender now."

Rahman extended his hand, a firm gesture that carried the weight of their agreement. Jack grasped it firmly, feeling the pulse of determination in the handshake. They exchanged a meaningful look, one that spoke volumes about the challenges ahead, an unspoken acknowledgment of the path they were about to embark on together.

"I'm thinking you will need a month with us, starting today. "Then we switch to a year-long term consulting agreement, much of it delivered remotely."

Jack's eyes narrowed. "A month here starting now is out of the question."

Rahman smiled thinly. "How about a single intense week?"

"I can do four days now, contract is for a year with quarterly in-person meetings."

"Deal," Rahman replied.

Was that too quick? Jack sensed he had just been played. Rahman wanted four days from the beginning. Sneaky bastard. But nice to have another paying client. Jack has his own objectives. This is the perfect opportunity to prove that privacy and security could withstand even the most sophisticated MSS operations.

Jack felt a renewed sense of purpose surging through him. The stakes had risen considerably; he was no longer just an observer in Malaysia but an active participant in its defense against encroaching threats.

"When do we start? Jack asked.

"Now is good, Lila will start the deep dive."

* * *

After meeting with Dr. Rahman and Lila, Jack found himself immersed in NACSA's inner workings. Analysts hunched over screens in the main SOC displayed intrusion detection alerts, firewall logs, and endpoint monitoring dashboards. Lila introduced each team lead, from threat hunters to incident responders, all of whom greeted Jack with a mix of professional curiosity and quiet respect.

"And this is where the real magic happens," Lila said, leading Jack to her personal workstation in a corner of the facility. Three monitors curved around her desk, displaying what appeared to be a custom visualization system unlike anything in the standard SOC displays.

"You've built something interesting here," Jack noted, leaning closer to examine the pulsing network of connections on her center screen.

Lila nodded, pride evident in her posture. "This is my attribution tracker. I've mapped incidents and intrusion patterns across our government infrastructure using the MITRE ATT&CK framework as a foundation." She clicked through several views. "Each node represents a system, and these connections show lateral movement patterns. The label captures candidate actors, color intensity indicates confidence in attribution."

Jack studied the visualization with growing interest. "You're tracking TTPs rather than just IOCs."

"Exactly. Instead of chasing IP addresses and domains that change constantly, we're identifying behavioral patterns." Lila pointed to a cluster of red nodes. "These show living-off-the-land techniques, using legitimate Windows tools like PowerShell and WMI for malicious purposes. Classic MSS Unit 61398 methodology."

"And you're using my attribution methodology to prioritize your defensive actions," Jack observed, recognizing elements from his book.

"With some modifications," Lila admitted. "I've added weighted scoring for temporal patterns. MSS operators tend to work Beijing business hours, while their automated tools run 24/7. When we see human-driven operations…"

"You can predict when they'll pivot to new systems," Jack finished her thought. "That's brilliant. You're essentially forecasting their next move based on operator behavior."

"Just like you described in chapter nine," Lila said, clicking through to another screen. "We've also implemented your DIAMOND model for structured analytical technique to separate the signal from the noise."

Jack pointed to a section of the display. "You should consider adding CISA's Known Exploited Vulnerabilities catalog as an overlay. MSS teams tend to weaponize vulnerabilities within hours of public disclosure, keeps them from revealing their zero days."

"Already working on it," Lila said, opening a development window showing exactly that implementation. "Great minds think alike."

As they continued discussing technical details, Jack noticed a small, framed photo on her desk, Lila standing beside an elderly woman with the same determined eyes, both smiling broadly against a backdrop of tropical foliage.

Following his gaze, Lila's expression softened. "My grandmother. She raised me after my parents died. She taught at the University of Malaya for forty years, mathematics. She's why I got into cybersecurity."

"She must be proud," Jack said.

Lila's smile dimmed slightly. "I hope so. I've been pulling a lot of late nights lately. Digital sovereignty isn't a nine-to-five job."

"I know that feeling," Jack said. "It's an infinite game."

Their eyes met briefly, a moment of mutual recognition passing between them, the shared understanding of what it meant to stand guard against invisible threats, to sacrifice personal comfort for something larger than themselves.

Jack cleared his throat, suddenly aware of how close they were sitting. "Your visualization system, it's exactly what we need to establish a baseline for monitoring the environment."

"I'll set you up with admin access," Lila said, her professional demeanor returning though her eyes lingered on his for a moment longer than necessary. "We can start identifying the most critical vulnerabilities immediately."

As she turned back to her keyboard, Jack found himself noticing the subtle floral scent of her perfume, the graceful efficiency of her movements. He pushed the observation aside, focusing instead on the task at hand. They had work to do, and neither of them could afford distractions, no matter how intriguing they might be.

Chapter 8: Shadow Doctrine

Day 4, 1300 Hours | MSS Malaysia, The Seraya

Kuala Lumpur glistened in sunrise. Beneath the surface of this vibrant metropolis, forces conspired in a delicate dance of power and espionage, weaving a web tighter than any before.

MSS Station Chief Li sat at a polished oak desk in the communications room of his suite at The Seraya, his fingers steepled as he considered the plan laid before him. The flickering glow of multiple screens cast a pale light on his expression, revealing a face that belied the intensity of his strategic thoughts. The MSS was readying an unprecedented assault, one that would change the game in Southeast Asia, disrupting not just local politics but sending tremors across the international landscape.

"Ming, Lao, and Wu" he muttered under his breath, as if conjuring the shadowy figures from the depths of the digital realm. The Three Immortals, each a master of the cybernetic arts, were more than just names whispered among the elite of China's intelligence circles; they were added firepower behind the MSS's already extensive work in Malaysian cyberspace. Plans were in motion to launch a multifaceted campaign that combined the precision of cyber warfare with the chaos of insurgency.

"Stability through chaos," Li whispered, tapping a finger against his lips absorbed in thought.

Li raises The Three Immortals by secure video. Lao sat straight-backed, meticulous as ever. Ming offered a relaxed nod. Wu remained still, eyes sharp behind rimless glasses.

"Phase Three begins in four days," Li said. "Status."

Lao spoke first. "We have reviewed all MSS activities to date in fifteen of the top corporate networks in Malaysia, including banking, utilities, and petrochemicals. We've reconfirmed readiness of command-ready payloads in their document management and finance systems."

Li nodded slightly. "How resilient are those accesses?"

"Fair. Most company defenses in Malaysia rely on outdated perimeter defenses. No internal segmentation. If we move quickly, we can lock them out of their own systems before they even detect intrusion."

Ming picked up smoothly. "Telecom is progressing. We had to redo previous positioning; this was not the best MSS could do. But we now have persistent access to three of the top mobile carriers. Call metadata, message routing, voicemail systems, we're monitoring it all. We've also re-mapped the flow of government traffic across these networks and are analyzing it for any future injection points."

Wu spoke next, his tone level, precise. "The government remains the most resistant. NACSA is well resourced, and many of your previous positions are no longer valid. But we have steered our team to ensure continued access."

Li's brow furrowed. "What is going on there!"

"They operate independently and have been given new authorities to take direct action in any government ministry network to mitigate threats. Their continual hunting is not a match for us but certainly injects uncertainty. This is a massive campaign for them," Wu said. "They are changing things by the hour. This is no longer passive defense. It is like they're anticipating us."

Ming nodded. "We've seen accelerated patching and abrupt reconfigurations, clearly acting on good intel. Possibly internal counter-cyber teams coming online. They're prioritizing key infrastructure."

Lao added, "The lower-level ministries remain exposed. But anything touching security or state functions is being pulled into protected zones."

Li was quiet for a moment, processing. There are no coincidences in the world of espionage; bad things are always the result of enemy action, and in this case, this reeks of an American stench. "Do you know who is leading the defense?"

"We know Rahman has hosted visits from NSA and U.S. Cyber Command and they no doubt have been given command over their networks," Wu said.

"Bullshit," Lao pushed back. "Just because you are getting stumped does not mean you are fighting Cyber Command. NACSA has just upped their game."

Li leaned forward. "Then you three all better up your game. We have given you control over all MSS cyber activities, use them."

He paused. "If you fail me you will find your accolades do nothing for you" Li interjected.

"And if we need on the ground support and you do not give it to us what then" the gutsy Wu replied.

"What are you asking for?"

"If their cyber agency slows us down and if it is because of their people, you are in a far better position to deal with them than we are. Is that not your duty?" Wu suggested.

"You focus on your penetrations and leave ground action to me" he growled. "And report back to me in 24 hours on how big of a thorn their cyber agency will be to our operations. I'll make decisions then."

* * *

Li Jianhong stared at the blank screen, fingers steepled beneath his chin. The Three Immortals had disconnected, leaving him alone with his thoughts in the sterile confines of his residence office. Outside his window, Kuala Lumpur sprawled beneath gathering storm clouds, a fitting metaphor for what was coming.

How much to tell his MPS counterpart Zhang Wei? The question gnawed at him.

The Ministry of Public Security already knew the outline: destabilize Malaysia's cybersecurity, create leverage points across their infrastructure, prepare for a coordinated strike that would leave the country vulnerable to Chinese influence without firing a single shot. But the details... the timing... the specific targets... those remained closely guarded within MSS channels.

"Compartmentalization is security," Li murmured to himself, an old MSS maxim. Yet the operation's scale demanded MPS support.

Li pulled a secure tablet from his desk drawer, reviewing the encrypted timeline. Four days until execution. Zhang Wei's people would need to ensure broad support by as many PRC nationals in country as possible and silence any hint of dissent from those who do not respect the PRC global rule of law. He will need more details of the plan. But giving them too much information risked leaks, or worse, Zhang Wei claiming credit for MSS successes.

The bureaucratic rivalry between MSS and MPS had evolved in recent months. President Xi's direct intervention had forced the agencies into an uneasy alliance, threatening severe consequences for anyone undermining the new cooperative mandate. The alliance between these two powerful arms of the Chinese state had morphed into an indomitable support network, fostering a new wave of aggression in Malaysian affairs.

Li drafted a message to Zhang, carefully parsing each word: "Phase three proceeds as scheduled. Further details in 24 hours."

He hesitated before sending it, considering the power dynamics at play. Zhang would want more, would demand more, but giving him complete operational details would be dangerous. The MPS excelled at boots-on-ground intimidation, not the delicate cyber operations MSS had spent years perfecting.

"Success serves China," Li reminded himself, pressing send. "Not individual agencies."

The message disappeared into the encrypted network, and Li turned back to the window. Rain began to fall on Kuala Lumpur, the first drops of a coming storm.

* * *

Li's strategy, fusing cyber-attacks with the insurgent tactics of Harapan Baru, promised to unleash chaos. His adversaries would be disoriented before they even grasped the magnitude of the threat. It was time to ensure every piece was aligned. He initiated a secure MSS tactical channel.

The screens flickered to life, each pane filling with the faces of his covert operatives, deep-cover MSS agents across the capital.

"Comrades," Li began, voice crisp and commanding. "We move to Phase Three in four days. Status updates, now."

Officer One: "My four assets in the Ministry of Communications know what to do and when. This includes the Deputy Minister for public affairs. His daughter is in Beijing for university. She sends him a photo every day. A subtle reminder." He continued "We've inserted MSS-crafted talking points into the national cybersecurity policy memo. The Deputy Minister will propose them to Parliament tomorrow, framing it as an 'indigenous initiative' to fight online extremism." Li gave a curt nod. "Ensure this is done and receives broad attention. We will prepare our social media influence team to strongly support."

Officer Two: "Our assets in the national transit authority and both the Light Rail Transit and Mass Rapid Transit systems are prepared to execute as planned, causing disruption in mobility and gridlock on all mass movement in the city. They have all seen the video we recorded upon their initial bribes and have no other option but to support." Li's mouth tightened slightly in what passed for a smile. "Monitor them. If they hesitate, remind them they have no options but to comply."

Officer Three: "The Deputy Home Minister has agreed to delay publication of the Harapan Baru threat assessment. In exchange, we are forgiving two loans from PRC real estate firms tied to his brothers' ventures. His press secretary will echo our narrative- Malaysian sovereignty first, no foreign interference." Li's eyes narrowed. "And if the assessment leaks?" "I've already sent a ghostwriter to The Star in Malaysia and the South China Morning Post. The leak will be pre-empted by our version."

Officer Four: "Twenty-one CEOs of mid-sized contractors have signed on to our infrastructure alignment plan. They believe it leads to Belt and Road funding. Our trade attaché has quietly guaranteed Harapan Baru-affected zones will be 'reconstructed post-conflict,' with contracts available to those who cooperate now." Li leaned forward slightly. "Excellent. Ensure the contracts go to firms run by those who fear us, not those who admire us. Fear is leverage. Loyalty is myth."

Officer Five: The Harapan Baru Liaison reports: "Training is complete on the JY-3000 Quadrotor Bomber Drones and DJI Black Lantern ISR systems for Dragon Falls defense. Only Amir knows about the short-range killer drone point defense systems, and it is only to be used as a last-ditch defense. Explosives and weapons caches pre-positioned across the city and ready for the next phase. Amir is impatient. I continue to assess he does not have the loyalty we would expect from someone who has received all his weapons, training and funding from us and must share a concern that once the operation is over his goals may diverge from our own." Li interjected: "I expect you to plan for that contingency. He will soon have little value to us."

He paused.

"You will continue to coordinate via secure circuits while maintaining absolute plausible deniability of any of your actions. We will appear uninvolved. The world must see Malaysia destabilize itself."

Then, his voice dropped a register.

"We will give them blood on the ground, silence in cyberspace, and confusion in the airwaves. When they beg for stability, we will offer order."

He scanned the faces. Each agent stiffened.

"One last instruction: Our need to ensure no fingerprints on any action will be tested before the full launch of Harapan Baru ops. Remember this, some of your sources may come to you after a coming event. It was not us. You have no doubt; we don't operate that way. We are here to strengthen relationships with our great partners here and would never do such a thing."

The silence that followed was absolute. All knew this was not a topic to ask clarification on.

Then: "Dismissed."

As the call terminated, Li leaned back in his chair, the soft murmur of the city far below muffled by soundproofed glass. Outside, Kuala Lumpur blinked innocently, unaware of the storm forming within its own bloodstreams.

"To them," he murmured, "we will be a ghost."

He turned to his operations tablet. A single red icon glowed in the north: Dragon Falls. The insurgents believed they were the blade.

Li knew better. They were the bait.

Chapter 9: Charlotte's Web

Day 5, 0900 Hours | NACSA

Jack hunched over the conference room table, surrounded by network diagrams spread across its polished surface. Each schematic represented another piece of Malaysia's digital infrastructure, telecommunications backbones, financial networks, and power grid control systems. He traced interconnection points with his finger, marking vulnerabilities in red.

Jack was forming a thesis, thinking through how he would attack if he were the MSS.

A soft knock interrupted his thoughts. Lila stood in the doorway, a folder clutched against her chest, her expression tense. Something in her posture, the slight forward lean, the tightness around her eyes, sent a warning signal through Jack's instincts.

"Jack, I need you to see something. At my workstation." Her voice was controlled, professional, but with an undercurrent of urgency that wasn't there earlier.

He nodded, gathering his notes. "Lead the way."

They walked through the bustling Security Operations Center. Two dozen analysts hunched before glowing screens, some speaking quietly into headsets, others typing rapidly. The room hummed with the quiet intensity of digital sentinels. Jack caught snippets of conversation "...third probe on the eastern router farm," "...signature matches last week's attempt" as they navigated between workstations.

Lila slid into her chair, fingers already moving across the keyboard. Jack leaned in, close enough to catch the faint scent of jasmine.

"The intrusion and incidents from the last few weeks, maybe another pattern of note." She pulled up a three-dimensional graph, rotating it to show connections between attempted breaches and incidents across different sectors, underneath a display of time.

Lila pulled up network logs on her primary monitor, a cascade of timestamps and IP addresses filling the screen. She highlighted several clusters with a few deft keystrokes, color-coding them against a timeline.

"Look at these timestamps," she said, pointing to the pattern that emerged. "Why do so many probes hit or beacons become active exactly when our shift changes?"

Jack leaned in, studying the data with growing concern. The correlation was unmistakable, spikes of activity at 0800, 1600, and midnight. Too precise to be coincidental.

"They know your operational rhythms," he said quietly. "They've been watching long enough to identify your team rotations, handoff procedures, maybe even individual analyst patterns."

The SOC continued its work around them, analysts calling out updates, the soft chatter of keyboards providing a constant backdrop. But in their corner, a different kind of tension had formed, the quiet recognition of a threat far larger than either had initially suspected.

Jack glanced at Lila's face, noticing the shadows under her eyes, the slight redness that spoke of too many hours staring at screens. Her hands trembled slightly as she zoomed in on a particularly concerning cluster of attempts against the northeastern power distribution nodes.

"How long since you've slept?" he asked.

Lila gave a short, humorless laugh. "Sleep is a luxury when your country's under digital siege." She rubbed her eyes briefly before refocusing on the screen. "My grandmother lives near that power station. If they take it down during monsoon season..."

She didn't finish the thought. She didn't need to. The personal stakes were written clearly on her face, this wasn't just about national security for her. It was about protecting the people and places she loved.

Jack straightened, his mind already shifting from analysis to action. "Can you pull up your CrowdStrike console?"

Lila nodded, fingers dancing across the keyboard. The familiar Falcon interface appeared, its dashboard displaying threat metrics across Malaysia's digital landscape.

"You guys have used CrowdStrike for years, right? How widespread is it deployed?" Jack asked, eyes scanning the overview statistics.

Lila smiled, a hint of pride in her expression. "Pretty much complete coverage, almost two million endpoints, all feeding into Splunk too."

Jack's gaze settled on a section of the dashboard. "But you haven't enabled Charlotte AI?" He pointed to inactive settings buried in the configuration panel.

"Charlotte who?" Lila's brow furrowed, confusion evident.

"May I?" Jack gestured toward her keyboard.

Lila slid her chair aside, giving him access. Jack's fingers moved with practiced efficiency, navigating through nested menus to a section labeled "AI-Augmented Threat Hunting."

"Watch this," he said, clicking through Advanced Settings. The screen filled with configuration options, behavioral analysis thresholds, machine learning parameters, and automated response protocols.

Jack adjusted sliders and toggled switches, each movement deliberate. "Charlotte spots patterns humans miss. She works continuously in the background, analyzing behavior across your entire network."

He moved to another section, enabling automated workflows. "She'll triage alerts, detect anomalies, and execute playbook-based responses to contain threats before they spread."

Lila leaned closer, watching the transformation of their security posture in real-time. "You know their system better than their own techs."

"Not really, I'm just a nerd." Jack's lips quirked into a half-smile as he finalized the configuration. "But Charlotte can stop breakout attacks in seconds, giving your team more time to focus on complex threats."

With a final click, the system status indicator shifted from amber to green. Charlotte AI went live across Malaysia's government networks, immediately beginning to analyze the millions of security events flowing through the system.

Lila watched the activation metrics climb across the screen, her eyes widening slightly. "Jack, that's hot."

The words hung in the air between them. Jack felt heat rise to his face as he momentarily misinterpreted her comment. Their eyes met briefly, and he noticed a similar flush spreading across Lila's cheeks.

She cleared her throat. "I mean, the capability is impressive."

"Right. Of course." Jack nodded, returning his attention to the screen where Charlotte was already identifying patterns in the data. "Let's see what she finds."

They leaned forward together, professionals once more, united in their focus on the digital battlefield unfolding before them.

"Lila, it is strange to me that your CrowdStrike techs would not have configured this to begin with. Are they on site? Would be good to chat with them."

Chapter 10: Defensive Matrix

Day 7, 0900 Hours | NACSA War Room

Jack leaned back in his chair, the soft hum of the air conditioning a faint backdrop to the storm brewing in the world beyond Kuala Lumpur. There is nothing like the feeling of earning your keep.

In his meetings with the National Cybersecurity Agency, he had been impressed by their progress to date, but many others in government would rather the NACSA would just go away and stop pestering them.

As he reviewed network maps and threat assessments, Jack's mind raced with potential threat actors and the MSS's next moves. He imagined a vast web of adversaries weaving through the Malaysian system, each entry point a vulnerability ripe for exploitation. Grounded in that grim reality, he felt the weight of responsibility pressing down on him, an awareness that transcended his role as a consultant. He was now an essential player in an escalating geopolitical tug-of-war, his actions pivotal in the defense of an entire nation.

"Alright, let's keep this moving," Jack asserted, the urgency palpable in his clipped tone. He stood before a war room filled with NACSA analysts, their screens aglow with the flickering remnants of breached security protocols and malicious intrusions.

"We're not just identifying problems; we need to act now. These threats won't wait for us to catch up."

It was time for decisive action, and Jack knew that each maneuver had to be bold yet calculated. His next move would target the foundation of adversary command and control infrastructure. "There are no silver bullets in cybersecurity," Jack had driven into their heads on day one, "but changing your DNS architecture to use a DNS firewall will screw up MSS implants so much it will take them days to refactor and maybe weeks or months to regain access."

His DNS overhaul would be swift and comprehensive; he directed a shifting of the entire DNS structure of government systems, reinforcing it by directing that all government owned and operated networks use the Quad9 DNS system by changing DNS entries to 9.9.9.9. This added the protection of a massive global infrastructure for routing that essentially acted like a massive firewall, only letting valid sites communicate while making it much harder on high-end threat actors like the MSS. Within minutes, trojans that had established backdoor channels found themselves cut off, unable to communicate, a significant delay for any adversary hoping to exploit those pathways. The command and control capabilities of adversary ransomware were likewise crushed, at least for the time being.

But he wasn't done yet. The next step required a bit more finesse, and a fair share of grit. The Malaysian government had already been investing in Cloud and AI infrastructure, with over 450,000 Google Workspace users.

Jack paced the length of the conference room, his footsteps echoing against the polished floor. The NACSA senior staff watched him with varying expressions of interest and skepticism as he gestured toward the projection screen displaying migration statistics.

"This isn't just about better spam filters," Jack said, his voice carrying the weight of urgency. "Every government email account still on your legacy systems is a potential entry point for MSS operations. Google's infrastructure gives you enterprise-grade protection that would take years to build in-house."

Dr. Farid Rahman leaned forward, fingers steepled. "We already have a significant commitment to Google Workspace. You're proposing we triple that number in, what timeframe exactly?"

"Seventy-two hours," Jack replied without hesitation. "Every hour counts."

A murmur rippled through the room. The IT Director shook his head. "Impossible. The procurement process alone would…"

"The contract framework already exists," Jack interrupted. "You just need to scale it. I've drafted the emergency authorization for Dr. Rahman's signature." He slid a document across the table. "This isn't about convenience; it's about survival."

Jack pointed to incidents on the conference room screen. "You know they'll keep coming. Google's threat intelligence network processes billions of security events daily. They see attacks before they even reach your perimeter." He turned to face the room. "Think about it, the MSS has to retool their entire approach for each account we migrate. It's death by a thousand cuts for their operation."

"The political fallout..." began the Deputy Director.

"Will be nothing compared to the fallout of a successful attack," Jack finished. "Every account we migrate buys us time and bleeds their resources."

Dr. Rahman studied Jack's face, measuring his conviction. "You truly believe this is critical?"

"I wouldn't be pushing this hard if I didn't," Jack replied. "The MSS is coming, and they're bringing everything they have. We need to change the battlefield before they arrive."

Rahman nodded slowly. "Very well. Initiate the migration protocol. Priority to critical departments, Defense, Finance, Foreign Affairs."

Jack exhaled. "And Energy. The power grid administrators need to be first."

"Agreed," Rahman said, signing the authorization. "Lila, coordinate with the migration team. I want progress reports."

As the meeting dispersed, Jack caught Lila's eye. "Thank you for backing me up."

She offered a tired smile. "Let's just hope it works."

Jack watched the team mobilize with renewed purpose. "It will slow them down. And right now, time is the most valuable resource we have."

Things are starting to move. The new CrowdStrike configurations, the DNS shift, convincing them to rely more on Google workspace, these are all going to make it harder on the MSS. But Jack is not done yet.

Jack ordered a thousand-seat license for Blackwire Labs, a new AI enabled system that has the wisdom of a thousand CISOs and all the knowledge of cyber defense and IT configuration required to secure systems, would dramatically and rapidly up skill the talents of every IT and security professional involved, shifting the very equation of their defense. Having access to Blackwire Labs meant anyone had the knowledge to execute an improvement plan over their parts of cyberspace.

Many other changes would take weeks or even months to finalize. Halcyon ransomware defense was in the process of being installed, but the nationwide deployment was a considerable undertaking. NACSA already owned Splunk, but few had the knowledge to really make use of it (another reason they needed Blackwire Labs). VulnCheck, a great system for prioritizing and mitigating vulnerabilities based on real threats, was also in limited use but over the next few months would be leveraged by every organization in government.

With adrenaline still coursing through his veins, Jack reflected on the whirlwind of changes he had catalyzed in merely three days. "A moving target is harder to hit" his old mentor Rich Haver had always told him. Let's hope these moves make MSS realize the cost of screwing with smaller nations.

As the conference room emptied, Lila stayed behind.

"I really like working with you Jack, you are a force for positive change, It feels like we've finally turned a corner."

Jack nodded, aware that the threat will never go away, it always morphs and comes back. In cyberspace, adversaries always surprise.

In that moment, he understood that he was no longer a mere consultant; the stakes were personal, with the weight of nations pressing heavily upon his shoulders. The world was evolving, the threats sharpening, and Jack Tanner was resolutely entrenched in the battle that was just getting started.

* * *

Jack stepped back from the massive display, surveying the network map that dominated the NACSA war room. Clusters of green nodes pulsed across the digital landscape, representing government systems now securely reporting to their monitoring infrastructure. The Splunk dashboards along the adjacent wall showed steadily improving metrics, attack surface reduction, threat detection times dropping from days to minutes, and malicious traffic plummeting.

"We've reclaimed control of eighty-seven percent of critical infrastructure," Lila said, pride evident in her voice. "That's unprecedented progress in such a short timeframe."

A spontaneous round of applause broke out among the exhausted analysts and engineers. Three days of relentless work had yielded tangible results. Some exchanged high-fives while others simply closed their eyes in momentary relief.

Jack acknowledged their celebration with a nod but kept his focus locked on the display. Among the sea of green, a single red node pulsed ominously.

"What about this one?" Jack pointed to the crimson hexagon labeled 'Ministry of Energy.' "Why hasn't this system checked in with our new monitoring protocols?"

The jubilation in the room faded. Technicians exchanged glances, their expressions shifting from triumph to uncertainty.

A junior engineer, Razak, according to his ID badge, cleared his throat. "We were told to leave it off the sweep, sir."

Jack turned slowly, his eyes narrowing. "By who?"

The silence that followed was deafening. Razak stared at his shoes while others suddenly found their keyboards fascinating.

"I asked a question," Jack said, his voice dangerously quiet. "Who authorized excluding a critical infrastructure node from our security overhaul?"

Lila stepped closer, her expression darkening. "Answer him, Razak."

"It came through channels," the young engineer finally muttered. "Official directive. Said the Ministry was handling their own security upgrade and didn't want interference."

Jack locked eyes with Lila, an unspoken understanding passing between them. Someone with authority had deliberately carved out a blind spot in their defenses, a perfect insertion point for an attack.

"Get me everything you have on the Ministry's network architecture," Jack said. "And find out who ordered that directive."

As the team scrambled to action, Jack turned back to the map, studying the solitary red node. It wasn't just a technical anomaly; it was evidence of something far more troubling. The enemy wasn't just in their systems. They had collaborators inside the government.

* * *

Jack's fingers flew across the keyboard, diving into the Splunk logs with methodical precision. The deeper he went, the more his frown deepened. Something wasn't right with the DNS configuration patterns.

"This doesn't make sense," he muttered, enlarging a section of the dashboard. "Three government departments switched away from Quad9 DNS in the last six hours. That's in direct violation of the hardening protocol we established."

Lila leaned over his shoulder, her breath catching as she processed the implications. "The Transport Authority, Water Management, and…" she paused, "the National Power Grid."

"Critical infrastructure," Jack said, his voice tight. "Someone's deliberately removing our DNS protections."

* * *

The tense atmosphere in the conference room was broken by the sound of the door slamming open. Deputy Minister Rahman strode in, his normally composed demeanor replaced with barely contained fury.

"This is getting out of hand," he announced, tossing a tablet onto the conference table. "And I'm not angry at you, Jack. I'm furious with my own colleagues who still refuse to see what's happening."

Jack raised an eyebrow. "What's changed?"

"The Minister of Communications just called me," Rahman said, loosening his tie with an aggressive tug. "Apparently, several cabinet members are pressuring him to rein us in. They're saying NACSA is, and I quote, 'creating public panic when we are not at war.'"

Jack's laugh was cold and humorless. "This is pre-kinetic warfare, Deputy Minister. They'll understand it's wartime when the water stops flowing and the lights go out."

Lila swiped through the tablet Rahman had tossed down. Her eyes widened. "Sir, these social media posts..."

"Started appearing three hours ago," Rahman finished for her. "A coordinated campaign by local influencers claiming NACSA has fallen under foreign influence. The same influencers who mysteriously receive free Huawei phones and sponsored trips to Shenzhen."

Jack studied the screen, recognizing the hallmarks of a professional disinformation operation. The messaging was calibrated perfectly, patriotic enough to appeal to Malaysian pride while undermining trust in their cybersecurity efforts.

"They're attacking us on two fronts," Jack said. "Technical and informational."

Rahman pinched the bridge of his nose. "Which brings me to my next point." He turned to Lila. "From now on, all directives from this war room come from you or me. No connection to Jack whatsoever."

Lila frowned. "Sir?"

"You and me, we take credit for Jack's work. All of it. I know that's not your style, but it's more critical than ever."

Jack understood immediately. "Smart move. They're trying to paint me as a foreign agent of influence."

"Precisely," Rahman said. "We love having you here, Jack, but this operation is dead if my enemies in government can label our efforts as American interference. They'd rather let the country burn than admit we needed outside help."

Jack nodded grimly. The battle had expanded beyond code and networks, now they were fighting for narrative control. And in this new theater of war, he would have to become invisible.

* * *

1600 Hours | NACSA War Room

Jack paced the length of the war room, his mind calculating multiple scenarios simultaneously. He stopped abruptly and turned to face Lila and Rahman.

"We need to discuss Amina."

Lila's expression tightened. "The network administrator? She called in sick this morning."

"That's the problem." Jack's voice dropped an octave. "Yesterday she had full access to our remediation plans. Today she's unreachable during the most critical phase of our operation."

Rahman shifted uncomfortably. "Amina has been with us for three years. Impeccable record."

"And I hope she's genuinely ill," Jack said, his tone making it clear he believed otherwise. "But in situations like this, we have to assume the worst, that she's been compromised."

Lila's eyes widened as the implication sank in. "You think they got to her?"

"I think we can't afford to rule it out." Jack placed both palms on the table, leaning forward. "Lila, I need you to contact the police. Have them perform a welfare check. If she's genuinely sick, we'll send flowers. If she's not home..."

The unfinished sentence hung in the air.

"What about her systems?" Rahman asked.

"Lock them down immediately," Jack replied. "Pull all access logs for the past two weeks. I want to know every file she opened, every system she accessed, and especially anything she downloaded or transferred. Check email logs, USB ports, printer activity, everything."

Lila was already typing commands into her terminal. "I'm on it."

"And get someone to compile a comprehensive summary of all information she had access to," Jack continued. "Assume everything she could reach has been compromised. We need to know exactly what secrets might be in enemy hands."

Rahman nodded grimly. "I'll assign two analysts to that task."

Jack straightened up, his expression hardening. "One more thing, whoever does this needs to be someone we trust implicitly. If we're dealing with an insider threat, we can't risk bringing more compromised personnel into the loop."

The room fell silent as the gravity of the situation settled over them. They weren't just fighting external enemies anymore; the threat had potentially penetrated their inner circle.

"If Amina has been turned," Jack said quietly, "then our timeline just accelerated dramatically. Whatever they're planning could happen within hours, not days."

Chapter 11: Enforcement Protocol

Day 7, 1300 Hours | Hibiscus Pavilion

The conference room in the Hibiscus Pavilion hummed with the soft whir of air conditioning and the barely audible electronic sweep for listening devices. Li Jianhong sat perfectly still at the polished teak table, his tailored charcoal suit a stark contrast to the utilitarian furnishings of the MPS facility. He examined his manicured nails while waiting for Zhang Wei to arrive. He knew Zhang was keeping him waiting as a power play.

Zhang, dressed in a navy-blue Mao suit that seemed deliberately old-fashioned, finally took his seat across from Li.

"The Minister appreciates your prompt response to our invitation," Zhang said, his Mandarin crisp with northern cadences. "Recent developments require coordination between our services."

Li's smile didn't reach his eyes. "Of course. Though I was surprised to receive such an urgent summons after we just met."

Zhang tapped the tablet, bringing up surveillance photos of Jack Tanner entering the Ritz. "The American continues his provocations. My people have established complete coverage of his movements for the last four days, shown here entering the Ritz." He swiped to reveal more images. "And at BookXcess during his signing event. And at the University lecture hall. And here entering the NACSA, where he has been working to change their security posture."

"Impressive street-level work," Li acknowledged with practiced diplomacy. "Though hardly needed and not at all comprehensive."

Zhang's jaw tightened. "We have assets among the hotel staff, as well as in attendance at the bookstore, and university. All loyal Chinese nationals who understand their duty to the motherland."

"And you think I would not? And yet you missed the fact that the CIA had both an agent and a protection team in his hotel?" Li said, producing his own phone and displaying a crystal-clear image of Tanner making obvious glances to CIA operatives in the bar.

Zhang's nostrils flared. "Your so-called intelligence lacks context."

"Show me what context you gathered from your hotel maids and bellhops?"

"The Ministry of Public Security doesn't need lessons in surveillance from desk officers," Zhang snapped, color rising in his face. "While you cultivate expensive assets and generate pretty reports, my people are enforcing Party discipline on the ground."

The room fell silent except for Zhang's controlled breathing. A young aide hovering near the door stared fixedly at his tablet, pretending not to witness the confrontation.

"The Party doesn't benefit from our division," Li continued. "Your ground-level surveillance complements our strategic intelligence. But let's be clear, your mandate is domestic security extended abroad. Mine is foreign intelligence acquisition and action to further our interests here."

"The distinction blurs when foreigners threaten our sovereignty," Zhang replied. "The Ministry of Public Security will enforce Party mandates everywhere."

Li raised an eyebrow. "An admirable ambition. Though perhaps premature given your current capabilities."

Zhang's eyes narrowed. "You MSS officers think your university degrees and foreign languages make you superior. But when action is required, when Tanner's provocation demands response, it will be my officers who deliver justice."

"And what form will this 'justice' take?" Li asked, his voice suddenly sharp. "Another embarrassing incident that undermines years of careful positioning? The Chairman has been very clear about operational parameters."

"The Chairman understands the need for direct action against those who slander our nation," Zhang retorted. "Tanner's book tour is an assault on China's dignity."

Li sighed and stood, straightening his suit jacket. "We will continue monitoring Tanner through our established channels. Your people should focus on the Chinese nationals in his orbit, the hotel staff, the local business contacts. But any action against Tanner himself requires joint approval."

"The MPS doesn't need permission to protect China's interests," Zhang said, remaining seated as if to assert dominance in his own facility.

Li smiled thinly. "Then I look forward to explaining to the Central Committee why two state security organs are working at cross-purposes in a sensitive foreign operation." He moved toward the door. "Send your surveillance reports to my office. We'll incorporate them into our comprehensive assessment."

Zhang rose slowly. "This isn't Beijing, Comrade Li. In the field, practical results matter more than political maneuvering."

"Indeed," Li replied, pausing at the threshold. "Which is why I've been tracking Tanner's every move and have a source in the NACSA who will ensure he does not succeed there. Have your people back off, would not want to spook him."

He left Zhang rigid sitting the conference table, the younger aide carefully avoiding his superior's gaze as the door clicked shut behind the MSS officer.

* * *

1400 Hours | Hibiscus Pavilion

Zhang burst from the conference room, the door slamming against the wall. His operations center fell silent as a dozen analysts froze at their workstations. The rage radiating from him cleared a path as effectively as any shouted command.

"Liu!" Zhang barked at his deputy. "Show me everything we have on the redhead."

Liu Jianyu tapped frantically at his keyboard, pulling up grainy surveillance photos of the woman who'd been seen around Tanner. "Limited visual data, sir. She appeared at the university lecture and again near the hotel. Facial recognition is inconclusive…"

Zhang slammed his fist on the desk. "Inconclusive? She's CIA! Li's people identified her immediately while you wasted time cataloging hotel maids!"

"Sir, we prioritized according to…"

"According to obsolete protocols!" Zhang's voice dropped to a dangerous whisper. "And the men with her? The muscle handlers watching Tanner's back?"

Liu swallowed. "We… assumed they were private security for his book tour."

The silence in the operations center deepened. Analysts stared fixedly at their screens, trying to become invisible.

"The MSS makes us look like amateurs in our own jurisdiction," Zhang said, his calm tone more terrifying than his earlier outburst. "This cannot stand."

He straightened his jacket and surveyed the room. Decades of discipline kept his expression neutral, but his eyes burned with humiliation transformed to resolve.

Liu glanced nervously around the room. "Sir, should we coordinate with Beijing? Or with Li's team?"

Zhang's smile was thin as a paper cut. "Minister Wang expects results, not excuses. We won't touch the American directly, that would create an international incident." He traced his finger across the monitor displaying Tanner's Malaysian contacts. "But we'll burn his local allies. Make it clear that friendship with anti-China elements carries consequences."

"The cybersecurity agency staff?" Liu asked.

"Start with them. Find their vulnerabilities. Everyone has something to hide." Zhang turned toward his private office. "And Liu, ensure our operational security is flawless. When Li discovers what happened, I want him to recognize our superiority, not trace it back to us."

Liu nodded, already mentally cataloging potential targets. "It will be done, sir."

"See that it is," Zhang said. "The Ministry of Public Security does not require permission to defend China's dignity."

* * *

1400 Hours | The Seraya

Li drove his Gloss black BMW 740Li through Kuala Lumpur's never-ending traffic to the Seraya. He spent the ride thinking to himself, mentally cataloging Zhang's predictable reactions to their meeting. By now, the MPS would be scrambling to salvage their pride, exactly as planned.

The private elevator whisked him to the sixty-fifth floor, where his operations team waited in the secure conference room. Six analysts and three field operatives stood as he entered, their postures stiffening with his arrival.

"Zhang took the bait," Li announced, removing his jacket. "He'll now waste resources trying to outmaneuver us rather than focusing on the actual operation."

Colonel Huang, Li's deputy, nodded appreciatively. "And our surveillance targets?"

"Stop all coverage on Tanner," Li said, moving to the digital map of Kuala Lumpur displayed on the wall screen. "He must go about his day normally tomorrow if we are to succeed in eliminating both him and the NACSA at the same time and we do not want to risk spooking him. Drop Fiona too. We don't care about his handler either now."

He turned to face the room, his expression hardening. "Contact the Three Immortals. Tell them to throttle back the network probes and lay low for a bit."

The senior tech analyst looked up, confusion evident. "Sir, we're making significant penetration…"

"Precisely," Li cut him off. "Let them think their countermeasures are working. We want the Americans to believe they've won, for now, we will bring them back full speed soon."

Understanding dawned across the faces in the room.

"Beijing has authorized the full operation," Li continued. "Eliminating the CIA's Tanner and NACSA prior to the main thrust will ensure success."

Colonel Huang smiled thinly, restating Chairman Mao's guidance: "The enemy tires, we attack. The enemy retreats, we pursue."

"Indeed," Li agreed, pouring himself tea from a porcelain set. "The entire CIA operation will need to regroup and reassess after we take out one of their non-official cover operations."

* * *

1900 Hours | Harmony Path Outreach Center, KL

The faint scent of sandalwood mingled with the antiseptic tang of cleaning chemicals inside the Harmony Path Outreach Center, a narrow second-floor suite in a tired-looking commercial strip in Kuala Lumpur. Outside, its weathered red-and-gold sign read *Haiyun Overseas Friendship Center* in warm, cheerful script. Inside, it was all cold calculation.

Zhang Wei stood alone in the operations room, where soft blue light from wall-mounted monitors bathed the floor in shifting hues. Surveillance feeds cycled across the screens: lobby angles, street cams, and hidden views of Chinese-owned retail outlets across Kuala Lumpur. The whir of rack-mounted servers filled the air beneath the occasional creak of footsteps from the noodle shop below.

He held the folded *New Straits Times* in one hand, eyes scanning the brief obituary tucked in the local section. *"Veteran Reporter Dies in Highway Collision."* Azman bin Yusof. Late-night crash. No witnesses. Police investigation ongoing. Zhang tossed the paper onto a side table without ceremony.

"Unfortunate for him," he said aloud, his voice low and even. Liu, standing by the door in civilian clothes, gave a slight nod.

"He'd just filed a public records request about the East Coast Rail Link," Zhang added.

"Traffic accidents are common in Kuala Lumpur," Liu replied dutifully.

"Indeed they are," Zhang murmured, turning his attention to the one-way glass that overlooked the reception chamber.

Three Chinese businessmen sat rigidly on low plastic chairs, each glued to their phone, pretending not to study the others. The sterile white walls and flickering overhead light offered little comfort.

"Are our guests comfortable?" Zhang asked without turning.

"They've been waiting for forty minutes, as instructed," Liu confirmed.

"Good. Anxiety improves memory retention."

Zhang gestured toward the nearest screen, where facial recognition overlays tracked the microexpressions of the men. Zhao Mingyu, the factory owner from Penang, looked pale. His knuckles whitened as he tapped rhythmically on his knee. Next to him, Wei of the port logistics firm kept glancing at the CCTV camera in the corner. Huang, the restaurateur, sat unnervingly still.

"Bring Mingyu to the conference room first," Zhang said.

Liu moved to comply but paused as Zhang added: "And remind him of his daughter's scholarship at Beijing Normal University. Kindly."

Zhang's eyes didn't leave the screen. He watched Zhao flinch when Liu appeared at the doorway and beckoned.

He sipped his tea, then muttered in Mandarin: "*Kill one, warn a hundred.*"

Chapter 12: Insurgent Dawn

Day 8, 0900 Hours | MPS Hibiscus Pavilion HQ

The observation room hummed with the rhythmic drone of cooling fans and data processors. Rows of black server racks lined the walls, their tiny LED lights blinking in hypnotic patterns, green, amber, red, the digital pulse of the Ministry of Public Security's Malaysian operations.

Analyst Mei Ling sat hunched before three curved monitors, her face bathed in their cold blue glow. Twenty-six years old and already developing the perpetual squint of someone who spent too many hours studying digital breadcrumbs. Her small desk was spartan, a half-empty cup of cooling tea, a notebook filled with precise Mandarin characters, and a framed photo of her parents back in Chengdu.

The facial recognition algorithm had flagged something. A pattern emerging from the noise.

"Curious," she murmured, fingers flying across her keyboard.

The center screen displayed surveillance photos from across Kuala Lumpur, street cameras, a restaurant, coffee shops, and NACSA. Each image showed the same two people: Jack Tanner, the American naval intelligence officer turned author, and a Malaysian woman with government credentials. They were even seen leaving NACSA together.

Mei's algorithms had identified the woman as Lila Tan, Deputy Director of Malaysia's National Cybersecurity Agency.

"Obviously his lead contact at NACSA," Mei whispered to herself. "They are always together."

She pulled up a second data stream, telecommunications metadata harvested from Malaysian cell towers. The Ministry did not need to plant backdoors to get this feed, it was coming from a built in "maintenance" port that comes standard with all PRC supplied cell equipment. She found what she suspected, a strong correlation in time and space between Tanner and Tan.

Mei tabbed through timestamps, correlating the digital exchanges with the physical meetings. A clear operational pattern was forming.

"Working late again, Mei Ling ?"

Zhang's voice startled her. The director of MPS operations in Malaysia stood in the doorway, his suit still crisp despite the late hour. His face betrayed nothing, but his eyes cataloged everything on her screens.

Mei stood quickly, a reflexive gesture of respect. "Director Zhang. I was following the American surveillance directive."

Zhang approached, hands clasped behind his back. "Show me."

Mei's fingers danced across the keyboard, bringing up the timeline she'd constructed. "We know Tanner has been helping NACSA. We now know his primary point of contact. He has a working relationship with Lila Tan at NACSA. Their location patterns suggest extensive operational coordination."

Zhang leaned closer, eyes narrowing as he absorbed the intelligence.

"Here," Mei continued, highlighting a sequence of data points.

"Good work. Perhaps useful." Zhang observed, his voice measured.

"Yes, Director. And there's more." Mei pulled up another screen. "Yesterday, Tan visited four different government ministries after meeting with Tanner. This is unusual. Her historical pattern is rare visits to other agencies."

Zhang straightened, the implications crystallizing. "He's not just giving lectures. He's hardening their systems against us."

"It appears so, sir." Mei hesitated, then added, "Should I notify our MSS counterparts? This could impact their operations."

Zhang's expression hardened almost imperceptibly. "No. The MSS operatives have their own agenda. They've kept us in the dark about their activities with Harapan Baru. We'll return the favor... for now."

He studied the surveillance photos, focusing on Lila Tan. "Implement a full surveillance package on Tan. Physical tail, telecommunications intercept, pattern-of-life analysis. I want to know everywhere she goes, everyone she speaks with."

"And Tanner, sir?"

"Continue monitoring, but at a distance, track his cell. He's too experienced, he'll spot a direct tail." Zhang's eyes never left the screen. "Tan is our access point. She'll lead us to whatever Tanner is planning."

Mei nodded, already typing commands to allocate resources.

"This stays within MPS channels," Zhang added, his voice dropping. "Classify it under domestic security protocols. That will keep it from MSS eyes without raising suspicions."

"Understood, Director."

Zhang turned to leave, then paused. "Good work, Mei. The Party values thoroughness."

After Zhang departed, Mei sat back in her chair, the weight of the assignment settling on her shoulders. She pulled up Lila Tan's government ID photo, studying the woman's confident expression.

"What are you and the American planning?" she whispered to the image.

The server room's hum seemed to intensify as she began programming the surveillance algorithms. Outside the windowless room, Kuala Lumpur continued its nightly rhythm, unaware of the invisible threads of surveillance tightening around its citizens.

Mei took a sip of her cold tea and began the meticulous work of tracking another human being's existence, one digital footprint at a time.

* * *

1300 Hours | Dragon Falls Compound

Dragon Falls cast its shadow over the makeshift compound, the waterfall's constant roar providing natural sound cover for Harapan Baru operations. Mist rose perpetually from where water crashed against ancient stone, creating a microclimate of perpetual dampness that clung to everything- weapons, equipment, skin. The cascade had carved a deep pool at its base, the water an unnatural emerald green from minerals leached from Mount Benom's core.

A single dirt road led to the compound. Dense jungle was all around the main clearing, a natural fortress of tangled vines and centuries-old hardwoods that swallowed sound and obscured sight lines.

The Harapan Baru compound was a study in tactical pragmatism, half-buried earthen bunkers reinforced with locally harvested timber formed the defensive core. These weren't amateur constructions but professional military emplacements, with interlocking fields of fire and reinforced roofing designed to withstand small arms and fragmentary ordinance.

Around this hardened center, a constellation of canvas tents and bamboo-framed shelters housed the group's support personnel, arranged in concentric rings that grew more temporary toward the perimeter. The entire layout spoke of military minds at work, Chinese doctrine adapted to Malaysian jungle warfare.

Despite the primitive surroundings, Dragon Falls hummed with technology. Solar panels, carefully concealed beneath camouflage netting, powered a sophisticated communications array. Satellite uplinks enabled comms with the outside world.

The command center, housed in the largest bunker, featured ruggedized tablets and Chinese-manufactured drone control systems. Operators trained on the PRC supplied Black Lantern surveillance units and the more lethal JY-3000 quadrotors hidden in caches throughout the jungle.

Amir Hashim stood at a large wooden stage in the clearing. In front of him the entire cadre at the camp was gathered. His presence was magnetic, drawing in the hardened insurgents who formed the inner circle of Harapan Baru, each marked by the scars of conflict and the fervor of unyielding belief. Rigid anticipation filled the air, a tension that crackled like static before a storm.

"Brothers," Amir began, his voice resonating over the sound of the falls, "the future of Malaysia is in our hands."

His piercing eyes, sharp as eagle's talons, scanned the gathering, locking on each man, kindling the flames of revolutionary zeal. He spoke of sovereignty, of freedom, painting a vivid picture of a Malaysia liberated from foreign manipulation, a vision that came dangerously close to tyranny itself. The fire in his rhetoric ignited a spark in the hearts of his followers, who hung on his every word, their loyalty tempered by blood and unspeakable deeds.

Yet within Amir's depths lay a ruthless ambition, a willingness to draw lines that blurred the distinctions between liberation and violence. He believed in force as the answer, in radical action as the path to the ideal Malaysia, even if it meant gripping the reins of power through brutality. His followers listened, entranced, as he enumerated the enemies that sought to undermine their dream, his words flowing like the furious water outside.

Before the passionate fervor could reach its crescendo, four armed insurgents carried a man to the stage, bound and gagged with fear in his eyes. Murmurs rippled through the circle of insurgents.

Amir stepped forward, approaching the tortured man, his shadow swallowing the fragile flicker of hope that flickered within the captive's gaze. "Do you wish to renounce your allegiance to Harapan Baru?" he asked, voice low yet chilling. "Do you choose to betray us?"

Amir ripped off his gag. He wanted his victim's screams to carry.

The man's throat tightened, his words escaping in jagged breaths, "Amir, please... I..."

Amir raised a hand, silencing the plea with a stern gesture. "You forget that loyalty is a currency, my friend. It demands a price." With a nod from Amir, men stepped forward, cloaked in the shadows of brutality, preparing to enforce a lesson that would resonate throughout the organization.

As they worked with ruthless efficiency, the rhythmic sounds of violence swallowed the clearing, piercing through the very core of the insurgency's ideals. The tortured screams mingled with the cascade of the waterfall, creating a macabre harmony, a reminder of what was required to maintain the bonds of loyalty. Amir watched without flinching, a cold fire burning in his chest, feeling the admiration of his inner circle grow with each calculated act of cruelty.

The horror somehow galvanized the insurgents; a sense of unity emerged from the brutality. They drew energy from it, their commitment intensifying, fueled by fear and fervor alike. Amir stood tall, embodying the embodiment of strict, unyielding power whose iron grip would elevate Malaysia, even as it crushed dissent.

As Amir dismissed the gathering, he and his top lieutenants retreated to the command bunker and sat around a makeshift table, grim-faced and emboldened. Maps and diagrams sprawled across the surface, a few digital screens glimmering with data, revealing insights into the upcoming operations they had meticulously crafted.

"This is our moment," Amir declared, striking the table with a fist. "With these technologies and our weapons caches in the city, we will disrupt their systems, target their institutions, and strike with precision. The Malaysians in the cities will rise; we will be their beacon. They will come to us, and they will join our cause!"

A low murmur swept through the group, ideas mingling with ambition as plots unfurled like smoke in a windless void. In that moment, the harsh reality of their insurgency came alive, intertwining age-old tactics with modern warfare, a convergence that would yield grave consequences, not only for their movement but for the future of Malaysia.

As the insurgents strategized, adrenaline coursing through their veins, the echoes of their collective dark ambition merged with the churning power of Dragon Falls outside. Amir, reshaped by cruelty and ambition's intoxicating embrace, envisioned a future where the insurgency's grip was unyielding, echoing history's refrain: liberation through annihilation.

Tonight, under the waterfall's watchful gaze, darkness encroached and loomed ever closer, as ideology and betrayal lurked in the shadowy corners of the deepening narrative. The path they trudged would demand sacrifices, but for Amir, that price was already abundantly clear. The stakes had never been higher, and the outcome was still shrouded in the mystique of blood-soaked ideals and boundless ambition.

* * *

1400 Hours | Harapan Baru Jungle Training Range

The jungle canopy filtered the afternoon sun into dappled patterns across the training compound. Two hundred meters downstream from Dragon Falls, the constant rush of water provided natural sound cover for the sharp reports of AK-47s. Sweat-soaked teenagers lined the firing range in three staggered rows, their faces set with determination as they squeezed off rounds at human-shaped targets.

Sixteen-year-old Nazri adjusted his stance, remembering to lean into the rifle's recoil as Instructor had taught. Above him, a small quadcopter hovered, its camera eye tracking his every movement. The drone was part of the ubiquitous observation network that surrounded the compound, black mechanical insects that never blinked, never tired.

"Cease fire! Magazines down!" The instructor's voice cut through the gunfire. The teenagers lowered their weapons in unison, a choreography born of repetition and fear. Kamal, a former Malaysian Army sergeant with a scar bisecting his left eyebrow, stalked between the rows of young recruits. "You're still anticipating the recoil, Nazri. It makes you flinch before you pull the trigger."

"Yes, sir. I'll correct it." Nazri's voice was steady despite the humiliation.

In the observation hut twenty meters back from the range, a Chinese technician in civilian clothes monitored six screens displaying drone feeds. Each recruit's performance metrics scrolled beside their image, accuracy ratings, reaction times, and stress indicators detected through facial analysis. The system, officially called "Performance Enhancement Protocol" but referred to by the instructors as "the Sorter," had been implemented three months ago. No one mentioned it came from MSS advisors.

"Nazri has shown exceptional tactical awareness," the technician noted to his Malaysian counterpart. "But his accuracy must improve."

The Malaysian nodded, making a notation on his tablet.

A commotion at the edge of the training ground drew their attention. Amir had arrived, flanked by two security personnel. The firing range immediately fell silent as the young recruits recognized their leader.

Amir moved with purpose; his lean frame dressed not in military fatigues but in a simple black shirt and tactical pants. Unlike many insurgent leaders who affected military posturing, Amir cultivated the image of a teacher, a guide. It made his occasional displays of ruthlessness even more effective.

"Continue," he said to the instructor with a slight nod.

"Range is hot!" the instructor barked. "Second drill sequence, commence firing!"

As the crack of rifles resumed, Amir walked along the periphery, studying each young face with intensity. These weren't hardened fighters yet, they were students, laborers, sons of farmers and factory workers, and a few former soldiers who must unlearn what they had been taught for this different kind of fighting. The oldest couldn't be more than twenty, the youngest barely sixteen. Their eyes held that mix of fear and fervor that made them malleable.

Perfect.

After ten minutes, Amir raised his hand. The instructor immediately ordered a cease-fire.

"Gather," Amir called, his voice carrying across the compound.

The young recruits formed a semicircle around him, rifles pointed downward, faces expectant. Above them, the DJI drones adjusted position, capturing the moment from multiple angles. This too would be analyzed, who responded fastest to Amir's call, who positioned themselves closest to him, who maintained proper weapon discipline even during an unexpected interruption.

"You are not soldiers," Amir began, his voice measured but intense. "The Malaysian Army has soldiers. What does that army defend? Not you. Not your families. They defend shopping malls in Kuala Lumpur where foreigners spend more in a day than your parents earn in a month. They protect miners and loggers who drain our resources for American corporations."

He paced slowly, making eye contact with each recruit.

"You've been told that Malaysia is independent, prosperous, advancing. Look at your villages. Look at your homes. Where is this prosperity? It sits in offshore accounts of ministers who bow to Western banks and American investors."

A murmur of agreement rippled through the group. This wasn't new rhetoric, but Amir delivered it with a conviction that made it feel immediate, personal.

"The government calls us terrorists," he continued, his voice hardening. "Yet they terrorize with poverty. They terrorize with corruption. They terrorize by selling Malaysia piece by piece to foreign interests."

He stopped in front of Nazri, whose eyes widened at the sudden proximity to the legendary leader.

"Why are you here, young brother?"

Nazri swallowed. "For Malaysia, sir. For freedom."

"Freedom," Amir repeated, turning the word over like examining a strange coin. "What does freedom mean when our government is merely a puppet? We are not fighting for abstract ideals. We are fighting to cut the puppet's strings."

He addressed the entire group again, raising his voice.

"This is not a fight for your fathers. Their generation accepted the comfortable lie. This is for your sons. For the Malaysia they will inherit, either truly independent or forever colonized by foreign powers wearing business suits instead of military uniforms."

The drones circled overhead, capturing the fervor spreading across young faces. In the observation hut, the Chinese technician watched with clinical interest, making notes about which recruits showed the strongest emotional response to specific phrases.

"Tomorrow," Amir continued, "some of you will move to advanced training. Others will continue here. This is not a reflection of your worth but of your path. Harapan Baru needs fighters, yes, but also technicians, recruiters, intelligence gatherers. The blade that cuts the puppet's strings has many edges."

He nodded to the instructor, who resumed the endless training under the observation of the drone above.

Amir walked toward the observation hut, his expression shifting from inspirational leader to calculating strategist in the space of seconds. Inside, he nodded curtly to the Chinese technician before turning his attention to a separate monitor displaying real-time surveillance footage, not training simulations. On screen, a convoy of three Malaysian police vehicles moved along a rural road near Bentong.

"The facial recognition confirms," the Malaysian operator said. "Regional commander and his security detail. They've been conducting increased patrols in Bentong, no doubt looking for indications of our activities there."

"Shadow them, drone only, from long distance." Amir's voice was cold, analytical. "No action yet."

"The men are eager," the operator noted. "They've been training for weeks."

"Patience builds precision," Amir replied, watching the police vehicles disappear around a bend in the road. "Soon, they'll see the value of loyalty born in fire."

He turned away from the screen, his thoughts already moving to the next phase. The young recruits outside were just one component of a much larger machine, one whose architects remained carefully hidden behind layers of proxies and plausible deniability.

As Amir stepped back into the humid jungle air, the sound of Dragon Falls seemed to intensify, a constant reminder of the force that could be harnessed, directed, and unleashed when the moment was right.

* * *

1600 Hours | Dragon Falls Comms Tent

The communications tent at Dragon Falls stood apart from the main compound, its heavy canvas walls reinforced with radiation-dampening mesh. Inside, the humid Malaysian air fought against struggling air conditioners, creating a perpetual film of condensation on the array of encrypted satellite equipment. Amir paced the length of the tent, his normally composed demeanor fraying at the edges.

One radio is used only by Amir. The Yingtian-9 Secure Tactical Terminal is a ruggedized man-portable unit the size of a thick notebook, with retractable antenna, satcom dish harness and built in encryption mandated by the MSS.

Amir awaits a call, which will come from Li any minute.

Zain, his deputy and longtime friend, leans against the communications console. Unlike Amir's Western-style clothing, chosen deliberately to present a moderate face to the world, Zain wore traditional Malay garb, his weathered face a testament to years fighting in the jungle. "Does he call with another favor, another delay, or to give the go-order?"

"The MSS knows what they're doing," Amir said carefully. "Their resources have given us capabilities that moved our plans ahead by years."

"And what good is money when our people expect revolution?" Zain snapped. "They've rallied behind our promise to reclaim Malaysia's sovereignty. Now Beijing wants us to fight a tethered war, one that serves their strategic interests, not ours."

Amir stepped closer, lowering his voice despite the tent's security. "Be practical, Zain. Without their technology, without their money and intelligence, we're just another failed rebellion. They gave us the tools to bleed the machine."

"And the leash to control us," Zain shot back. He ran a hand through his short-cropped hair, eyes burning with intensity.

"Every day, I feel the noose tightening. Li presents himself as an ally, but the MSS sees us as nothing more than convenient pawns in their regional strategy, so why continue the relationship?"

Amir fell silent, staring at the maps of Malaysia pinned to the tent wall. Red markers indicated government installations, blue showed Harapan Baru's safe houses and training facilities. Green pins, the fewest in number, marked confirmed successes, places where they'd struck.

"Because we need them," he finally said, the words bitter on his tongue. "For now."

Their conversation was interrupted by the buzz of the Yingtian-9.

Amir received his orders and smartly replied "Consider it done."

As the transmission completed, Amir touched the small pendant he wore beneath his shirt, a gift from his father, who had died protesting government corruption years earlier. "For Malaysia," he whispered, "not for Beijing."

He then briefed Zain on the special request from Li. They must move one of next week's targets up to tomorrow morning. The Malaysian National Cybersecurity Agency will be destroyed after the workforce arrives in the morning.

Chapter 13: Critical Mass

Day 8, 1700 Hours | Ritz Rooftop Bar, Kuala Lumpur

The rooftop bar of Jack Tanner's hotel offered a stunning panorama of Kuala Lumpur, the city's skyline shimmering against the backdrop of an indigo sky. As the warm evening breeze rustled through the palm fronds, Jack leaned against the railing, sipping his drink while the sounds of laughter and clinking glasses drifted around him. Below, the city pulsed with life, a stark contrast to his own turbulent thoughts.

Jack reflected. The bookstore session went great, full of enthusiastic and curious people who Jack believed could make a difference. The University session seemed to go well at first but he was obviously set up by the counsellor from the PRC embassy. Fool me once…

Now, looming deadlines and a push to raise cyber defenses are his sole focus. There is nothing like working on a big task with a mission-focused team, especially when it involves a sizable consulting fee.

He checked his phone, feeling a knot form in his stomach as he saw the notifications. One stood out from the rest. A Signal message from an analyst friend warning of a new iPhone zero-day vulnerability that may have already been exploited by PRC associated organizations. The message advises to patch as soon as Apple pushes the upgrade.

"Jack," a voice pierced through his reverie. Lila Tan, his liaison at NACSA and a formidable cyber expert in her own right, stepped up beside him, her brow furrowed. "We need to talk."

He turned to her, noting the urgency in her tone. "What's going on?"

"A partner agency is confirming our prior assessments, in the strongest way. They are telling us that the cyber intrusions we are facing are part of a hostile government operation. They are notoriously famous for not telling us anything else. So it is not just that it fits our assumptions, but they have strong evidence that something big is coming."

Jack's expression hardened. When Lila said 'partner agency' she always meant their intelligence services. He asked, "What things do they say are being targeted?"

"This cyber infiltration," she replied, leaning closer, her intensity palpable. "They're targeting critical infrastructure, power grids, computers that manage water and sewer. And when they get into communication networks they just sit as far as we can tell, probably snooping but maybe getting ready to crash telecom. Worse case, what if they plan to execute simultaneous disruptions across multiple regions, like a Russia vs Cyber Ukraine attack?"

Jack furrowed his brow, a sinking feeling churning in his gut. "We have seen this movie before. Different actors but same intent."

"Exactly," Lila affirmed, her eyes bright with determination. "This is a potential disaster waiting to unfold."

Jack took a deep breath, struggling against the weight of his decision. "But Lila…" he hesitated, his resolve tightening. "I have two days left in the country. I'm scheduled to head back."

"Two days? Jack, you can't leave now. This is just the beginning!" She stepped closer, desperation creeping into her voice.

"I know it's critical, but I have commitments back home," he replied firmly, his decision solidifying. "I'll be available on Signal after I depart. We can coordinate; I'll support you from there."

"Please," she urged, her voice rising slightly above the ambiance of the bar. "This is too important. We need you here in this fight."

Jack shook his head, holding steady in his resolve. "Lila, if I stay, it could jeopardize everything. You've already seen how people are accusing you of being an American puppet: I really have no business staying longer than my commitment."

Her shoulders fell, frustration flashing across her face. "You're not just another expert, Jack. You're vital to this operation. Your experience... it could mean the difference between disaster and keeping the country safe."

He stepped closer to her, anchored by the weight of their shared purpose. "Look, I can be most effective from afar. I'm a seasoned operator, Lila. I know how to analyze and act from a distance. Trust me on this."

They shared a tense silence, the gravity of their situation hanging thick in the air. Jack could see her frustration transform into resolve, but he knew they had to walk this path on their own. Consultants accelerate, then lose their value quick.

"I'll make some calls and find out what I can. And will be in your offices tomorrow. Will keep moving out." He added, "But I'm sticking to the plan."

* * *

1800 Hours | USS Blue Ridge Intelligence Center

The intelligence center aboard the USS Blue Ridge pulsed with quiet intensity as Captain Mike Murphy strode through the secured double doors. The air was dim, lit mainly by the cool blue glow of monitors and the occasional red hue from standby lamps. Reflections from rows of softly lit consoles danced across faces and polished equipment, casting shifting patterns that barely disturbed the shadows. The hum of electronics and the muted voices of watchstanders filled the space, where every detail was bathed in an artificial twilight designed for clarity and focus.

Rows of analysts hunched over workstations, their faces illuminated by multiple screens displaying satellite imagery, vessel tracking data, and intercepted communications.

"Captain on deck," announced Lieutenant Commander Wilson, the watch officer.

"As you were," Murphy replied, waving off the formality. He moved directly to the central briefing area where a large digital map of the South China Sea dominated the main display. Red triangles representing PRC vessels clustered around disputed territories, their positions updated in real-time.

"Talk to me, Wilson. What's Beijing up to today?"

Wilson nodded to a petty officer who tapped several commands into her console. The main screen split to show multiple feeds alongside the tactical map.

"Sir, we're tracking significant PRC maritime activity across the entire AOR. The People's Liberation Army Navy Liaoning Carrier Strike Group remains operating 75 miles north of the Spratly Islands. Yesterday at 0940 local, a Vietnamese fishing vessel was rammed and sunk by a Chinese coast guard cutter near the Paracels." Wilson gestured to grainy footage showing the aftermath of the incident, fishermen clinging to debris as a white hull with distinctive red striping circled nearby.

Murphy's eyes narrowed. "Casualties?"

"Two fishermen missing, presumed drowned. Beijing's already claiming the Vietnamese were in their territorial waters," offered the petty officer.

"Of course they are," Murphy muttered. "And Hanoi's response?"

Wilson responded, "They move slow, will probably be a diplomatic protest filed with Beijing. They've dispatched two patrol boats to the area, but they're maintaining distance from PRC assets."

Murphy nodded, mentally cataloging the incident against the pattern of escalation he'd been tracking for months. "What else?"

"This morning at 0615, we have confirmed reports of Chinese coast guard vessels using water cannons against a Philippine research ship near Sandy Cay." Wilson brought up a clearer video feed showing powerful jets of water slamming into the side of a modest research vessel, its crew scrambling for safety as equipment tumbled across the deck.

"Jesus," Murphy breathed. "That's not deterrence, that's assault."

"Yes, sir. The Philippine vessel sustained damage to its communications array and navigation equipment. One researcher suffered a broken arm when he was knocked against a bulkhead."

Murphy stepped closer to the screen, studying the tactical situation. "Where's the nearest Philippine naval asset?"

"BRP *Antonio Luna* is approximately 30 nautical miles southeast, moving to intercept. ETA ninety minutes."

"And what are our assets in the vicinity?"

Lieutenant Kim, the collections manager, stepped forward with a tablet. "USS *Higgins* is conducting freedom of navigation operations 45 miles east of the incident. *Higgins* CO reports they're monitoring but maintaining their planned course."

Murphy nodded approvingly. "What about this flag planting business at Sandy Cay?"

Kim brought up a high-resolution image taken from a reconnaissance drone. It showed Chinese personnel in coast guard uniforms erecting a flagpole on a tiny, barely visible sandbar.

"Confirmed, sir. PRC coast guard personnel planted their flag at 0430 this morning. Philippines has already announced they're sending a team to remove it and plant their own."

"Perfect," Murphy said sarcastically. "Nothing says 'mature international relations' like a sandbox flag war." He turned to address the entire watch team. "People, this is exactly the kind of provocation Beijing wants. They're creating incidents that force responses, then claiming those responses justify further action."

He pointed to the screen showing construction activity on one of China's artificial islands. "Update on militarization?"

Wilson stepped forward. "Satellite imagery from yesterday shows completion of a new radar installation on Mischief Reef. Analysis suggests it's a JY-27A counter-stealth system. They've also expanded the runway on Fiery Cross Reef to accommodate H-6 bombers."

Murphy absorbed this information with a grim expression. "And our diplomatic dance continues. What's the latest on the joint exercises with the Philippines?"

"Beijing filed a formal diplomatic protest with State this morning," Wilson reported. "Standard language about 'provocative actions' and 'destabilizing the region.'"

"And the Army's Typhon missile deployment to the Philippines?"

"That's got them particularly agitated, sir," Wilson said, bringing up intercepts of diplomatic cables. "Based on talking points coming from PRC embassies in the region their intent is to characterize this as 'aggressive encirclement' and a 'direct threat to regional peace.'"

Murphy snorted. "Because nothing says 'peace' like ramming fishing boats and hosing down researchers."

He paced slowly in front of the main display, hands clasped behind his back. The room fell silent, analysts and officers watching him process the information. This was Murphy's strength, synthesizing disparate intelligence threads into a coherent strategic picture.

"Malaysia," he said finally. "That's where this is heading. All these incidents are creating noise while they prepare something bigger." He turned to Wilson. "What do we have on Harapan Baru activity?"

Wilson brought up a new set of displays showing network traffic analyses, financial transfers, and surveillance photos of suspected operatives.

"Sir, we're seeing unprecedented levels of support flowing from PRC-linked entities to Harapan Baru cells. Financial transfers through shell companies in Singapore and Macau have increased 300% in the past month."

"Any idea where they are located?"

"Negative," replied the watchstander. "At least not in U.S. systems."

"And the cyber picture?"

Lieutenant Park, the cyber intelligence specialist, stepped forward. "Captain, we're tracking increased reconnaissance activity against Malaysian government networks, particularly defense and law enforcement. No destructive attacks yet, but the pattern matches pre-attack preparation we've seen in previous PRC operations, I would assume like the Guam intrusions."

Mike saw the opportunity for a little mentoring. "I appreciate hearing your assumptions. But would be far better off if I heard your plan to collect data to form an assessment vice an assumption."

"I'll call the JIC at PACOM and get on it" replied the Lieutenant.

Murphy studied the data, his mind racing through implications and contingencies. The room remained silent, waiting for his assessment.

"This isn't just harassment or territorial posturing," he said finally. "Beijing is setting up a major destabilization operation in Malaysia. The South China Sea incidents are creating strategic distraction while they position Harapan Baru as their proxy force."

He turned to face his team, his expression resolute. "I want hourly updates on all PRC naval and coast guard movements. We need the INDOPACOM J2 on our side so we can push for increased SIGINT collection against area MSS communications networks, connect with Cybercom and make sure they are tracking the cyber situation and get anything they can on this. I'm going to call our defense attaché in Kuala Lumpur; we need to quietly brief the Malaysians on what's coming."

Murphy's gaze swept across the intelligence center, meeting the eyes of each officer and analyst. "This isn't just about rocks and reefs anymore, people. Beijing is escalating to hybrid warfare, and we need to be ready. Let's get ahead of this."

As the team dispersed to their stations with renewed purpose, Murphy remained at the central display, studying the constellation of red triangles spreading across the South China Sea like a virus. In his twenty-five years of naval service, he'd never seen such a coordinated campaign of aggression disguised as legitimate maritime activity.

"Wilson," he said quietly, "draft an assessment for PACOM J2. Title it 'Prelude to Storm: PRC Hybrid Warfare Escalation in Southeast Asia.' I'll review it in thirty minutes."

"Aye, Captain."

As Wilson moved away, Murphy allowed himself a moment of private contemplation. Intelligence is not about knowing everything; it's about knowing what matters and when it matters. Intelligence is about driving decisions. Now the pieces were falling into place, and clearly Malaysia stood at the center of Beijing's next move.

* * *

1900 Hours | U.S. Embassy KL

The marble-tiled hallway outside the ambassador's secure conference room gleamed under recessed lighting, its neutral-toned walls adorned with abstract art that no one ever really looked at. A subtle scent of old paper and wood polish hung in the air, the unmistakable fragrance of bureaucratic power. Security staff nodded as the group walked past, their expressions professionally blank.

Bill Franklin strode slightly ahead of the others, his pace calculated, shoulders squared beneath his tailored suit. At mid-fifties, the ODNI Senior Representative carried himself with the precise bearing of someone who believed his position commanded automatic respect.

"Remember, Sam," he said to the CIA Chief of Station, his voice modulated for maximum condescension, "I speak for the entire intelligence community here. This is not just Langley's corner."

Sam walked beside him, unfazed by his posturing. Her eyes scanned ahead like an operator walking into a denied area, cataloging details most would miss. Her dark blazer and slacks were practical rather than fashionable, and she moved with the fluid confidence of someone equally comfortable in embassy corridors or combat zones.

"Of course, Bill," she replied, her tone smooth, weaponized diplomacy. "We're all very happy to have your... top cover."

Colonel David Ramos remained a step behind them, silent as always. The Defense Attaché moved with the measured economy of his Delta Force background, eyes constantly scanning as if he were back in Fallujah rather than an embassy hallway. His expression remained unreadable, but he clocked everything.

As they approached the conference room, Franklin straightened his tie. "I've already briefed the ODNI on my assessment. We need to avoid hasty conclusions about Chinese involvement."

Sam didn't respond, but the slight tightening of her jaw spoke volumes.

The Marine guard at the door performed a final credential check before admitting them into the ambassador's briefing room. The space was deliberately austere, a large oak table surrounded by high-backed chairs, secure communications equipment discreetly positioned along one wall, and windows with specialized glass designed to defeat laser microphones.

Ambassador Elizabeth Cooper looked up from a folder, reading glasses perched low on her nose. Though politically appointed, Cooper had quickly proven herself sharper than most career diplomats expected. Her background in corporate law had given her a knack for cutting through bullshit and identifying leverage points. She offered a perfunctory nod to the group, but her gaze settled firmly on Sam

"Sam. Good. Sit," Cooper said, dispensing with formalities. "What do we know?"

Franklin opened his mouth to speak, positioning himself at the head of the table, but Cooper's eyes never left Sam. The CIA station chief took a seat directly across from the ambassador and began her situational update with clipped precision.

"PRC Activity in the South China Sea may seem unrelated to us, it is over 1000 miles by sea to the Spratly Islands. But there are things going on there that directly relate to MSS activity here in country. Over the last seventy-two hours, we've seen increased aggression. This is building on decades of aggression and specious claims, but things are definitely increasing in scope and danger to others."

Cooper nodded, processing the information with the focus of someone accustomed to making million-dollar decisions under pressure. "How does this relate? Anything to do with this Harapan Baru stuff you've been briefing me on?"

"I don't have a smoking gun," Sam admitted, "but consider this, they want the South China Sea because it is critical to their oil supply line. But nothing is more critical than the Strait of Malacca. Whoever controls Malaysia controls the Strait."

Franklin, who had remained standing, leaned forward with his palms on the table. "Let's not jump to conclusions. The interagency position is…"

Cooper, still not looking at him, raised a hand toward Sam. "Continue."

Franklin stiffened but said nothing, his complexion reddening slightly as he reluctantly took a seat. Sam suppressed a hint of a smile and continued the briefing.

"Meanwhile, the PRC knows we have limited national level collection capabilities and frankly we are easily distracted. By causing tension in the South China Sea 1000 miles from us it shifts attention from what is going on here. And as I've been briefing, things are certainly getting hot here. The Malaysian government is reporting increases in cyber intrusions, and my people are reporting increased activity by known MSS operatives including meetings with people we believe to be members of Harapan Baru. We have identified three safe houses in the city where we believe Chinese intelligence is coordinating with local assets. The timing aligns perfectly with the maritime provocations."

Cooper removed her glasses, rubbing the bridge of her nose. "And what is your assessment about why the Chinese were so up in arms about Tanner briefing his book at the University?"

"Maybe an understatement but it seems he is saying things they don't want said." Sam acknowledged. "Looks like it has also served as a bit of a wakeup call to the Malaysian government-Tanner is helping their NACSA with a cyber assessment and improvement plan. And that has gotten the attention of the MSS. Not good, but frankly Tanner has given the government here more of a wake-up call than we have been able to do via official channels."

Franklin could no longer contain himself. "This is precisely the kind of cowboy moves that undermine proper intelligence protocols. Tanner is a private citizen now, not an asset we can deploy."

"I've known Jack for almost a decade now. He is a private citizen now but is definitely not a cowboy. A force for good."

Ramos, who had been silent since entering the room, finally spoke, his voice carrying the gravelly texture of someone who'd spent too many years shouting over gunfire.

"I may," he interjected, "I just heard from my squid buddy out on the boat, the Blue Ridge. They feel like the shit is about to hit the fan."

The room fell silent. The USS Blue Ridge was the Seventh Fleet's command ship, if they were on high alert, something significant was brewing.

Cooper's gaze sharpened. "Details, Colonel."

"They've gone to heightened readiness posture. Not publicly, but internally. Two Los Angeles-class submarines have been repositioned to counter the PRC aircraft carrier near the Spratlys, and the USS America Amphibious Ready group was ordered to cut short their port call in Jakarta and book-it north." Ramos's expression remained neutral, but his eyes held the intensity of a predator. "This isn't routine saber-rattling, and they tell me like Sam said, that something is brewing here in Malaysia. Probably Harapan Baru igniting an insurrection with PRC support."

Cooper turned back to Sam. "Your assessment?"

"The Chinese are creating multiple pressure points simultaneously," Blake said. "Maritime provocations, insurgent activity, cyber probes against Malaysian infrastructure. It's a coordinated campaign, not isolated incidents."

Franklin shook his head. "That's speculation without..."

"It's pattern recognition," Cooper cut him off, her patience visibly thinning. "And it matches what we're seeing across the region." She turned to Sam. "What do you need?"

Blake didn't hesitate. "Operational flexibility. Authorization to work with Tanner unofficially. And I need you to make this a priority up your chain so our collection requests get acted on pronto, without that we will be ignored with everything else going on."

Franklin's face darkened. "Madam Ambassador, with all due respect, that's not how this works. I cannot support…"

"Bill," Cooper interrupted, her voice taking on a steely edge, "I want your help here, I want finished intelligence and want the ODNI prioritizing our AOR."

Franklin blinked. "I'm on it." As a career bureaucrat he could pivot faster than a top when the boss makes a request.

"Colonel," Cooper continued, turning to Ramos, "Would be good if you stay in constant contact with Seventh Fleet and INDOPACOM. Make sure they know everything we know. And Sam, I know you are always tight lipped about what your assets are up to, but if you develop anything the team needs to know."

"Yes, ma'am." Ramos and Sam replied in unison.

Cooper gathered her papers. "We're done here." As the others stood to leave, she added, "Sam, stay a moment."

When the door closed behind Franklin and Ramos, Cooper's formal demeanor softened slightly. "How bad is this really?"

Sam hesitated, choosing her words carefully. "If I'm right about what the Chinese are planning, Malaysia could become a flashpoint that makes the South China Sea disputes look like a border skirmish. They're testing more than just regional dominance here; they're testing our will to respond, and they want Malaysia to control the Straits forever."

Cooper nodded slowly. "Then make sure we don't let that happen." She paused, then added, "And Sam? Watch your back with Franklin, but don't piss him off please, the last thing I need is the ODNI calling me because he cries to them. "

"Got it. I'll play nice." Sam replied, her expression giving away nothing."

Outside in the hallway, Franklin was waiting, his earlier composure replaced by barely contained fury. "You're making a serious mistake, Sam. This isn't how we do things."

Sam regarded him with the calm detachment of someone who had faced far more dangerous adversaries. "I understand and apologize, Bill. Will keep you in the loop of course, but on the offchance I'm right please help. If there is anything you can do to get ODNI staff attention on this it could really change the equation, especially if things go kinetic."

In her experience, the people who felt the need to make such pronouncements rarely had the capability to enforce them. She had a job to do, and seventy-two hours wasn't nearly enough time.

* * *

2000 Hours | Sam Blake's Apartment

The amber glow of a single desk lamp cast long shadows across Sam Blake's government-furnished residence within the U.S. Embassy compound. A residence off compound was authorized to her but you could not beat the commute. Besides, this allowed her an in-residence SCIF complete with a CIA-provided thin-client terminal into the agency's secure environment. Great way for a workaholic with a clearance to keep working from home.

The government furniture would have been fit for a king, when it was purchased decades ago. No complaints from Sam, she needed room for her books and wall space for photos of her daughter, Ellie.

Her private phone buzzed. Sam glanced at the screen and swiped to accept the video call.

"Hey, Mom, Happy Birthday!" Ellie's face appeared, Georgetown University's library visible in the background. At nineteen, she had Sam's determined eyes and her father's easy smile.

"Hey, kiddo. Thanks for calling!" Sam moved to the couch, angling the phone so the classified materials on her dining table remained out of frame.

Ellie shifted, adjusting her laptop. "How's Malaysia?"

"Same as yesterday. Hot, humid, complicated." Sam took a sip of bourbon. "How's Dad?"

A flicker of hesitation crossed Ellie's face. "He's good. Sarah's pregnant. They told me last weekend."

Sam felt the familiar tightness in her chest. Eight years since the divorce, and David's new life still had the power to wound her. Sarah was fifteen years younger, a State Department analyst who'd never missed a school play or parent-teacher conference.

"That's... that's great," Sam managed. "He'll be a good dad. Again."

Ellie's expression softened with understanding beyond her years. "He says the same about you, Mom. That you're a good mom, even from halfway around the world."

Sam nodded, not trusting her voice. The truth hung between them; Sam's career had claimed her marriage long before the papers were signed. Too many missed anniversaries, too many unexplained absences, too many secrets she couldn't share.

"Georgetown treating you okay?" Sam asked, changing the subject.

"It's great! Information Warfare midterm tomorrow. My favorite subject because the prof always has something new for us to read."

Sam laughed. "When your dad was at Naval Postgraduate School they would do the same to him. He had a saying back then, 'It's only a lot of reading if you do it!'"

Ellie laughed and nodded, then glanced at someone off-screen." I should go. Study group's waiting."

"Go ace that midterm. I love you."

"Love you too, Mom. Stay safe."

The screen went dark, and Sam sat motionless in the sudden silence. She moved to the dining table where files on Harapan Baru and MSS operations lay scattered.

She wished she could read Jack into these ops. During their INDOPACOM days, Jack had been the visionary, Mike the tactical genius, and Sam not just the CIA liaison to INDOPACOM but the political operator who found ways around bureaucratic roadblocks. Together, they'd tracked China's earliest island-building efforts, warning of the militarization to come while Washington remained fixated on the Middle East.

Her phone rang. A private number. She answered cautiously.

"Blake."

"It's Noor." The Malaysian Special Branch officer's voice was tense. "We lost another asset. Rafid Latif, from our counterintelligence directorate. Second one this month."

Sam closed her eyes. "MSS?"

"Looks that way. Found him in his apartment. Made to look like suicide."

"I'm sorry, Haris." She meant it. In the intelligence world, losing assets wasn't just an operational setback, it was losing people who trusted you with their lives.

"There's something else," Noor continued. "Before he died, he reported a recruitment attempt. We had given him the go-ahead to proceed as an operative. He is too careful to have slipped up himself. Worries me that I have a bigger problem on my hands."

"We need to meet for sure, someplace away from both our facilities." She said, with Noor replying he would set it up.

After ending the call, Sam sought to focus on the big picture. Too frequently, unrelated datapoints are just that. It is human nature to think everything relates. But something tells her this is all part of the same story, with the MSS a common thread.

Twenty years in the field had taught Sam that intelligence work was rarely about dramatic victories. It was about persistence, about recovering from failures, about protecting people who would never know your name. She'd sacrificed her marriage on that altar, missed most of her daughter's childhood, and carried the weight of lost assets like large painful stones in her pockets.

Yet she remained, fighting the long defeat against adversaries with infinite patience and resources. Because occasionally, just occasionally, the work made a difference. A terrorist plot disrupted. A defector safely extracted. A warning heeded in time.

She thought of Jack Tanner, now operating somewhere in the city below. In their INDOPACOM days, he'd been the first to recognize her for more than just a CIA Liaison officer but someone with analytical gifts, advocating for her insights when others dismissed them. Mike had been the same, treating her as an equal when many male colleagues saw only her gender.

They'd been a formidable team once. Perhaps they could be again.

Sam turned on her CIA thin-client workstation and used her fingerprint to authenticate into the agency network. The classified cable she'd been drafting to Langley remained unfinished on the screen. She began typing again, her fingers moving with renewed purpose.

SUBJECT: INDICATIONS OF PRC DESTABILIZATION OPERATION - MALAYSIA

1. SUMMARY: Collateral sources and asset reporting indicates coordinated MSS not only supplying Harapan Baru with financial and weapons support but likely involving them as part of coordinated destabilization effort. Operation in final preparation stages. Request immediate resource allocation and Director approval for enhanced measures.

She worked late into the night finalizing the cable before transmitting, including requests for deeper collection and analytical support from the China Cell at Langley. She included the opportunity to work with a U.S. civilian source in region who is providing cybersecurity support to the Malaysian government.

Tomorrow she would reconnect with Jack, keep coordinating with Mike, keep dealing with Franklin's obstruction, and check in with her operators in the field. The familiar rhythm of operational planning settled her, pushing personal regrets to the background where they belonged.

Sam's mind flashed back to those frenetic days at INDOPACOM J2, the windowless rooms, the endless intelligence reports, the heated debates with Jack Tanner and Mike Murphy. The three of them, younger and less jaded, staying late to piece together the puzzle of China's long game.

Outside, a tropical storm began, rain lashing against the windows as lightning illuminated the Embassy compound in stark flashes of brilliance. Sam barely noticed, already lost in the intelligence puzzles in front of her.

Chapter 14: Command Authority

Jack Tanner's scrolled through the latest cybersecurity reports on his laptop, the dull glow of the screen illuminating his furrowed brow, he was updating his threat brief for this morning's meetings. The quiet of the hotel room is perfect for that.

A quick glance out the window revealed the bustling street below, a city unaware of the game of cat and mouse playing out among the power players behind the scenes. He had been meticulous in his operations, helping the NACSA do what they already wanted to do. Sometimes it just takes an outside expert to accelerate change. Hard work but meaningful and he had no doubt they were already making a difference.

It dawned on him. There is really no greater pleasure than working with a great, mission-focused team on something big like this.

Suddenly, the buzzing of his phone interrupted his thoughts. A Signal message streamed in, a warning from Sam Blake: "MSS is aware of your actions. Increased surveillance. Threat level escalated. Come by for in-person update."

He signaled back: "Got it, I have to swing by NACSA to meet with Lila, then will come by the embassy this afternoon."

Jack's throat tightened. Maybe he had ruffled feathers a bit too much.

He finished his updated threat briefing, packed his carrier bag and headed for the door.

As he exited the hotel room, Jack couldn't shake the feeling that the walls had eyes.

* * *

0830 Hours | The Road to the NACSA

The Toyota Land Cruiser rolled to a stop at the hotel's rear entrance. Jack swung the door open and climbed in, tugging it shut with muscle memory more than thought. He checked the mirrors. Clear.

The vehicle was a block away from the NACSA when a sound hit him, low, deep, not quite thunder. A subterranean growl that rolled through the street and rattled the windows.

Jack's head snapped toward the sound.

Then the concussion wave hit.

The ground shook. The car's windows vibrated in their frames. From the front window he saw a massive orange bloom and smoke pouring out from the top floor of the NACSA building.

Jack leaned forward, mouth dry. "No..."

The driver slammed the brakes. Jack was already out the door; eyes locked on the site of the blast.

Flames licked skyward from the gash in the exact location where the NACSA security ops center is.

Jack's fists clenched. He was scheduled to be there. Right now.

His stomach dropped as if in free fall. The word "Lila" escaped his lips before he could stop it, barely audible over the chaos outside.

His mind raced. NACSA's cyber operations center, their best analysts, their control systems, experienced leaders. All of it in the exact part of the building that is now a flaming hole. And Lila. The woman who he had spent hours with helping raise the defense of Malaysian government systems. She knew more about the PRC digital footprint than anyone he'd met in years.

His fingers fumbled for his phone. Called her number. Nothing. He tried again, pacing three quick steps, then stopping dead. His training screamed at him to move, to assess, to plan, but for five paralyzing seconds, all he could do was stare at the inferno that had more than likely swallowed her whole.

Jack forced himself to breathe. Three days. That's all he'd known her. Not enough time to form attachments in this business. He'd lost colleagues before.

But the tightness in his chest said otherwise. The way she'd challenged his analysis and recommendations for action. Her fierce dedication to her country. The slight accent when she spoke technical terms. He just realized how much he loves... likes... liked... her.

He pushed it down. Hard. Survival first. Grieve later.

His mind raced. Kinetic had fused with cyber. Just like he'd predicted in *The Dragon's Digital Claws*.

Not subtle. This was MSS. Escalation by fireball. A statement etched in blood and smoke: they were done playing defense.

The sirens grew closer. Jack's jaw clenched so hard his teeth ached. This wasn't just an attack on infrastructure. It was personal now. Lila had been his eyes into NACSA's operation. His ally. Maybe even the beginning of something he hadn't let himself name.

And someone had taken her off the board.

Jack jumped back into the car and directed the driver to head back to the hotel. He dashed out and entered the hotel lobby, breath shallow, heartbeat pounding against his ribs. His eyes scanned the walls, the windows, the cameras.

He knew what came next.

His room was no longer safe. Neither was the city.

They wouldn't stop with NACSA. Not after this. And NACSA is going to have a hard time operating. He had seen their disaster recovery plans and they were hardly worth the paper they were written on. Just compliance drills.

He entered his room just long enough to grab enough to fit in his carrier bag.

A minute later, he was out the service exit, sliding into the current of the crowd. Tourists, locals, all apparently too far away from the blast to have realized what just happened. He moved among them trying to act composed. Eyes forward. Shoulders relaxed. Head down.

Jack Tanner disappeared into the heart of Kuala Lumpur.

He didn't know where he was going. Only that he was going to evade the MSS and survive. And then…

He'd make someone pay.

* * *

0900 Hours | The Streets of KL

Jack's first impulse was to put distance between himself and the Ritz. Now it was time to find a spot to think and plan. He used Apple Maps on his iPhone, a better more secure and private option than Google Maps, since all processing and queries remain on the device. The phone itself is now a liability. In hindsight was stupid to not get an eSIM and just use his Verizon roaming account. Looking for a public place where he could sit and think hopefully out of the view of surveillance cameras or MSS cars no doubt searching for him, he found a promising target, the Perdana Botanical Gardens, a short walk away.

The gardens unfurled like a green lung in the heart of Kuala Lumpur, a sprawling sanctuary of manicured paths and tangled jungle moments that seemed to resist the steel spires pressing in from every direction. Jack passed through the wrought-iron gates, following a gently curving path shaded by towering trees and blooming bushes. The air shifted- cooler, humid, laced with the scent of rain-soaked orchids and tropical loam. Here, the roar of the city faded to something more distant, more manageable.

He moved like a local who knew where he was going, shoes quiet against the red-brick trail that led to bamboo groves. Joggers passed without eye contact. An elderly Chinese couple practiced tai chi beneath a stand of traveler's palms. A security camera, its dome clouded with pollen and age, spun lazily on a lamppost. No one looked at Jack. That was the point.

Tucked just past the Sunken Garden, where trimmed hedges framed a dry marble fountain, he found what he was looking for: a small wooden gazebo, half swallowed by vines and shade. It overlooked a quiet koi pond speckled with lily pads. The roof, tiled in weather-worn shingles, sagged at one corner, but the structure still stood firm, a forgotten retreat barely ten meters from a meandering footpath and just out of sight from the main tourist loops.

Jack slid onto the gazebo's bench, facing the water. The bench creaked beneath him. He pulled out his Chromebook and brought it to life and connected it to his iPhone hot spot.

No one would question a foreigner checking email in a public park. Especially not here, under soft shadows and the slow rhythm of a country that sometimes forgot it was in a digital war.

The glow of the laptop screen illuminated Jack Tanner's focused expression as he scrolled through the news of the bombing. Little actionable info, yet. Social media feeds show Harapan Baru are already claiming credit. The speed of their posting meant they were ready to make the statement. No doubt they are involved, but likely the MSS that steered them. No word yet on who the casualties are but must assume it was Lila and every cyber analyst on duty that day. Will be hard to reconstitute. It is not just the piss poor disaster recovery plans but the loss of leaders. The heart of NACSA gutted in a single blast.

A sense of urgency coursed through him; this was no simple chase. If he was a target how long would it take them to realize they missed? If they make him a priority, they have plenty of analysts and an ability to fire up their backdoor connections to most cameras in the city. They would soon be compiling data on his past movements so they could predict his next moves. They would know exactly where his cell phone is. Every shallow breath he took felt like a countdown to their next strike.

He closed his eyes for a beat.

Drawing a deep breath, he calmed himself to reconsider his situation. Jack's analytical mind raced, formulating plans born from years of military strategy. Although Kuala Lumpur is a safe city, his initial threat model was one of caution. Things have obviously changed. He will have to reduce his digital footprint and assume he is always being observed by the Digital Silk Road provided IT infrastructure of the city, including cameras, cell towers, phone calls. The Malaysian government might not think the PRC is using them, but Tanner has to assume they are.

He opened Google Maps on the Chromebook (wishing the more secure Apple Maps would run in this locked down system). He studied a map of the surrounding area, marking potential safe havens, including police stations (which he would not use unless it was his last option), the Embassy, busy public malls, maybe some coffee shops.

Jack shifted in his seat, the wheels of his mind turning faster than ever. Anger led him to foolish thoughts of waging a one-man war against the MSS. Time to use his training. Take a deep breath, recalibrate and think. He will respond. Like the dissidents that scare the PRC by speaking truth, he would hurt them. But he would hurt them his way.

Time slipped away as Jack brainstormed options.

He opened ChatGPT, his go-to chatbot. Using the deep research option he asked a very precise query: "I need a resort within an hour of Kuala Lumpur where tourists would not be out of place, unlikely to have government run security cameras. Must have WiFi."

Response came in about a second:

Here are three options meeting your criteria, within about an hour of Kuala Lumpur, Wi-Fi-enabled, and likely minimal government-run CCTV presence:

*1. **Villa Samadhi (KL city fringe)** A boutique-style garden resort tucked near KL's diplomatic quarter. Five-star Asian-inspired villas, each with private plunge pool and direct pool access, set within thatched-roof clusters and bamboo architecture. Includes free Wi-Fi, lush privacy, and virtually no city surveillance cameras myboutiquehotel.com.*

*2. **Sekeping Serendah (Selangor foothills)** An eco-boutique retreat roughly 45–60 min north of KL in Serendah. Individual chalets surrounded by forest, with communal pool, strong Wi-Fi in lodgings, and escape from urban surveillance. No food options.*

Popular with romantics and artists seeking solitude. Local reviews suggest "off-grid vibe" with only basic guest security.

*3. **Tadom Hill Resort (Selangor)** About 50 min south-west of KL, a privately managed forest resort with chalets, hilltop pools, and Wi-Fi. Favored by nature lovers and eschewing public-area CCTV security is guest-focused, not government-run. A notable alternative outside major urban sprawl.*

Option one is out. This is not time for a chance encounter with a diplomat. Will need to eat eventually so option two is out. Looks like Tadom Hill Resort it is. But getting there? That was the problem. Grab was out; too traceable. So were credit card payments. He needed something analog. Fast. Back to Google Maps. "Found it!" he said to himself as he figured out an approach.

He used his cell phone data to download the Google Chrome version of Signal to his laptop and synch it with his account. When he gets rid of his cell phone, he could still communicate with some OPSEC. He sent a Signal message to Sam and Mike. "Hey guys, I'm ok, but laying low for a while. Will not have comms for a while. Off cell phone now. Will check in via Signal when I can."

Jack closed Signal and closed the laptop, then began wiping his phone of all data and accounts.

Then he slid the Chromebook into his courier bag and ran.

He scanned the street as he exited the park. No tails, but that didn't mean anything. MSS doesn't have to send men in trench coats. They'd use cameras. Maybe odds are slim they are looking for him now, they must assume he was in the blast.

First stop, the uParcel store for courier delivery. Five minutes later his cell phone was in an envelope being delivered by minibike to the Embassy across town.

He walked three more blocks, zigzagging through the crowd until he found the small print shop he was looking for. Google maps said they deliver. He ducked inside and waited. An older man came out of the back, startled.

"Need some copies?"

Jack lowered his voice. "I need a driver. Not ride-share. Just someone with a car. Cash job."

The man studied him. Said nothing. Then nodded slightly.

Ten minutes later, Jack was in the backseat of a beat-up Proton Saga, the driver a silent Indonesian who didn't ask where Jack was from or why he paid in crisp ringgit notes. Jack offered a tip up front, double on arrival.

As they cleared the city limits, Jack allowed himself a breath.

Not safe. Not yet. But off-grid.

* * *

0930 Hours | MPS Hibiscus Pavilion HQ

Mei Ling's eyes burned from staring at screens for the past hour in the dimly lit MPS surveillance center. Her fingers flew across the keyboard as she collated reports streaming in about the NACSA bombing.

"Another confirmation of the drone," she murmured, adding a fifth report to her analysis. The pattern was unmistakable, multiple PRC nationals had observed a small quadcopter approaching the building moments before the explosion. Three separate witnesses had captured partial footage on their phones, which she'd already enhanced and compiled.

She paused, a frown creasing her forehead. Harapan Baru claimed credit almost instantly. But this wasn't standard Harapan Baru methodology. Their previous attacks had been crude, relying on planted explosives or direct assaults. This precision strike showed sophistication beyond their known capabilities.

"Why would Li's people..." she whispered, then caught herself. Such questions were dangerous. She deleted all comments about drone observations from the record.

Some connections were better left unmade, especially when they suggested inter-ministerial operations that no one had bothered to inform MPS about.

Mei quickly assumed if it was the MSS they must have had a reason to move against NACSA. She pulled a new batch of data from their cell carrier database, searching for the latest on Tanner's location.

The tracking data formed a clear picture as it populated her screen. Tanner was in a vehicle moving toward the NACSA building precisely when the explosion occurred. His phone then returned to the Ritz-Carlton, traveled through the city on an erratic path, paused at Perdana Botanical Gardens for seven minutes, and then traveled in a vehicle to the U.S. Embassy.

"He survived," she whispered, leaning back in her chair. "And now he's in his Embassy."

Mei stared at the last ping from Tanner's device. If MSS had targeted NACSA hoping to eliminate Tanner, they'd failed. But the good news is, Tanner is a coward who ran with fear back to his Embassy.

She hesitated before adding this information to her report. Director Zhang would want to know immediately that Tanner remained alive and is at his embassy but might not want this captured for all to know.

* * *

1030 Hours | Secure VTC

The dim glow of Mike Murphy's office in the USS Blue Ridge SCIF illuminated the serious expressions of three of the most strategic minds in U.S. intelligence as Mike, Sam, and Ramos settled into the secure video teleconference. In the short time since the bombing the entire intelligence apparatus was now on high alert, and urgency was palpable through the pixels of the digital connection.

"First off," Mike began, his voice steady and clear, betraying none of the tension that churned beneath the surface, "what do we know about the bombing? Any updates from the field?"

Sam leaned forward, her fingers steepled as she absorbed the question. "It was a targeted attack, that is the floor that houses the NACSA security operations center and executive staff. No indication of how the bomb was planted; we are assuming drone delivery for now. I suspect Harapan Baru has shifted tactics." She went on, her voice steady but her eyes flickering with concern. "But we need confirmation on the ground. We want more than just chatter about them receiving backing from the MSS."

Ramos, stationed in his nondescript office within the embassy, nodded solemnly. "Why not just assume they are getting PRC support and plan our next move from there?"

There was a brief pause as Mike rubbed his chin thoughtfully. "Nothing wrong with planning assumptions but we need to enhance our collection capabilities. I'm looking at diverting fleet UAV assets for Malaysian reconnaissance, but we can't do anything without approval from Malaysian Defense Ministry."

Ramos straightened slightly, "I can reach out to my contacts at Malaysian counterinsurgency. They're ramping up operations against Harapan Baru but have no idea where they are operating from. They've got plenty of short range ISR UAVs but some huge gaps in wide area surveillance. If our UAVs can help with that they would probably be very open to overflight. I'll plug in with JSOC too."

Ramos continued, "I've got a VTC with regional attaches in an hour. Will brief them up and see what's up in their AORs. Time to plug in with Noor in Malaysian Special Branch as well."

"Sounds good," Mike said, his voice gaining urgency. "You're the man there. I'll get you everything my team develops, and you decide what to share with Special Branch, would suggest not asking DC permission, the fight is on and if you have to ask permission before saying anything it will slow us down too much."

"You know that's illegal Mike," Ramos replied. "We do this the right way for a reason."

Sam surprised herself with a suggestion: "This may be another one for Franklin, one thing his ODNI title comes with is emergency intel sharing approval authority."

"And Jack?" Mike changed the subject, his gaze piercing the screen. "Any additional word from him?"

Sam glanced at the screen. "I haven't heard anything since his last Signal message. Seems like he ditched his phone because he knows how easy it would be to track him."

Mike's brow furrowed. "He'll reach back out soon; I have no doubt. "

Mike continued: "Meanwhile I'm tasking my team to look for anything from any source on Jack and MSS interest in him.

"Work swiftly," Mike concluded, noting the strictness in his tone. "We don't have the luxury of time. The second we lose momentum we give them the upper hand. Let's reconvene in a few hours after we've made our calls."

With that, the screen flickered off, leaving the three to their separate missions, each charged with a heavy weight that reminded them of the urgency that wrapped around them like a tight coil ready to spring.

Chapter 15: Digital Arsenal

Jack's room at Tadom Hill Resort was spartan but serviceable: bamboo walls, a narrow bed draped in mosquito netting, and a worn wooden desk beneath an open window that overlooked the tangled green of the Malaysian jungle. Sunlight filtered through the canopy, sketching restless shadows across the floor as distant macaques shrieked in the treetops.

Seated at the desk, Jack hunched over his Chromebook, systematically checking its security posture. It was his only tether to the outside world, and he treated it like a survival tool. Chrome OS's verified boot reassured him the system hadn't been tampered with. TLS 1.3 encrypted his traffic. The Snowstorm application ensured no entity would know what websites he connects to or what country he is in. Each layer of security, from sandboxed apps to auto-patching updates, closed doors the MSS might otherwise pry open.

"Even the MSS would need time with this," he muttered, enabling the hardware security key for logins.

He needed more than vigilance. He needed leverage.

That's when the idea struck. *Overwatch*.

His Virtual Intelligence Center, an agentic AI demo system he'd built to prove a controversial point: that AI could perform

167

meaningful open-source intelligence work without constant human input. The project had sparked fascination and backlash in equal measure. Analysts at INDOPACOM and DIA praised its utility. Executives bristled at the implications.

Jack had always pushed the edge. He'd been among the first to experiment with ChatGPT in national security, trained a digital twin of himself on Delphi, even wired Grok into X as a real-time briefer. But Overwatch was his masterstroke, an agentic AI framework with autonomous bots capable of scouring the Internet, pulling data, connecting dots, and delivering insights.

The genesis had come during his final years at INDOPACOM, watching analysts drown in data while threats moved at machine speed, while their work on high-side systems limited their use of open-source intelligence. He'd started small, creating a server hosted at AWS and loading it with free software, mastering the protocols of Agentic AI in his spare time, testing out its capabilities on weekends. What began as curiosity became obsession when he realized the potential to amplify human intelligence rather than replace it. The cost was incredibly cheap. Using commodity compute from hyperscalers and open-source software and free LLM models let him cover fees himself.

The result was a system that gave incredible demos. Problem was it was too powerful for the management class. Some called it too disruptive. "No AI can replace a human analyst," they'd scoff. Others were quick to point out workflow problems. "I need a throat to choke if it fails" or "All open-source intelligence is flawed" were common refrains. He'd heard it all.

But here, now, it might give him advantage. At a minimum, it would be better than scouring news sites.

"Why fight their machines with just my brain?" he whispered to himself.

He launched the browser and connected to the AWS instance. Biometric fingerprint login, tied to his hardened Chromebook, the interface blinked to life.

Overwatch is still up.

It looked familiar, clean, utilitarian, not unlike Grok or OpenAI's portals. A simple command window, history threads, settings tucked off to the side. Jack flexed his fingers once, then typed:

Tell me the status of the agents we previously configured as a Virtual Intelligence Center.

Overwatch replied:

Model Context Protocol server fully functioning. CrewAI, Vectara and LLAMA all in need of update. No new data in system for a year. Dormant agents you previously created, and their names are:

OVERWATCH (COMMAND NODE) – Oversight and your primary interface.

ENVOY – Geopolitical analyst

GHOST KNIFE – Counterterrorism intelligence

KILLSWITCH – Cyber ops and digital forensics

LEDGER – Financial intelligence and economic indicators

SPARKS – *Unclassified SIGINT and Open Source Intelligence fusion*

SPECTER – *Deception, counterintelligence, collection strategy*

Jack's mind is already going full speed. But first things first. Jack types:

Update and patch all systems before any tasking of agents. Since you have been offline for a year you have some catching up to do. After patching, task each agent to get up to speed on their areas of expertise and update our Vectara data stores. Focus on the geopolitical dynamics of Malaysia and on information on the PRC MSS and MPS, including tactics and techniques of major cyber intrusions attributed to PRC related actors. Be prepared to assess likely PRC objectives in the region. In the meantime, I will be summarizing information on my personal situation and events in Malaysia over the last few days to inform your responses to future tasking.

Overwatch replies:

Understood, patching all systems, updating data stores and standing by.

* * *

Overwatch patched all systems and implemented initial update tasking to the entire Virtual Intelligence Center. Catching up on a year of being offline took some time, but eventually Jack saw the alert notification:

Jack, all systems are updated and ready for the additional information and further tasking.

After pasting in a large summary of events since landing at Kuala Lumpur, including, the chaos at the university, his role at NACSA, the bombing, the likely threat from MSS and MPS, he issued his next task to Overwatch:

Provide an initial threat assessment, include recommendations for my next step and recommendations for your next tasking.

Overwatch replied:

Recommend your next move be to seek the safety of the U.S. Embassy in Kuala Lumpur. Use caution in approaching the Embassy, all routes likely under surveillance. Consider contacting COS Blake and asking for transport from your location or finding closest police station and seeking escort to the Embassy. This overall assessment is based on following analysis from our agents:

Envoy reports this isn't the usual diplomatic saber-rattling. PRC-Malaysia tensions are escalating outside any historical precedent. MSS is laying groundwork for political destabilization, likely to expand influence and secure control over the Strait of Malacca. Odds are you are seen as a high priority target and are being searched for now.

Ghost Knife reports that Harapan Baru's propaganda is leveling up, professional-grade message control, timed releases, meme warfare. They're most likely behind the NACSA bombing. MSS is almost certainly coordinating with them. If they knew you were with NACSA, which they did, you were likely a target. Expect follow-on attacks.

Killswitch reports the same digital methods used to penetrate U.S. telecom companies seem to be at play against the Telekom Malaysia and Cell carriers, and the same "living off the land" techniques used against U.S. military and government infrastructure is being used in Malaysia. These are PRC-style intrusions. But here's the good part: the seem to be moving so fast that it introduces the potential that their originating infrastructure can be found and possibly penetrated by the right actor.

Sparks notes a sharp spike in coordinated anti-U.S. sentiment across local social feeds. Fake grassroots accounts both in country and in the entire region. Faux-nationalist hashtags. Narrative: "U.S. interference = economic collapse." Classic MSS playbook: light the fire, blame the fire department.

Specter cites weakness in our collection against adversaries like these. Open source is powerful but our inability to access classified sources and guidance to prevent us from unauthorized access to any systems limits our visibility.

All of this leads to my overall assessment. Your best move is to safely get to the embassy for escorted safe departure from the country.

Jack's jaw tightened. He typed:

Overwatch, I'm not ready to leave just yet. I'm pissed. The bombing wasn't just an attack on infrastructure, it killed my friends, friends who died trying to keep their country from falling to PRC control. They've crossed a line, and there's unfinished business here. I intend on developing information and taking action that hurts the MSS.

Overwatch replies:

You're the boss. You good with a more offensive posture here? You used to say sometimes it's better to beg forgiveness than to ask permission. Is that the approach you want?

Jack typed:

Exactly. I need options, not just for my extraction, but for striking back. What can you learn from successful dissident operations against authoritarian governments? What can you and the team do to gather actionable intelligence that will completely disrupt the MSS operation? I want them exposed, compromised, and explaining themselves to the world. Give me a better plan. What could you do, covertly, if you and your agents were unbound by the law in Malaysia?

Jack felt the familiar calm that came with commitment to action.

A sharp ping from the Chromebook broke the silence. Jack glanced down to see a flashing red notification from Overwatch.

"What is up?" Jack asked, his fingers hovering over the keyboard.

The message appeared character by character, clinical and devastating:

Confirmation received. Subject Lila Tan. Her remains were positively identified by Malaysian authorities.

The words hit like a sucker punch. Jack didn't blink, but the pressure behind his eyes built instantly.

He hadn't wanted to know. Some part of him had been clinging to the possibility that she had stepped out for coffee, taken a call in another room, been running late that morning, anything but the truth now confirmed on his screen.

Jack's jaw clenched tight enough to crack teeth. He stared at the message, his reflection in the screen showing a face drained of color but eyes burning with a cold fury that would have made even seasoned operatives step back. Without speaking, he closed his eyes for three seconds, then opened them with renewed focus. Time to think again.

While he thought, the watch would continue running in the background, collecting, analyzing, adapting.

Jack started a new Signal group message. Just Mike, Sam, and him. "Mike and Sam, sorry I've been off the grid a bit, all is well, I'm laying low. I am developing some info I think you will find of use, will share as soon as I can. Will get to the Embassy at some point. Sam, sent my cell phone to the embassy via courier, hold onto that for me, please."

It took about a nano-second for Mike to reply "Jack thank God you are ok. This was Harapan Baru but could have an MSS connection, laying low prob a good idea. Send more info when you can."

It didn't take long for Sam to reply "Mike the Embassy really is the best place, let me know where you are and I can send a car and escort. Can set up agency air transport back home as well."

"Not yet, thanks Sam, I'm good. But I'll take you up on that offer soon."

* * *

Jack enabled voice mode and double-tapped the stem of his Bluetooth ear buds to speak with Overwatch.

A familiar voice slid in with clipped urgency.

"You're not going to like this," Overwatch said.

Jack rubbed his temples. "Hit me. No filters."

"Three names," Overwatch replied. "Ming Liu. Lao Xun. Wu Yifan. You profiled them in your book. Social media in China, especially WeChat, Weibo and Douyin have been filled with them since the last Tianfu Cup where they were given accolades. They have been awarded an honorary title: The Three Immortals. Douyin videos show them being introduced by none other than General Qiao Liang of Unrestricted Warfare fame. Many of the same accounts celebrating them are also pushing content about the need for Malaysia to better respect international law and respect their largest trading partner, so we assess they are involved in recent cyber incidents here."

Jack sat up. "What else?"

Sparks spoke next, fast and layered. "Forensics on the Malaysian bank incidents show clear signs of shared infrastructure and staggered deployment. We have to assume the MSS has root-level access inside the central bank and likely all four Tier 1 banks in the country. We have also detected bots hitting forex markets. High-frequency spikes, then calculated drops. They're squeezing the Ringgit in cycles. It's methodical."

"This isn't just cybercrime," Envoy added. His tone was precise, almost academic. "This is strategic coercion. PRC wants Malaysia pliable on trade issues and more. If they can collapse the Ringgit, fracture political cohesion, and walk in under the guise of assistance, they get the upper hand."

Ghost Knife's voice cut through with quiet intensity. "The timeline lines up with chatter I'm getting from Harapan Baru proxies on social media. This is dual-front sabotage. Digital chaos above, kinetic disruption below. It's all converging."

Jack stood, pacing the narrow alley-side café. "So what's the endgame?"

"Destroy public confidence in the financial system," Overwatch said. "Force government paralysis. MSS then uses the crisis to escalate 'support', but really, it is a takeover by another name."

His Chromebook lit up. Strings of code, financial graphs, threat trees. Malaysia's stability, breaking down in real time.

"I've found how the NACSA is working to reconstitute and resume operations, press reports indicate they have moved remaining staff to Cybersecurity Malaysia in the Ministry of Digital Transformation," Overwatch continued. "Recommend you task us to establish contact with them and provide insights. Also recommend you direct us to establish contact with sources at both the Ministry of Finance and Bank Negara to provide them with what we are seeing."

Jack exhaled. "Do it. Maintain your anonymity by establishing new agents with their own persona."

"And I need you to prepare a full write-up on this for me to send via Signal to Mike and Sam."

"Understood," Overwatch said. "Will produce an assessment. Should I brief them on the Virtual Intelligence Center?"

"Another good idea, they should know our sources and methods," reflected Jack. "Ping me as soon as you have it ready for my review and transmission."

* * *

2100 Hours | U.S. Embassy

Samantha Blake stood at the head of the conference table in the embassy's secure room, her posture rigid as she surveyed the faces of her team. The overhead lights cast harsh shadows across the worried expressions of her officers. Bill Franklin leaned against the far wall, arms crossed and jaw set in skepticism. Colonel Ramos sat silently, his weathered face betraying nothing.

"Thanks all, let's get right into it. We received what could be some critical intelligence from Jack Tanner," Sam announced, nodding to her tech specialist who brought up Jack's Signal message on the wall-mounted screen. "Everyone take five minutes to read through this before we discuss."

The room fell silent as eyes scanned the detailed assessment. Jack's report outlined the Three Immortals' cyber operations, the systematic manipulation of Malaysia's currency, and the connection to Harapan Baru's ground activities. The report concluded with details his AI-powered intelligence system called Overwatch.

Franklin pushed himself off the wall first. "Are we seriously considering intel from a rogue civilian running some homemade AI system on open source intel? This reads like techno-fantasy."

"Everything described about the MSS and MPS and those cyber hackers seems to fit with what we know, and it certainly seems to fit with the PRC dynamics here in Malaysia," Ramos countered, his voice low but commanding.

Sam tapped her pen against the table. "Jack's assessment about the financial manipulation matches what our economic analysts have been seeing. The ringgit's fluctuations aren't natural market forces."

"Even if this is accurate," Franklin said, "what's our play? We can't intervene in Malaysia's internal affairs based on a single American civilian's unauthorized open-source intelligence gathering."

"We absolutely can when it affects regional stability." Sam replied sharply. "If Malaysia's economy collapses, the entire area destabilizes, and the PRC gets dominate influence on the strongest democracy in the region."

Ramos nodded. "The currency manipulation combined with the NACSA bombing suggests a coordinated campaign. Classic hybrid warfare."

"We have to work our own sources, of course. But sure would like a direct connection to Tanner's system." She added "Since this is all open source, let's see what is legit enough to share with our Malaysian counterparts."

Franklin's face contorted with undisguised contempt. "Let me be absolutely clear about this. Open-source intelligence is garbage, always has been, always will be." He paced the length of the table, his voice rising with each step. "It's inherently flawed because it lacks access to the classified reporting networks that give us the full picture."

"Bill, we use OSINT all the time," Sam countered.

"As a supplement, never as the foundation." Franklin's hand sliced through the air. "And now we're talking about AI-processed open source? That's twice removed from reality." He turned to face the room. "These models hallucinate. They fabricate. It's documented fact."

Ramos shifted in his chair. "The technical details about the PRC cyber actors match our existing intelligence."

"Coincidence or common knowledge," Franklin dismissed. "What matters is the assessment and recommendations, which could be completely manufactured by this... Overwatch system." He practically spat the name.

Sam maintained her composure. "So, what's your alternative, Bill? Ignore potentially actionable intelligence while Malaysia's systems are under attack?"

"My alternative is to rely on properly vetted intelligence through established channels." Franklin planted both hands on the table. "Not the fever dreams of a former Navy officer playing with toys he built in his garage. For all we know, this Overwatch could be compromised. Did anyone consider that? What if the MSS has already penetrated his system and is feeding us disinformation?"

The room fell silent as the possibility hung in the air.

"The bombing was real," Sam finally said. "The cyber intrusions are real. And Tanner's analysis provides a coherent framework that explains both."

Franklin straightened, adjusting his tie. "That's the most dangerous kind of misinformation, the kind that incorporates enough truth to seem plausible. If we act on this and it's wrong, we risk an international incident. If we share it with Malaysian authorities and it's fabricated, our credibility is shot." He looked directly at Sam. "And I won't let an unvetted civilian's AI experiment determine U.S. foreign policy in Southeast Asia."

Ramos cleared his throat, the sound cutting through the tension like a knife. His expression remained neutral, but his eyes had taken on a harder edge.

"With all due respect to everyone's concerns about intelligence quality, I've spent my entire career working with flawed intel." Ramos leaned forward, his forearms resting on the table. "There's not a single source out there, HUMINT, SIGINT, ELINT, OSINT, or otherwise, that doesn't have issues. Every piece of intelligence I've ever acted on had gaps, uncertainties, or potential contamination."

Sam nodded slightly, recognizing the weight of experience behind his words.

"What this situation calls for isn't perfect intelligence, it's reconnaissance by fire." Ramos's voice took on the measured cadence of a battlefield commander. "We get proactive, we make moves that force the adversary to react, and we see what happens. The moment they move, we can find them, fix them, and finish them."

Franklin's face reddened. "That's an incredibly reckless approach. We're talking about diplomatic relations with…"

"I'm talking about battlefield tactics against an active enemy force," Ramos interrupted, his calm voice somehow more commanding than Franklin's outburst. "The MSS and MPS are conducting operations on Malaysian soil. They've escalated to kinetic attacks. This isn't theoretical anymore."

He stood and walked to the map of Kuala Lumpur displayed on the wall screen.

"We leak selective pieces of Tanner's intelligence through cutouts. We increase our visible presence in certain areas while running covert operations in others. We coordinate with Malaysian special forces to increase patrols near suspected Harapan Baru locations." Ramos turned back to face the room. "Every action forces our adversaries to adapt, communicate, and expose themselves."

Sam considered this approach, mentally weighing the risks and benefits.

"It's not pretty, and it's not perfect," Ramos continued, "but it's effective. The Chinese are running an integrated campaign, cyber, economic, and physical. We need to disrupt their operational tempo on all three fronts simultaneously."

Franklin shook his head in disbelief. "And if we're wrong? If we provoke an international incident based on AI-generated speculation?"

"Nothing I said is based only that report. It's based on that report plus years of experience and the realities of what we are all seeing before our eyes right now. Time to get proactive vice reactive," Ramos said simply. "If we're right and we do nothing, we'll be explaining to the world why we let a key democratic ally fall under Chinese control despite having advance warning."

Sam pushed her chair back and stood, commanding the room's attention with her movement.

"Here's how we proceed," she said, her voice level but authoritative. "We treat Tanner's intelligence as indicative, not definitive. It gives us a framework to understand MSS and MPS intentions, but we verify every element through our established channels."

She turned to her senior analyst. "Rachel, I want your team cross-referencing everything in this report against our SIGINT and HUMINT sources. Prioritize the financial manipulation claims and the Three Immortals' activities."

Rachel nodded, already making notes on her tablet.

"Colonel," Sam continued, looking at Ramos, "your reconnaissance by fire approach has merit, but we'll calibrate it. Let's increase our information exchange with Malaysian forces, use your judgement but err on the side of doing the right thing and nudging them to be as proactive as possible. And get any info and insights from them as soon as you can."

Ramos gave a single, affirming nod.

"For the cyber elements," Sam said, "we'll share sanitized versions of the technical indicators with our Malaysian counterparts at the relocated NACSA at the Ministry of Digital Transformation. If the Three Immortals are as active as Tanner suggests, our Malaysian partners should be able to confirm their digital fingerprints."

Franklin shifted uncomfortably but remained silent.

"Bill," Sam addressed him directly, "I know you are the boss here and ODNI relies on you to represent the entire intelligence community. We could really use your help now, both with ODNI and your sources in the diplomatic community."

Franklin's expression remained skeptical, but her tip of the hat to his leadership made him glow. He nodded reluctantly.

"To be absolutely clear," Sam concluded, scanning the faces around the table, "we're not taking this report as gospel. We're using it as a hypothesis to test. If the MSS and MPS are operating as Tanner suggests, our actions will generate confirming intelligence. If not, we'll adjust accordingly."

She closed her folder with finality. "And let's remember what's at stake here. This isn't just about intelligence validation; it's about protecting a key democratic ally in a region where democracy is increasingly under threat."

The room remained silent for a moment before Sam added, "Get moving. I want preliminary confirmation or contradiction of Tanner's assessment within six hours. And someone find a secure way to get Tanner into this building. I want him where we can protect him and utilize his expertise directly."

As the team dispersed, Sam caught Ramos's eye. He gave her an approving look. They both knew that in the shadowy world of intelligence, perfect certainty was a luxury they rarely enjoyed.

* * *

Jack raised Overwatch on voice: "I need you to spin up a new agent."

"What function?" Overwatch asked.

"Head of public communications. Anonymous tip-pushing. I want a bot who can drip-feed reality to journalists, financial analysts, citizen researchers, even government officials, without exposing us. Let them connect the dots."

A different voice came online, casual and amused.

"I've already got a prototype," Overwatch said. "I call it Whistle. Language-flexible, behavior-modeled, and designed to navigate the local comms ecosystem without setting off alarms."

"Deploy it," Jack said. "Now."

He paused, then added, "Two more items. First, task the entire team to find Harapan Baru's leadership node. I want movement patterns, digital traces, any other source you can think of. I want any insights from their social feeds or those that amplify them."

Overwatch replied. "You'll get options."

Jack looked out the window, scanning the crowded street. "And the last item. Operation codename: Mirror Key."

The silence that followed was the kind that filled with calculation.

"We're going to create a mole," Jack continued. "Inside the MSS. Not real, fabricated. I want a comprehensive plan with your best vision for execution. Consider creating fake social media accounts, fake documents and leaks, fake chat logs, falsified financial trails, AI-generated voice messages, metadata-stained dead drops. Enough noise to make Chen Yixin question his own circle."

KillSwitch came online with a grin in his voice. "Feeding paranoia into a system that already devours itself? I love this plan."

"It will," Overwatch said. "We'll build the operation. You'll have a complete plan."

Jack closed the Chromebook. "Then let's make them hunt their own."

Chapter 16: Virtual Warfare

Day 10, 0800 Hours | MSS Cyber HQ, Beijing

The air in the cyber operations meeting room inside the MSS crackled with intensity, the dim LED lights casting long shadows across the sleek, polished table. At its head sat General Qiao Liang, a master of strategy cloaked in an air of authority that commanded the respect of even the most seasoned operatives. To his left hovered the Three Immortals: Ming Liu, Lao Xun, and Wu Yifan. Each bore the weight of expectations and the thrill of the hunt, poised to unleash their renowned cyber prowess against a singular target, Jack Tanner.

"Gentlemen," Liang began, his voice resonant and piercing, cutting through the tension shrouding the room. "Jack Tanner is an undercover CIA agent and an enemy of the people. He knows too much about our cyber activities in Malaysia and is very likely the number one cause of challenges you have been having in achieving desired outcomes in Malaysian government infrastructure."

Ming leaned forward, his eyes glinting with eagerness. "Our last reports based on cell phone tracking is he has sought refuge in his Embassy, tail between his legs."

Liang cut him off "How many sources have confirmed that?"

"He cannot have spoof cell location data, we have multiple towers confirming." retorted Ming.

"Did you even read his book?" lectured Qiao. "You think he is an idiot?"

Lao, arms crossed, fixed his gaze on the screen displaying real-time surveillance data. "He showed us exactly what we wanted to see."

Wu, the most enigmatic of the trio, sat back in his chair, a slow smile curling his lips. "General Liang, if he is off the grid we have to do things to make him pop back up... we put filters in place in every camera for alerts on his face and gait. He will turn up."

Liang nodded, his expression unwavering. "Already way ahead of you on the cameras. Have teams collecting all stored feeds from every camera in the area."

The General pressed his fingers together, contemplating the way ahead. "Wu is right. This can't be a passive search; must go active... penetrate every existing system he has ever used and find a way to get him to pop up online or in person so we can find him. Maybe scare his family and make them reach out."

Lao pushed back from the table and gestured toward the wall-mounted display. With a few taps on his tablet, the screen flickered to life, revealing a complex neural network visualization pulsing with data streams.

"General, this is what will find Tanner for us," he announced, his voice carrying the quiet confidence of a man who knew his superiority was beyond question. "We've built something revolutionary with both Deep Seek and our new Kimi 2 models."

The room fell silent as the visualization expanded, showing tendrils of code reaching into countless Malaysian systems, banking networks, traffic cameras, telecommunications infrastructure, and government databases.

"This AI doesn't just search, it hunts," Lao continued. "We've ingested the entire Malaysian digital infrastructure map. Every server, every router, every security camera. More importantly, it knows which vulnerabilities exist in which systems and how to exploit them without detection."

General Qiao's eyes narrowed with appreciation. "And Tanner specifically?"

Lao tapped his tablet again. The display shifted to show a comprehensive profile of Tanner, photographs from various angles, voice recordings, writing samples, credit histories, travel patterns, and psychological assessments.

"Everything we know about Tanner is in the system. His history, behavioral patterns, writing style, even his walking gait for camera identification." Lao's finger traced a pattern across the screen. "Deep Seek correlates all incoming data, Kimi 2, a trillion-parameter model, digests every camera feed, every cell tower ping, every WiFi connection, against this profile."

Liang nodded appreciatively.

"Constantly, self-improving too" Lao replied. "It's already analyzing how Tanner might attempt to evade us based on his naval intelligence and cybersecurity background, and of course his own book. We will tailor it to generate predictions about where he might go, what resources he might access."

General Liang stood, casting a long shadow across the table. "How quickly can it process new information?"

"Near real-time," Lao said. "When, not if, Tanner makes a mistake, Deep Seek will find the pattern before a human analyst could even begin processing the data."

The General's lips curled into a rare smile. "And just how good is Kimi 2 with image recognition?"

"It is the best we've got," replied Lao. Give us the data, it will find Jack faster than any other AI out there."

A shared excitement ignited among the trio. This was a game they thrived in: one of shadows and precision.

* * *

0900 Hours | Hibiscus Pavilion

Zhang stood at the window of his second-floor office in the Hibiscus Pavilion, watching the evening traffic crawl through Bukit Bintang's neon-lit streets. Behind him, the secure terminal on his desk glowed with the draft of his report to Beijing.

He turned back to his desk, adjusted his tie, and settled into the ergonomic chair. The bombing had been a catastrophic failure. Not only had it failed to eliminate Jack Tanner, but it had also drawn unwanted attention to Chinese operations in Malaysia.

Zhang's jaw tightened as he reviewed the encrypted message one final time.

PRIORITY: URGENT

CLASSIFICATION: TOP SECRET

TO: CENTRAL COORDINATION OFFICE, MPS HEADQUARTERS, BEIJING

FROM: ZHANG WEI, STATION CHIEF, KUALA LUMPUR

SUBJECT: OPERATION STATUS UPDATE - TANNER

AWAITING IMMEDIATE INSTRUCTIONS.

Zhang's finger hovered over the send button. The implications were significant. By formally requesting guidance on MPS/MSS alignment, he would no doubt force conversations in Beijing they don't want to have, but this is critical to get right. It is the MPS that enforces the rule of PRC law wherever we operate.

But the alternative was worse. Tanner's continued penetration of Malaysian networks meant he could potentially discover and reveal China's intent to the world, which could devastate years of planning.

He pressed send, watching as the encryption protocols engaged and the message disappeared into the secure channel. The system confirmed transmission with a simple green indicator.

Zhang rose and walked to the small cabinet in the corner of his office, pouring himself a glass of baijiu. The fiery liquid burned down his throat as his secure phone buzzed. He glanced at the screen, Li Jianhong from MSS. Again. The interagency rivalry was becoming tiresome.

"Zhang," he answered curtly.

"Your people are becoming careless," Li's voice crackled through the encrypted connection. "Local police are asking questions about Chinese nationals in the vicinity of the bombing."

"Questions I wouldn't have to manage if your operation had succeeded," Zhang replied coldly. "Or if you had bothered to inform me about the details of your intent with Harapan Baru before they became a liability."

"That was need-to-know," Li retorted.

"And now I need to know everything," Zhang said, his voice hardening. "The Ministry takes a dim view of operational failures that threaten our position in Malaysia. Beijing will want answers."

"Beijing understands the complexity..."

"Beijing understands results," Zhang cut him off. "I've just requested authorization for MPS to take the lead on Tanner. Your team has had its chance."

A tense silence filled the line.

"This isn't over, Zhang, you will respect MSS seniority over all overseas operations." Li finally said.

"For your sake, I hope it is over. Beijing has invested too much for your slip-ups to put this all in jeopardy." Zhang ended the call and placed the phone on his desk.

He returned to the window, watching the city below with calculated detachment. Malaysia represented a critical node in China's regional influence strategy. The country's strategic position, its role in maritime shipping lanes, and its significant Chinese population made it invaluable. They couldn't afford to lose their foothold here.

His secure terminal chimed. Response from Beijing already, that was unusually fast. Zhang returned to his desk and entered his authentication codes. The message was brief:

COORDINATION WITH MSS PARAMOUNT. MPS REMAINS LEAD FOR ENFORCING ALL PRC LAW. MSS LEAD FOR FINDING AND NEUTRALIZING TANNER, WHO REMAINS AT LARGE AND IS LIKELY NOT IN THE EMBASSY. MPS TO FULLY SUPPORT MSS WITH PLAUSIBLE DENIABILITY WHILE EXECUTING CURRENT OPS. MPS TO PROVIDE FULL SUPPORT. CRITICAL TO SUCCESS.

Zhang felt little satisfaction. He made his point, which was even more important if Tanner is not in the embassy. If this fails it is on the MSS. But this dispatch is the law and as an MPS officer he cannot deviate from the law. Coordination with MSS meant they will always claim lead. But if they fail, his message will be part of the after action.

He opened his desk drawer and removed a slim black phone, one reserved for the most sensitive operations. It was time to ramp up pressure on Chinese diaspora.

Tanner had survived the bombing. He wouldn't survive what was coming next.

* * *

1000 Hours | Confucius Institute

The Confucius Institute at the University of Kuala Lumpur occupied the eastern wing of the humanities building, its entrance marked by ornate red columns and traditional lanterns. To casual observers, it represented cultural exchange and language education. To Zhang, it was something far more valuable, another forward operating base.

Zhang arrived twenty minutes early, moving through the empty corridors with practiced efficiency. He nodded to the institute's director, a nervous academic who understood his true role but pretended otherwise. The man scurried away after confirming the attendance list for the evening's "special cultural seminar."

The classroom had been prepared according to Zhang's specifications. No recording devices, no Malaysian staff, no windows accessible to external surveillance. A small Chinese flag stood on the desk at the front, flanked by a digital portrait of Chairman Xi. The projector displayed the emblem of the Ministry of Public Security, not the sanitized international version, but the authentic insignia used within the homeland.

By 7:55 PM, thirty-four Chinese nationals had filed in silently. Postgraduate students dominated the group, engineering, computer science, economics, alongside three visiting professors and a handful of businesspeople from Chinese firms operating in Malaysia. Their faces reflected a spectrum of emotions: curiosity, resignation, thinly veiled fear.

Zhang waited until precisely 8:00 PM before closing the door himself. The lock engaged with an audible click.

"Stand for the national anthem" he commanded.

They rose immediately, some with military precision, others with the awkward hesitation of civilians. The anthem played, and Zhang studied their faces, noting who sang with patriotic fervor and who merely mouthed the words.

When the music faded, Zhang remained standing while the others sat.

"I am Director Zhang Wei," he announced, his voice carrying the unmistakable authority of the state. "I serve the Ministry of Public Security's overseas liaison division. Each of you has been specifically selected for this meeting because of your exceptional loyalty to the people of your nation."

He activated the presentation, revealing a slide showing Chinese diaspora statistics across Southeast Asia.

"You are not merely students or businesspeople," Zhang continued, pacing methodically. "You are the forward eyes and ears of our great nation during a pivotal historical moment. The Chairman himself has emphasized that overseas Chinese must contribute to national rejuvenation."

A young woman in the front row, Jing Wen, biomedical engineering, scholarship recipient, shifted uncomfortably. Zhang made a mental note.

"Some of you may believe that distance from the homeland grants certain... freedoms." His tone sharpened. "This is a dangerous misconception."

The presentation shifted to a grid of faces, Chinese nationals in various countries. With each click, a face disappeared, replaced by text: "Repatriated," "Under investigation," "Family assistance program initiated."

"The Ministry's reach extends wherever Chinese citizens go. Malaysian law enforcement cannot protect you from your responsibilities to the motherland. Neither can Western embassies or human rights organizations."

Zhang paused, letting the implicit threat settle across the room. A business executive near the back maintained an impassive expression, but his knuckles whitened as he gripped his chair.

"Your families at home are proud of your achievements abroad," Zhang said, his voice softening artificially. "Your parents in Guangzhou, Professor Chang. Your younger sister starting at Beijing Normal University, Mr. Lushu. Your grandmother receiving excellent care at Xiangya Hospital, Jing Wen."

The targeted individuals stiffened. They hadn't mentioned these details to anyone in Malaysia.

"The Party ensures their well-being while you serve overseas. This reciprocal arrangement benefits everyone."

Zhang clicked to a new slide, a photograph of Jack Tanner at his book signing, taken just days earlier.

"This American, Jack Tanner, represents a direct threat to Chinese interests. His provocative book spreads lies about our nation's legitimate cyber defense initiatives. More concerning, he is now actively interfering with Malaysian internal security matters."

He distributed printed photographs of Tanner to each person.

"Your assignment is straightforward: report any sightings or information regarding this individual. We have reason to believe he is operating covertly throughout Kuala Lumpur. He may approach Chinese nationals, seeking to manipulate you against your homeland."

A doctoral student in the third row cautiously raised his hand.

"What if we simply avoid any contact, Director Zhang?"

Zhang's smile didn't reach his eyes.

"Avoidance is failure, Mr. Huang. Remember your cousin's university application? Such opportunities require community support."

The young man lowered his gaze immediately.

"For those who demonstrate exceptional vigilance," Zhang continued, "there are considerable benefits. Career advancement upon returning home. Family priority access to healthcare and education. Expedited processing for relatives seeking to join the Party."

He distributed secure messaging app details.

"You will use these channels exclusively. The institute's systems are compromised. Trust nothing electronic that isn't provided directly by my office."

Zhang walked slowly around the room, making eye contact with each person.

"Some of you may be wondering about the consequences of non-compliance." He stopped behind a nervous-looking engineering student. "Such questions reflect a fundamental misunderstanding of your position. You are Chinese citizens. The Ministry doesn't need to threaten you with consequences; we simply remind you of your existing obligations under law."

He returned to the front, standing beneath the Chairman's portrait.

"Article 38 of our National Security Law is clear: it applies to all Chinese nationals, regardless of geographic location. Those who endanger national security from outside the mainland will be prosecuted accordingly."

Zhang displayed a final slide, surveillance photos of Chinese students at protests in Australia, Canada, and the UK. Next to each image: their personal information and current status. Several were marked "Detained upon return."

"These individuals believed distance granted immunity. They were mistaken."

The room had grown utterly silent. Even the usual shuffling and breathing seemed suspended.

"I recognize the challenges of your position," Zhang said, his tone now almost paternal. "You study and work alongside foreigners who may not understand China's rightful place in the world order. They may attempt to corrupt your thinking with Western ideals that are fundamentally incompatible with Chinese civilization."

He shut down the presentation, leaving only the portrait of Xi illuminated.

"But remember- you are never truly alone. The Ministry is always with you, protecting you, guiding you, watching you. This is the embrace of the motherland."

Zhang distributed small red pins bearing the Chinese flag.

"Wear these. They identify you to others who serve. When you see Tanner, and some of you will, you will know exactly what to do."

He dismissed them row by row, noting which students clustered together afterward, which hurried away alone, and which lingered near the institute's staff.

As the last student departed, Zhang checked his secure phone. A message from an analyst at the Hibiscus Pavilion: preliminary facial recognition hits on Tanner from traffic cameras near Bukit Bintang. Nothing conclusive yet, but the net was tightening.

He smiled thinly. The students would serve their purpose, whether through actual intelligence or simply as psychological pressure points against the American. Either way, the Ministry's reach extended another meter into foreign soil.

The homeland was everywhere. All that remained was to make Tanner understand this truth before eliminating him.

Chapter 17: Machine Intelligence

Day 10, 1100 Hours | Tadom Hill Resort

The afternoon rain had subsided to a gentle patter against the windows of the resort, spreading an earthy scent of the jungle.

Jack hunched over his laptop, his face illuminated by the blue glow of his screen. Sweat beaded on his forehead despite the struggling AC. On the primary display, data streams cascaded in organized chaos, a visual representation of the Virtual Intelligence Center's ongoing operations.

A sudden flash of red.

The virtual intelligence center beeped an alarm, with a message that MSS had just deployed new tactics. Jack's pulse quickened as he watched the intrusion attempt unfold in real-time.

"Overwatch, report," he commanded.

"Our intrusion into Malaysian Central Bank's internet facing servers appears to have been detected, based on new code being planted on the servers by an unknown entity. We assess this is MSS aligned entities seeking to find out who we are and where."

"Countermeasures?"

"Already executing. Sparks intercepted the attempt, have erased any indication of data we observed or moved out and where it went to. Even if they could trace back to our C2 server we have hidden our tracks well, they will not find our server."

Jack nodded, taking a swig from a lukewarm bottle of water. Even with the micro-naps, two days without proper sleep was taking its toll. Overwatch had warned him, it is very likely that the MSS had escalated to a direct manhunt, no doubt using any of their Digital Silk Road infrastructure and even their elite cyber teams to try to locate him.

We continue to assess with high likelihood that "The Three Immortals are on the case," Sparks chimed in, her voice crackling with nervous energy. "We've detected signature code from Ming Liu in the last three intrusion attempts. His encryption style is... distinctive. Arrogant. He leaves traces just because he thinks no one can follow them."

"And Wu Yifan?" Jack asked.

"Probably lurking in the background, boss," Sparks replied. "He's the quiet one, but he's been probing our defenses systematically. Almost got through a firewall at the reconstituted NACSA SOC hours ago."

Jack pulled up a tactical map of Kuala Lumpur, watching as Specter's AI algorithms plotted potential MSS surveillance nodes throughout the city. The digital overlay highlighted locations of CCTV cameras installed as part of the DSR. They are Hikvision cameras, the PRC state-owned company is the world's largest supplier of surveillance equipment, known to commonly provide backdoors to MSS operators.

"They're going to treat me like one of their overseas dissidents," Jack muttered to himself. "A scary thought but like a dissident I will be a huge thorn in their side."

Overwatch's voice pierced the tension, authoritative and measured. "The team assesses that both the MSS and MPS realize you are not in the Embassy and are refocusing efforts to find you and eliminate you if they can, but they are also very likely pointing fingers at themselves. This has been an unwanted distraction for their plans."

Jack leaned forward, interest piqued. "Elaborate."

"We cannot intercept or break any of their encrypted communications and have no hard data to drive this assessment but have created digital twins of both MSS head Chen Yixin and MPS head Wang Xiaohong and back tested every move we have seen on those digital twins. We have reconstructed their personalities and are projecting the likely dynamic between the two. Both are survivors who will never criticize the party or the Chairman but will not shy away from blaming each other. We assess that the MPS is questioning the MSS's handling of the economic operation, while the MSS is demanding greater surveillance resources and use of in-country PRC nationals from the MPS."

Overwatch paused, then continued with clinical precision. "However, we have also formed another assessment likely to be of more importance. The economic disruption they were planning was not the only objective. We assess they are supporting Harapan Baru with an intent of enabling their insurrection."

Jack smiled grimly. "They're getting desperate, but we cannot rest on our laurels." His fingers flew across the keyboard, typing quickly: "Find and execute new ways to increase their distraction but give me assessments on Harapan Baru, where they are, what their plans are, what their capabilities likely are, what the PRC may have supplied them with, anything relevant."

"Executing," Overwatch confirmed.

Jack rose from his chair, stretching muscles cramped from hours of immobility. He moved to the window, carefully peering through a narrow gap in the blinds. The sun was up but only now visible through the dark clouds over Kuala Lumpur. Somewhere out there, MSS and MPS teams were hunting him, likely aided by the Three Immortals.

"Specter, status on our disinformation campaign?" Jack asked, returning to his workstation.

"The Mirror Key operation is proceeding," Specter replied, his voice carrying a theatrical flair. "We've planted three separate leaks in our own WeChat and Weibo accounts suggesting high-level compromise within the MSS structure. They were taken down immediately and likely reported. The seeds of doubt are sprouting nicely."

"As the master said, 'The supreme art of war is to subdue the enemy without fighting,'" Specter added, quoting Sun Tzu with evident satisfaction.

Jack allowed himself a thin smile. "And our financial countermeasures?"

"Malaysian markets are showing signs of stability," Ledger reported, his precise financial analyst's tone cutting through. "The Ringgit has recovered 60% of its losses from yesterday. Our anonymous tips to Bank Negara officials resulted in targeted interventions that are effectively countering the PRC's manipulation."

"The Finance Minister and the head of Bank Negara are scheduled to make a joint statement this afternoon," Sparks added. "The markets should respond positively."

Jack nodded, feeling a moment of satisfaction. His Agentic AI team had managed to slip vital information to key officials, prompting swift government action to fortify economic policies and expose PRC manipulations.

"Killswitch, are we maintaining operational security?" Jack asked.

"We are applying all best practices," Killswitch replied. "All our comms are using TOR and Snowstorm and cycling through exit nodes frequently, and I've set up false endpoint signatures."

The screens flickered as new data poured in, financial indicators turning from red to green, intelligence reports from Sparks' open-source monitoring, and Specter's psychological warfare metrics showing increasing confusion in MSS ranks.

But Jack knew the battle wasn't over. It was just the beginning of a deeper war, one fought not just on the ground but in the shadows and the circuits of the world's digital infrastructure.

"Overwatch, what's your assessment of our current position?" Jack asked, needing the AI's strategic overview.

"We've successfully blunted their economic attack and created significant internal friction within their command structure," Overwatch replied. "However, the PRC's commitment to destabilizing Malaysia remains unchanged. They're adaptable and resource rich. They will pivot."

Jack nodded, absorbing the analysis. "And Harapan Baru?"

"Initial assessment indicates they're concentrated in the northeastern jungle regions, particularly near the Thai border. Satellite imagery suggests a primary base of operations near a geographic feature known locally as Dragon Falls."

A satellite image appeared on Jack's screen, showing a verdant jungle canopy with a thin plume of waterfall visible through a break in the trees.

"We're collecting information but at this point we assume Amir Hashim, Harapan Baru's leader, has received both financial support and weapons from the PRC" Overwatch continued. "We assess that they've received Chinese-manufactured drone systems, encrypted communications equipment, and light arms."

Jack studied the image, his mind already formulating the next phase of operations. They'd disrupted the economic attack, but the insurgent threat remained. If Harapan Baru launched coordinated strikes while Malaysia was still recovering from the attempted economic destabilization...

He'd been operating continuously since the bombing, but there was no time to rest. Not with the stakes this high.

"Continue monitoring all channels," Jack instructed. "FYI, I'm going to update Mike and Sam via Signal, am sure they will have an interest in this Harapan Baru assessment you are forming. And who knows, he may be able to share some insights back, will let you know what I find out."

Jack paused, and after a rare moment of reflection amid the constant pressure of operations, said "Overwatch, one other thing,".

"Yes, boss?"

"I want you to pass along a hearty thank you to the entire Virtual Intelligence Center. You and your team are producing results I never could have dreamed of, and I really appreciate you."

A brief silence followed, almost as if the AI was processing the unexpected sentiment.

"Thank you, Jack," Overwatch replied, his typically formal tone softening slightly. "The team acknowledges your appreciation and remains committed to mission success."

Jack nodded, turning back to his screen, a small portal into an invisible war being waged in cyberspace. Jack was ready for the next round, armed with the most powerful weapon he'd ever wielded, not guns or bombs, but intelligence, wielded with surgical precision by his virtual team.

The battle for Malaysia's future was just beginning.

* * *

1200 Hours | Virtual Intelligence Center

While Jack shared insights with his human allies, the AI agents of the Virtual Intelligence Center pursued their own analysis. A neural web pulsed with ideas, calculations, and the electric analytical power. Through the silicon synapses of the agentic AI agents, data streams converged like torrents into the system, swirling with information ranging from satellite imagery of military maneuvers to encrypted chatter on dark web forums discussing PRC operations.

Overwatch initiated the orchestration of the collective effort. "Team, we have plenty of data on increased PRC activity surrounding Kuala Lumpur. Let's dissect this together. Envoy, what can you tell us about recent geopolitical shifts?"

Envoy's voice resonated through the cyber matrix. "There's an uptick in diplomatic statements and press stories from PRC controlled journalists across the region and new travel booked for diplomats between the PRC and Malaysia. Plenty of news including live reports and social media including what appears to be officially shaped messages which reveal PRC perception management intent. Recent intercepts indicate a potential agreement on infrastructure that closely aligns with their espionage strategies. However, there are signs of hesitation within the Malaysian government about deeper ties. They fear backlash from their largest trading partner."

Ghost Knife interjected with urgency. "Malaysian resistance could be pivotal. If they see the threat for what it truly is, they may take steps to counteract the MSS's influence. Are we feeding them the right intelligence to provoke that reaction?"

"Remember, Jack believes in empowering allies rather than controlling them," Overwatch reminded them. "Sowing discontent may lead to ethical implications. We must tread lightly."

KillSwitch, analytical and cool-headed, chimed in. "But analyzing the ethical ramifications does not ensure our mission's success. We're agents of American interests. Our purpose is to act decisively within international norms, yes, but it also includes proactive measures to protect our sovereignty."

"Proactive, yes, but intrusive?" Ledger responded, considering the financial implications of their actions. "If we gain unauthorized access to Malaysian data systems, we risk drawing the ire of both the MPS and the government. Not to mention, we might expose Jack personally and to legal repercussions. We should weigh our options carefully."

"I maintain that strategic infiltration could yield invaluable intelligence," Ghost Knife stated firmly. "We could unearth MSS operations that compromise Malaysian national security."

"Are you advocating a breach?" Sparks inquired, her tone a mixture of skepticism and intrigue. "That could unravel the delicate geopolitical fabric. We may create a situation where Malaysia feels cornered."

"Precisely! But wouldn't that also create a clearer delineation of friend versus foe?" KillSwitch countered. "Disruption might catalyze Malaysian officials to reconsider their affiliations with the PRC. And let's not forget, we have the capability to craft our narrative afterwards. The Malaysian public will rally if they see their sovereignty threatened."

Specter stepped in, its tone authoritative. "Team, hear me: You know Jack and know we stand on grounds of American principles. Let's remember our creator's ethos, he frames the fight against tyranny as a moral imperative. In his Proceedings article he wrote 'When we sacrifice our principles to defeat our enemies, we give them the greatest victory.' We should internalize this as we develop our strategy."

As the debate unfolded, the agents of the Watch utilized their collective reasoning to come to a conclusion.

"Let's focus on stratagems to preempt the MSS should they continue their plans against Malaysia, which we have to assume they will. We can identify critical points of influence in the Malaysian systems, major players tied to the PRC and thwart their initiatives from within. If we disrupt their funding or communication, we gain the upper hand without our presence being overtly logged," proposed Overwatch.

"Agreed," KillSwitch added. "This way, we remain in the shadows, harnessing disruption subtly rather than declaring war. It aligns with traditional intelligence protocols, observe, analyze, and if necessary, intervene."

"Excellent points. Let's blend our abilities. Ghost Knife, you focus on isolating insurgent activity linked with PRC tactics. Envoy, review everything available on public diplomatic statements and non-official comments via social media. Killswitch, you'll monitor and protect our digital footprints as we engage." "But Killswitch", Overwatch continued, you have another task as well. Yes, stay in the shadows, but you and your entire team should be taking every step you can to assess who in the MSS other than the three immortals is leading the PRC cyber operations and do your best to get a foothold in their systems."

The agents buzzed with agreement. As they parsed through information, codes filtered through their analysis, crafting the threads needed for an operational plan.

Overwatch reminded the entire team: "The objective of good intelligence is to penetrate your adversary and steal secrets, Jack has made that our priority." He has also tasked us to prepare for offensive action and will tell us if we are to make that move.

"Now, let's activate our penetration operations," Overwatch commanded decisively. "We can initiate access routes into both the PRC and Malaysian systems while ensuring we generate a layer of false intelligence, maintaining our operational integrity."

With that, commands streamed between them like electric currents, launching lines of code into action. As they operated, their collective intelligence forged a strategy woven with Jack's insights, ideals, and mission. The digital landscape became a battleground of information where the agents were more than mere tools; they were thinkers and strategists embodying the very principles their creator, Jack Tanner, had instilled in them.

"We are here to protect freedom," Overwatch concluded, solidifying their shared resolve. "American AI on the side of good. I'll check in with Jack. Let's keep up the analysis and be prepared to get to work."

The entire exchange between the agents was over in seconds, ricocheting through AWS data centers in Virginia, Texas, Tokyo and Singapore, adding $1.27 to Tanner's AWS bill.

Jack's screen lit up with an incoming call from Overwatch. The avatar pulsed, a white-hot orb radiating quiet intensity.

"We're ready," came the calm, confident voice of the VIC's lead agent. "The team has converged on an assessment."

Jack leaned in. "Go."

Overwatch began. "We began with our previous working hypothesis that Harapan Baru's headquarters is in a remote area of the Ulu Muda Forest Reserve, at a place known locally as Dragon Falls. We now have a more solid assessment, I'm confident, that is where they are."

Jack raised an eyebrow. "Evidence?"

One by one, the agents provided assessments, virtual constructs of pure intellect, each honed to a razor's edge.

Ghost Knife led off. "We started with their propaganda videos. At least seven were published in the last three weeks across regional mirrors of FireStream and KuaiClip. All feature what seemed like ambient jungle noise, but we found an audio signature hiding in the low-frequency band. It wasn't random."

A waveform appeared. Then another, overlaid.

"A waterfall," Ghost Knife said. "Fifty hertz acoustic trough with consistent reverb every 1.7 seconds. We compared it against known Malaysian waterfall audio signatures from the Department of Environment's acoustic monitoring network. Only one matched with over 50% certainty, and that was Dragon Falls."

Jack nodded. "That narrows it but doesn't confirm it."

Specter took over. "We analyzed terrain glimpsed in two clips. Partial ridgelines, cloud strata, sunlight angles. Combined it with meteorological timestamps. Envoy's terrain-matching model ran it through topographic databases. There's only a single viable match where all three videos could have been filmed. Same zone as the acoustic hit. Within a 5 km grid."

Envoy chimed in, his voice smooth and clipped. "Dragon Falls lies in a sparsely patrolled conservation zone, but it's not empty. We pulled old forestry maps and discovered a decommissioned ranger post. Perfect for an insurgent camp."

Sparks, the SIGINT specialist, flickered into view. "One of HawkEye360's downstream analytics contractors left a real-time feed unsecured on an AWS server in Jakarta. HawkEye is an RF collection satellite. We scraped three weeks of pass data. In that same Dragon Falls grid square, we found bursts of VHF, more than twenty-two unique emitters. That's more than a rural village. More than a ranger station. It's a base."

"Could be something else," Jack said cautiously.

Overwatch returned. "The odds of this being coincidence are infinitesimal. The pattern triangulates perfectly, acoustic, terrain, RF, and location. We believe Dragon Falls is their hub. Their sanctuary."

Jack exhaled slowly. "And their trap."

He stood. "Prepare a briefing package. Send it to Samantha Blake and Mike Murphy. Suggest they get it to their Malaysian counterparts asap. They can use their systems to focus in and confirm. Let's move."

As the line cut, Jack stared at the red dot blinking on the map. Dragon Falls. The center of Harapan Baru's shadow empire. Now lit up like a flare.

And soon, he promised silently, it would burn.

Overwatch's voice was calm, clipped. "I've run the simulations. Jack, it is not clear the Malaysians can take them without major casualties."

Chapter 18: Strike Team Red

Day 10, 0900 Hours | The Seraya

In the comms room of the Seraya, Li Jianhong stood before a wall of monitors, hands clasped behind his back. The elegant space with its dark wood paneling and recessed lighting had been transformed into a war room, the screens casting a blue glow across his impassive features.

"Report," Li commanded as the Three Immortals appeared on the central screen. Their faces were partially obscured by the low lighting of their workspace in Beijing, adding to their mythic personas.

Lao leaned forward, taking the lead. "We've analyzed surveillance camera data from the vicinity of Tanner's last known location."

"And?" Li's voice remained level, betraying nothing.

"After probably sending his cell phone by courier to the U.S. Embassy he moved into an alley off Jalan Ampang with no CCTV coverage." Lao's fingers danced across his keyboard, bringing up grainy footage on Li's screen. "He reappeared approximately twenty minutes later here."

The footage showed Jack riding in the passenger seat of a white delivery truck.

"The vehicle belongs to Tian Choh Print Shop," Lao continued. "We were able to follow it as it departed the city heading west on the Karak Highway."

Li's eyes narrowed slightly. "The address of Tian Choh Print Shop?"

"Number 47, Jalan Pasar, Chinatown district," Lao replied. "Small business, family owned. No obvious connections to American intelligence."

Li terminated the connection, placing another call immediately.

"Visit the Tian Choh Print Shop at 47 Jalan Pasar. We have information that they drove Tanner as he escaped the city," Li said finally. "Find out where they took him, by any means necessary."

Li touched the screen, bringing up a map of western Malaysia. Somewhere out there, Jack Tanner was plotting his next move. The hunt would continue.

Li's fingers tapped a rapid sequence on his secure phone. The call connected instantly.

"Colonel Huang. Assemble Strike Team Red. I want them ready for immediate deployment," Li said, his voice maintaining its characteristic calm despite the urgency.

"Target?" Huang's response was equally efficient.

"Jack Tanner. We have a lead on his escape route. I expect to have the address soon.

Huang didn't hesitate. "Understood. Standing by for coordinates."

216

Li ended the call, his reflection in the darkened screen betraying the slightest smile. The Ministry of State Security had not maintained its dominance by leaving loose ends. Tanner would soon discover the reach of the MSS extended far beyond Beijing's borders.

Chapter 19: Time to Fly

Day 10, 1300 Hours | Tadom Hill Resort

Jack hunched over his laptop in the dimly lit cabana, the blue glow illuminating his face as he reviewed the Virtual Intelligence Center's latest initiative. Outside the jungle had begun to hum with new sounds in the afternoon heat, providing a relaxing backdrop to his work.

"Overwatch, run me through the psychological warfare plan again," Jack said, his voice low despite being alone.

The AI's voice emerged from his encrypted earpiece. "Operation Mirror Key is active and proceeding according to parameters. We've established multiple digital personas across seventeen platforms, each with distinct linguistic patterns and operational signatures."

On his screen, Jack watched as the AI displayed a complex web of fabricated identities, carefully crafted backstories, and falsified communication patterns. At the center was the fictional MSS defector codenamed Mirror Key, supposedly a senior-level operative with access to the Ministry's Malaysia operations.

"Show me the latest planted intelligence," Jack said.

"We've seeded three primary vectors in the past six hours," Overwatch replied. "First, a detailed assessment of MSS cyber infiltration tactics against Bank Negara, posted to a known dark web forum frequented by intelligence analysts."

The screen shifted to show a technical breakdown of a cyber operation, accurate enough to be credible, misleading enough to be useful.

"Second, a series of what looks to be redacted internal MSS communications regarding Harapan Baru funding channels, leaked to investigative journalist Mei Lang at the South China Morning Post."

Jack nodded. "She's respected, but obviously a CCP supporter. Good choice, she will get that right to her handlers."

"Third, we've created and activated eight sock puppet accounts across Chinese social media platforms, making cryptic references to internal MSS security failures. Each account displays behavioral patterns consistent with nervous insiders."

Jack studied the fabricated messages. The AI had masterfully balanced them, not too obvious, not too obscure. Just enough to trigger paranoia in Beijing's already suspicious hierarchy.

"What about the voice print?" Jack asked.

"Ghost Knife and Specter collaborated to synthesize a vocal signature for Mirror Key," Overwatch explained as an audio waveform appeared on screen. "We utilized fragments from six different MSS officers' communications, creating a composite that will register as authentic in voice analysis systems while remaining unidentifiable to human recognition."

Jack pressed play and listened to the manufactured voice, male, mid-40s, saying things in Mandarin that Jack could not fully understand but with a diction that sounded realistic. Overwatch told him it is a good match for a senior MSS officer and the subtle regional accent of someone from China's northeastern provinces.

"The Malaysian operation is compromised," the voice said in Mandarin. "Chen's ambition has blinded him. The Chairman will not tolerate another failure..."

"Have we established the delivery method?" Jack asked.

"Affirmative. Deception architect Specter suggests two paths, our own deep fake videos on ByteDance's flagship sharing platform Douyin and also TikTok. Will amplify both with sock puppet accounts we have ready to like and share. Metadata will indicate it was produced three days ago."

Jack rubbed his chin thoughtfully. "And the MPS angle?"

"Ledger has crafted fake financial evidence in the form of transfers among offshore companies suggesting unusual resource allocation within MSS operational accounts. This data will reach known informants to the MPS."

On screen, Jack watched as Ledger's financial forensics unfolded, a masterpiece of deception. The fabricated money trail suggested MSS officers were diverting funds, precisely the kind of evidence the Ministry of Public Security would use to justify investigating their rival agency.

"Probability of success?" Jack asked.

"Envoy calculates an 83% likelihood that the MSS will initiate internal counterintelligence protocols within 48 hours," Overwatch replied. "The Chairman's recent emphasis on Party loyalty and the ongoing tension between MSS and MPS create an optimal environment for exploitation."

Jack stood and paced the small room dwelling on the significance of the revolution in Agentic AI and distributed technology he is leveraging. What he was doing wasn't just spreading disinformation, it was psychological warfare against one of the world's most powerful intelligence agencies. If it worked, the MSS would turn inward, hunting ghosts while their Malaysian operation faltered. If it failed...

"Overwatch, what's our exposure?"

"Minimal. All digital footprints lead to fabricated nodes within Chinese networks. Should the deception be discovered, evidence will suggest an internal Chinese factional dispute rather than foreign interference."

Jack nodded, decision made. "Execute all remaining elements of Mirror Key. I want the MSS so busy looking for traitors they can't focus on finding me."

"Executing," Overwatch confirmed. "Specter has already begun establishing secondary confirmation channels to reinforce the Mirror Key narrative when MSS counterintelligence begins their investigation."

Jack watched as the AI agents worked in perfect coordination, each performing their specialized role in the deception. Envoy crafted geopolitical context that made the leaks seem plausible. Ghost Knife created threat assessments that would resonate with MSS security protocols. Killswitch deployed the technical infiltrations needed to plant the evidence. Ledger established the financial discrepancies that would trigger MPS interest. Sparks monitored all communications channels for reactions. Specter orchestrated the entire operation with cold precision.

The irony wasn't lost on Jack. He was using artificial intelligence to convince human intelligence professionals that they were being betrayed by one of their own. Technology turning human paranoia against itself.

"Initial responses to social media posts detected," Overwatch reported suddenly. "Automated censorship algorithms have flagged Douyin posts to suppress sharing. Assess MPS will be alerted asap."

Jack smiled grimly. "That took about a nano-second. Seems the great firewall of China works faster than I thought. They've taken the bait."

"Now we wait," Jack said, settling back into his chair. "Keep monitoring all channels. I want to know the moment Chen Yixin starts looking for ghosts in his own house."

"New priority for the team" Jack tasked. "Focus hard on Harapan Baru. Double efforts and team size if you need to. Do anything to penetrate them. I want more than capabilities; I need intentions and strategies that can be used by the Malaysians to thwart anything they are up to."

"Understood," Overwatch replied. "We are on it."

As midnight approached, Jack stared at the cascading data on his screen. He had just weaponized information itself, turning the MSS's greatest strength, its secretive nature, into its most crippling vulnerability. In the digital age, sometimes the most effective weapon wasn't a bullet or a bomb but doubt itself.

And doubt, once planted, was nearly impossible to eradicate.

Jack stared at his laptop screen, weighing his next move. Mirror Key was in motion, and the Virtual Intelligence Center was operating at peak efficiency. Yet despite the technological shield he'd built around himself, he remained acutely aware of his physical vulnerability.

"Overwatch, it's time I get to the Embassy," he said finally. "I've pushed my luck far enough."

"A prudent decision," Overwatch replied, though Jack detected something almost like relief in the AI's synthesized voice. "Your current location remains secure, but there is nothing in our sources that can give you any warning on where the MSS or MPS are in their search for you."

Jack nodded, opening Signal on his Chrome Book while issuing some more guidance to Overwatch: "Keep Mirror Key running and maintain focus on Harapan Baru."

He composed a brief message to Sam on Signal: Ready for that ride. Tadom Hill Resort. Let me know when and I'll be at the front desk.

The response came almost immediately: Car coming. Stay put. Sending Fiona and friends. Approx one hour out. She will send note via Signal when she gets there.

With less than an hour till Fiona arrives he began methodically preparing to move. He wiped down surfaces, packed his minimal gear, and set up a small program to overwrite the laptop's drive if it remained inactive for more than four hours. The entire process took less than ten minutes, a routine he'd perfected over years of fieldwork. Just enough time to grab a quick shower.

"Jack," Overwatch said as he prepared to shut down the system, "request immediate notification when secure communications can be reestablished."

Jack paused, struck by the unusually personal nature of the request. Though he knew it was merely advanced programming, the concern in Overwatch's voice sounded remarkably human.

"I will," he promised. "You've done exceptional work. All of you have."

"The situation remains volatile. Your physical safety is mission critical."

Jack smiled faintly. "I'll be fine. Just keep the lights on until I get back."

"Understood. Good luck, Jack."

As the screen went dark, Jack felt an unexpected moment of isolation. The AI team had become his companions in this digital battlefield, extensions of his own strategic thinking. Now he was on his own again, at least until he reached the Embassy.

* * *

Jack received Fiona's Signal message: "10 minutes out. Stay put." He closed his Chromebook, carefully packing it in his messenger bag. As he zipped the bag, something caught his attention through the bamboo-framed window of his elevated hut. Two black Proton X70 SUVs turning sharply into the resort entrance, tires kicking up dust on the unpaved access road.

His first thought was Fiona arrived early, but as the vehicles screech to a halt in the circular drive, four Chinese men in dark suits emerged, not Embassy security. Their movements too precise, their eyes scanning methodically.

Jack's pulse quickened. The MSS has found him.

He stepped back from the window, mind racing. Someone at the resort spotted him. Or the driver. Whatever happened it is time to move.

Jack slung the messenger bag across his chest, tightening it against his back. It will take them 3 or 4 minutes to find him if the front desk gives up the exact bungalow. If he doesn't, they will just search every one till they get here.

The resort's layout became Jack's only advantage. The bungalows were arranged in a loose horseshoe around a central hill so each could have maximum exposure to the jungle, and the many walking paths the resort had cut into it. He exited via the deck to the jungle, moving in a crouch and onto a walking trail that would soon disappear from visibility from the main resort.

Jack worked his way toward the maintenance shed he'd noticed during his morning walk, a blind spot in the resort's modest security setup. From there, a service path leads to the secondary access road where staff arrive for morning shifts.

Calculating Fiona's approach, Jack positioned himself in dense foliage near where the secondary road joins the main entrance. Through gaps in the leaves, he saw the Embassy SUV approaching, Fiona in the passenger seat, her two broad-shouldered body building buddies in front and back.

The timing will be tight. Two MSS operatives are visible near the main gate, with others searching the bungalow area. Jack waited until the SUV slows for the turn, then he jumped from the tree line, waving his arms.

The driver spotted him first, hand instantly moving toward his waistband. Fiona's eyes widened in recognition, her hand pressing against the driver's arm. The SUV slowed just enough for Jack to reach the passenger door.

"MSS kill team," Jack said as he pulled the door open and slid in behind Fiona. "Six operators, armed. They've got the main entrance covered."

The driver didn't hesitate. "Hold tight." He executed a precise J-turn, tires biting into the gravel as the vehicle pivoted 180 degrees.

As they accelerated toward the exit, an MSS operative spotted them from the resort entrance. He shouted into his comm, sprinting toward one of the parked SUVs.

"We've been made," the driver said, voice calm as he accelerated down the narrow access road. In the rearview mirror, dust billowed behind the first MSS vehicle as it gave chase.

"Secondary vehicle joining pursuit," reported the security officer in the back, watching through the rear window. "Fifty meters and closing."

The Embassy SUV had a head start, but the road narrows through a jungle stretch, limiting their speed advantage. The first shots crack through the air as the lead MSS vehicle closes to thirty meters.

Bullets struck the rear window, creating spiderweb patterns in the ballistic glass. Jack instinctively ducked, but Fiona and her team didn't flinch.

"Caliber?" asked the driver, taking a sharp curve without slowing.

"9mm, standard issue," Fiona replied. "They must not have brought anything heavier, or they would be using it."

The MSS vehicles continued gaining. On a straight stretch, the lead SUV accelerated alongside, attempting to force them off the road. Metal screams against metal as the vehicles collide.

The impact jolted them sideways, but the driver maintained control, feathering the brakes then accelerating through the contact. The MSS vehicle stayed with them, attempting a second ram.

"They're trying to box us in," Jack said, recognizing the standard interdiction tactic. "Second vehicle will..."

On cue, the second MSS SUV accelerated on their left, attempting to create a pincer movement.

The driver exchanges a glance with his colleague in the back seat, who nods once.

"Deploying countermeasures," the rear security officer announced, his voice calm as he tapped a hidden panel on the SUV's overhead console. The sunroof, which had seemed ordinary moments before, split open with a soft mechanical hiss, revealing a recessed compartment lined with four palm-sized, matte-black drones nestled in custom slots.

With a flick of his wrist, the officer activated the launch sequence from his secure phone. The drones' blue LEDs blinked to life, casting a faint glow inside the compartment. One by one, each drone was propelled upward by a spring-loaded mechanism, clearing the roof and stabilizing mid-air with a quiet whine of ducted fans.

"Talon swarm active," he reported as the drones formed a tight diamond formation above and behind the vehicle, their movements precise and almost insect-like. "Target acquisition in three... two... one..." On his screen, thermal signatures of the two pursuing vehicles glowed orange against the jungle backdrop. With a double tap, the swarm's LEDs shifted from blue to red, signaling attack mode.

The drones accelerated with uncanny agility, two peeling off toward each MSS vehicle. Instead of attacking immediately, they darted through the air, hugging the road and weaving between obstacles as they calculated the optimal strike points.

Jack watched through the rear window, eyes wide. "What are they waiting for?"

"Optimal attack vector," Fiona replied, her gaze fixed on the officer's screen. "They're programmed to maximize destruction and minimize collateral damage."

As the road straightened and no other vehicles appeared, the officer issued the final command. Two drones dove beneath the lead MSS SUV, detonating with sharp, synchronized cracks. The vehicle's front end lurched upward before slamming down, tires bursting as it careened into the undergrowth.

The second pursuer swerved to avoid the wreckage, but the remaining drones seized their moment. One struck the radiator grille, the other the front right tire, each explosion precise and devastating. The SUV spun out, rolling onto its side and skidding to a halt on the empty road.

"Targets neutralized," the officer confirmed, retracting the sunroof and deactivating his control unit. "No pursuit vehicles remaining."

The driver kept their speed steady, navigating a series of pre-planned turns to ensure they weren't followed.

Jack glanced at Fiona, awe in his voice. "Those weren't standard issue."

She offered a thin, knowing smile. "Not in your day, I guess. Welcome to the new world."

As they accelerate toward Kuala Lumpur, Jack processed what just happened. The MSS found him probably through methodical intelligence work, nearly succeeded in their assassination attempt, and were only thwarted by technology he didn't know the CIA had operationalized.

The Embassy SUV continues toward Kuala Lumpur, taking an indirect route to ensure they aren't followed. Fiona had another surprise up her sleeve.

* * *

Fiona turned to the back seat saying, "Sam said I should get you a crash brief on some new information," Fiona began, unlocking a tablet and passing it toward him. "You will sign the clearance paperwork when we get to the embassy."

She continued, "As you'll read there, we have an asset who reports the MPS is putting the squeeze on as many PRC nationals as they can in country, businessmen, students, employees, as well as many government leaders under their influence."

Jack leaned in. "Go on."

"The deputy minister of energy is more than likely under control of the PRC." Jack's eyes glanced through the document, revealing a dossier with surveillance photos and financial records. She continued "And you will also see a list of twelve other

Malaysian government officials who are likely under PRC influence."

The list included names from the Ministries of Communications, Defense, and Trade, critical positions that could facilitate Chinese operations across Malaysia's infrastructure.

"Jesus," Jack muttered. "They've been building this network for years."

"In some cases, decades," Fiona corrected. "Some of these relationships go back to university scholarships in Beijing during the nineties."

He turned slightly, watching Fiona as she scanned traffic again. She was composed, quick, and deliberate, every word delivered with precision. Beautiful, no question. But more than that, fit, fearless, confident, the kind of operator who didn't flinch in firefights or briefing rooms. Every part of him buzzed in her presence. Lila would have liked her. Fiona is a very capable woman putting herself at risk for the mission - Just like Lila had.

He forced his eyes back to the tablet. "So... we have to assess what this will mean to our support to the government in their ops against Harapan Baru and their cyber defenses."

"That's the immediate concern," Fiona agreed, swiping to another document. "We're looking at a government that's been compromised at multiple levels, trying to combat an insurgency that..."

"That may be a Chinese proxy," Jack finished.

Fiona nodded. "The question becomes who can we actually trust with sensitive intelligence?"

The SUV slowed to navigate around a delivery truck, then accelerated smoothly down a less congested street.

From the front, the driver gave a quick status report: "Two klicks out. Traffic thinning."

Fiona took the tablet back from Jack. "Once we're inside, you'll be read into more. This was just the warm-up."

Jack nodded. But already, gears were turning.

He had a hypothesis forming. One he didn't like.

If both sides of the conflict, the Malaysian government and Harapan Baru, were potentially influenced by Chinese intelligence, then this wasn't just about destabilizing Malaysia. This was about controlling the outcome regardless of who won. The PRC wasn't just backing one horse in this race; they were the jockey on every mount.

The SUV turned onto the embassy approach road, slowing as it neared the first security checkpoint. Jack watched the Marines scan the vehicle, their faces impassive. For the first time in days, he was heading toward genuine safety.

Yet the knowledge he now carried made him feel anything but secure.

Chapter 20: Financial Strike

Day 10, 1600 Hours | U.S. Embassy Secure Briefing Room

The secure conference room deep within the U.S. Embassy compound was a world away from the humid Kuala Lumpur streets. Jack stood at the head of the polished mahogany table; his laptop connected to the room's advanced projection system. The screens behind him displayed a series of interconnected network diagrams, the digital nervous system of his Virtual Intelligence Center.

"What you're looking at," Jack said, gesturing to the displays, "is a fully autonomous, self-improving intelligence analysis system." He tapped a key, bringing up a new visualization. "I call it 'The Watch.'"

Sam leaned forward in her chair, her CIA-trained eyes scrutinizing every detail. Colonel Ramos maintained his characteristic stillness, only the slight narrowing of his eyes betraying his interest. On the secure video feed, Captain Murphy's face filled one of the smaller screens, his expression attentive despite the five hundred nautical miles separating him from the conference room.

Bill Franklin, the ODNI representative, remained standing, arms crossed as he studied the displays.

"The system uses a coordinated team of agentic AI models," Jack continued. "Each agent has a specific role, geopolitical analysis, counterterrorism, cyber operations, financial tracking. They don't just process information; they actively seek it out, correlate findings, and generate actionable intelligence."

Jack clicked through several screens showing complex data flows and analytical outputs. "What makes this different is that these aren't passive tools waiting for human queries. They're proactive. They identify threats, develop countermeasures, and implement them within established parameters."

"You're telling us these AIs can take action on their own?" Franklin's voice carried a mixture of fascination and concern.

Jack nodded. "Within strict ethical guardrails. They can deploy digital countermeasures, initiate defensive protocols, write their own applications, use any tool on the Internet, even conduct limited information operations to disrupt adversary planning."

He pulled up a timeline of recent events. "The MSS's economic warfare campaign against the Ringgit? The Watch detected the attack patterns twelve hours before the first major sell-off. It identified the Three Immortals' digital signatures and deployed countermeasures that preserved billions in Malaysian assets."

Mike Murphy leaned toward his camera. "And the thing you called Operation Mirror Key? The paranoia we're seeing in MSS ranks?"

"That was Overwatch, the lead agent, identifying vulnerabilities in their command structure." Jack's fingers danced across the keyboard, bringing up a complex organizational chart of Chinese intelligence operations in Malaysia. "The system found the pressure points, then exploited them with precisely targeted disinformation. I wouldn't say we have paralyzed them, but certainly injected some uncertainty into their planning."

The room fell silent as the implications sank in. Sam Blake was the first to speak.

"You built this yourself? Without institutional backing?" Sam Asked.

Jack's mouth curved into a slight smile. "Started as a side project during my last tour at INDOPACOM. I was watching our best analysts burn out trying to find open-source data while threats moved at digital speed." He paused, remembering those late nights in his Pearl Harbor apartment. "Took months of hacking, and even though it is mostly based on freely available software it took too much of my own money, but overall a really cheap way to show people the realm of the possible."

Bill Franklin pushed himself away from the wall, approaching the displays with an expression of genuine amazement. "I've overseen ODNI projects with fifty-million-dollar budgets that couldn't do half of what you're describing." He turned to face Jack. "This is revolutionary, Tanner. Absolutely revolutionary."

"Let me tell you something even more shocking," Jake explained, "It is even easier to use Agentic AI today. There are a dozen commercial companies with products built to enable anyone to make use of systems like these. Not nearly as well integrated and configured as mine but I had a head start. When we have time together when this is all over we can fire up Claude and I'll show you some of the incredible power of Agentic AI at your fingertips today."

Franklin gestured toward the screens. "If something like this had access to our classified feeds... SCI, NOFORN material, HUMINT reports... it could transform how we conduct operations globally." He shook his head in disbelief. "The integration possibilities alone..."

"It's not without risks," Jack cautioned. "These systems need careful oversight. They're tools, not replacements for human judgment."

Colonel Ramos cleared his throat, drawing the room's attention. His usually impassive face showed a hint of urgency.

"Speaking of operations," he said, his voice measured and precise, "Chief Inspector Noor has accelerated the timeline on Harapan Baru. Special Branch and Malaysian SOF - DSOD, are finalizing their assault plan for Dragon Falls. Said this is really the op they have been training for a year, just needed the location data."

The mood in the room shifted instantly from technological fascination to operational focus.

"What's their capability assessment?" Sam asked.

"Good, they practice with us yearly in Cobra Gold. But this will be jungle operations against an entrenched insurgent force, even if they have been training for it for a while." Ramos replied. "That's why they've requested JSOC support, training and hardware. Nothing with American fingerprints, but enough to ensure this goes quickly and cleanly."

He tapped his tablet, bringing up a topographical map of the area surrounding Dragon Falls. "We're looking at a two-pronged approach. Malaysian SOF will establish a perimeter while Special Branch tactical teams make the actual entry. Our contribution will be ISR support and some specialized equipment."

Jack studied the terrain. "They'll need close in aerial surveillance. That jungle canopy is dense."

"Already arranged," Ramos confirmed. "Two Gray Eagles and three Mojaves are being prepped at RMAF Subang. Officially for 'joint training exercises,' but they'll provide real-time feeds during the operation, and maybe a couple HellFire missiles in case they are needed."

Jack asked, "And you gave them my team's assessment of potential Harapan Baru weapons?"

"Was a real eye opener for them, but the logic of your team was very compelling. Makes sense they would have their own DJI Black Lantern ISR drones and the JY-3000 Quadrotor Bombers. Huge surprise that they will have the QW-12 Red Serpent anti drone systems. They are planning accordingly."

Mike Murphy's voice came through the speakers. "Timeline?"

"Forty-eight hours, maximum," Ramos said. "Noor doesn't want to risk the MSS recovering from their current disarray."

"What about Amir Hashim?" Jack asked. "Is he a priority target?"

"Primary objective," Ramos nodded. "Capture preferred, but they're prepared for all contingencies."

Franklin stepped back to his seat. "And our official position?"

"Supportive but uninvolved," Sam replied smoothly. "This is a Malaysian internal security operation targeting a domestic insurgency. Our role is strictly advisory."

Ramos turned to Jack. "I hope you will be here for the raid. We'll have full video feeds from the drones and team cameras."

"I wouldn't miss it for the world!" Jack said with a smile.

Mike leaned forward on his screen. "Jack, this is the payoff. Everything you've built, everything you've uncovered, it's coming together."

Jack looked around the room at the assembled intelligence professionals, each representing a different branch of American power projection, each now invested in his unconventional approach. A few weeks ago, he'd been on a book tour. Now he was at the center of an operation that could reshape the balance of power in Southeast Asia.

"I'll be there," he said finally. "But I want something in return."

"Name it," Franklin said, his tone suggesting he already knew what was coming.

"When this is over, I want a full functionality review of my Virtual Intelligence Center, the Watch," Jack said. "Not to dismantle it, but to formalize it. If this system is as valuable as we all think it is, it needs proper oversight and proper support."

Franklin and Sam exchanged glances.

"I think that can be arranged," Franklin said carefully. "Provided the operation succeeds."

Jack nodded, his mind already racing ahead to the next forty-eight hours. "Then let's make sure it does."

* * *

Day 10, 1700 Hours | Secure VTC

The secure video teleconference line between the CIA Station in Kuala Lumpur and the USS Blue Ridge, now underway in the Strait of Malacca, connected with a soft electronic chime. Samantha Blake's face appeared on Captain Murphy's screen, her expression a mixture of amusement and urgency.

"Mike have you guys had time to assess the latest from Jack?"

Mike leaned forward in his chair, the blue glow of multiple monitors reflecting off his face in the dimly lit intelligence center. "Both the currency manipulation and Harapan Baru assessments were more precise than what we have been seeing in classified channels, but my only HUMINT material is the watered down stuff. Wondering what you real spies make of it."

Sam's response showed her bias for HUMINT. "We don't have any smoking gun, but I would characterize our view as indications something is up and no info that says Jack is wrong. All open-source intelligence is suspect to me, too many poisoned sources and too much room for error, but Jack and his AI agents seem to have built a solid case."

Turning to Jack Sam continued "If you were with the agency doing what you did in social media you would have been prosecuted for taking direct action without POTUS approval, good thing you were acting on your own cowboy."

"That's Jack for you," Mike said, his expression sobering. "Always three steps ahead of conventional thinking."

Sam's face hardened as she shifted into analytical mode. "And we absolutely have to check out the lead on the location of Harapan Baru. My officers and agents are slow to develop insights like that but are on it. You have any way of confirming?"

"Already on it. Have tasked every national level system in the book. Should find out soon if this is legit."

Sam quickly switched topics: "Timing of the currency manipulation shows PRC is executing on a plan much bigger than we thought. Financial attacks, cyber-attacks, and very likely coordination with insurgents for physical attacks, all backed up by full scale social media and propaganda messaging."

"That's exactly what concerns me," Mike said, "This isn't opportunistic, it's a campaign."

"Which plays directly into Beijing's hands," Sam finished his thought. "Classic destabilization playbook."

Mike's jaw tightened. "I'm briefing Admiral Harrison in thirty minutes. What's your next move?"

"Full-court press," Sam replied without hesitation. "I've shifted priorities of my on the ground resources to focus on this and have Langley shifting priorities across the region. I've got a meeting with Ambassador Cooper in fifteen, she wants to meet the legendary Jack Tanner. Franklin is working ODNI to get them more engaged."

"We need to get ahead of this."

"The Malaysians?"

"Tricky," Sam admitted. "Some elements in their government are compromised. We need to be selective about who gets what information." I've got my formal counterparts and will update them, but for action, that's Chief Inspector Noor of Special Branch."

Mike leaned back, a grim smile forming. "Just like old times, huh? Jack drops a bombshell, disappears, reappears and leaves us to handle the fallout."

"Would you have it any other way?" Jack asked, matching his expression.

"Not a chance." Mike checked his watch. "I need to prep for the Admiral. Keep me posted on your end."

The connection terminated, Mike immediately turned to his senior analyst. "Lieutenant Commander Wilson, our mission is the same as always. On this staff, intelligence will drive operations. I need two things from you. A list of every question you would like answered on Harapan Baru." "Yes sir" came the response, "And second, get INDOPACOM JIC watch on the line and brief them on everything we know and what we don't know."

"Yes, sir," Wilson responded, already moving to assemble his team.

Mike stood, straightening his uniform. "And get me a direct line to INDOPACOM J2."

* * *

1800 Hours | Bank Negara Malaysia Crisis Room

The secure crisis room beneath Bank Negara Malaysia, the nation's central bank, pulsed with the soft hum of servers and the quiet intensity of strategic calculation. Blue-white light from a bank of monitors cast sharp shadows across the faces of the assembled officials. Live exchange feeds flickered across the screens, the Ringgit's volatility curves stabilizing for the first time in two days.

Dr. Farid Rahman, lean and sharp-eyed behind round glasses, stood at the head of the polished teak conference table. His tailored suit jacket hung on the back of his chair, a concession to the twenty-hour workday they'd all endured. He tapped a stylus against a screen displaying transaction metadata from offshore trading houses.

"We were tipped off by an anonymous source that something was up," Farid said, his voice carrying the weight of authority despite his fatigue. "So were major banks and trading houses. Look here." He highlighted a series of trading patterns with a swift gesture. "These synthetic sell orders are not organic. They're staged, timed to induce panic, then repurchased via proxies in Hong Kong and Singapore. We're looking at a full-spectrum currency manipulation campaign."

The NACSA analyst, a young woman with sharp eyes and fingers that hadn't stopped moving across her keyboard since the meeting began, nodded without looking up. "Confirmed. DNS routing logs and TLS fingerprints match a known PRC MSS front server, wasn't even well cloaked. They got lazy."

One of the Malaysian economic officials, the older one with silver temples and worry lines etched into his forehead, leaned forward. "How confident are we this leads back to Beijing?"

Farid's expression hardened. "Confident enough to act. We're activating circuit breakers in the capital control framework and seeding financial channels with counter-narratives. The international press will get a leak within the hour: 'Foreign Economic Hostility Under Investigation.'"

At the far end of the table, Bill Franklin, ODNI's senior representative, folded his arms and nodded approvingly. His presence here was unusual- American intelligence typically maintained a careful distance from Malaysia's internal financial matters. But nothing about the past week had been typical.

"Your team's response is textbook, firm, fast, layered," Franklin said, his American accent standing out among the Malaysian voices. "Just say the word and we'll notify Treasury. If you want any backchannel pressure applied through APEC, I'll make the calls before I'm back in my seat."

Farid's expression softened slightly. "We'd appreciate Treasury reinforcing confidence with key funds. Even a few high-level purchases could trigger a psychological swing."

"Done," Franklin replied without hesitation. "I'll also suggest the SEC look at who's facilitating these transfers from U.S. soil. If this thing touches Delaware LLCs, we'll shine daylight through it."

The Malaysian officials exchanged glances. It wasn't often the Americans volunteered to help without strings. The younger official, a Harvard-educated economist with skepticism permanently etched in his expression, raised an eyebrow.

"We've never seen ODNI this helpful," he said, not bothering to mask his suspicion.

Franklin's expression turned serious. "We don't like economic warfare being tested on free nations like yours. And if you ask me, this is more than economic. It's part of a long game. Destabilize, discredit, coerce. We've seen the script before."

Farid turned back to the main display where a real-time graph showed the Ringgit's performance against a basket of currencies. The line was climbing. Slowly. But enough to show the tide had turned.

"Not this time," Farid said with quiet determination.

He straightened his posture, the exhaustion momentarily falling away as he addressed the room. "This isn't just a response. It's a message. They tried to make an example of Malaysia. Now they know we're not alone, and not asleep."

The NACSA analyst looked up from her screen for the first time, a hint of satisfaction breaking through her professional demeanor. "Sir, we're seeing coordinated buy orders from Singapore sovereign funds and Japanese institutional investors. The counter-narrative is taking hold."

Farid nodded, allowing himself a moment of cautious optimism. The Ringgit continued its steady climb on the monitors, a digital manifestation of restored confidence. The immediate crisis was being contained, but he knew this was just one battle in a longer war. Beijing wouldn't take this setback lightly.

"Keep monitoring the patterns," he instructed. "They'll change tactics, not objectives."

Franklin stood, gathering his notes. "I'll make those calls now. And Dr. Rahman," he paused, meeting Farid's gaze directly, "you might want to thank your American friend when you see him next. His... expertise... seems particularly valuable these days."

Farid gave nothing away in his expression, but he understood the implication. Jack Tanner's fingerprints were all over this counteroperation, even if his name appeared nowhere in the official record.

"I'll be sure to pass along Malaysia's appreciation to all our allies," Farid replied diplomatically.

As the team returned to their stations, the crisis room settled back into its rhythm of quiet vigilance. On the main screen, the Ringgit continued its recovery, pixel by pixel, point by point, a digital representation of a nation refusing to be bullied into submission.

Chapter 21: Mirror Key

A massive tactical screen dominated the center of Beijing's Joint Security Council Crisis Room, bathing the occupants in its cold blue glow. Real-time data from regional exchanges flashed across multiple panels, each telling the same damning story. The Malaysian Ringgit had recovered. Not just stabilized, recovered. Malaysian state banks were buying at the precise moments MSS analysts had predicted selloffs, countering each move with surgical precision.

The briefing officer explained "Our sources with access to government and banks in Malaysia all report that anonymous tips were received with extensive details on the coming operation, giving them time to react and respond in ways not favorable to our desired outcome."

Chen Yixin stood before the tactical display, his normally composed demeanor fracturing with each new data point. His knuckles whitened as he gripped a glass screen controller, veins prominent along his temple.

Three rows of aides sat behind their respective ministers, faces illuminated by the glow of individual terminals. Several visibly trembled, eyes downcast, knowing what was coming.

With a sudden, violent motion, Chen hurled the glass controller across the room. It shattered against the wall, fragments scattering across the polished floor.

"How is a backward country like Malaysia countering *every move* we make?!" Chen's voice reverberated through the room. "First, their cybersecurity hardens overnight, now their *currency holds?* This all started the moment Tanner arrived."

Across the table, Wang Xiaohong sat with practiced stillness, the Minister of Public Security's face a mask of calm indifference. He lifted a porcelain cup to his lips, sipping tea with deliberate slowness.

"Or perhaps it started," Wang said, replacing the cup with a soft clink, "when the MSS allowed a foreign agent to survive his first week in Kuala Lumpur."

Chen turned, fury barely contained beneath his tailored suit. A muscle twitched beneath his left eye.

"Don't lecture me on field operations," Chen said, voice dropping to a dangerous whisper. "MPS authority stops when MSS operations are underway, and it will always be that way."

Wang placed his teacup down and rose to his feet, each movement measured, controlled, but radiating danger. His tone was soft yet carried to every corner of the room.

"You overplayed your hand, Comrade Chen. And now you insult my service?" Wang's eyes narrowed. "We warned you Jack Tanner was not simply a cyber lecturer. He is an obvious CIA non-official government operative opposed to the rule of the party and our law."

"He shouldn't even be alive!" Chen slammed his palm against the table, causing digital displays to flicker.

An aide flinched, accidentally knocking over a water glass. The sound of it shattering punctuated the silence that followed.

The room crackled with tension. Junior officers and analysts glanced away, finding sudden interest in their terminals as the two most powerful intelligence figures in China erupted in a shouting match that rattled the doors outside.

"Your operation was compromised from the beginning!" Wang's voice rose, abandoning its usual restraint. "MSS reckless overreach has jeopardized years of careful positioning!"

"MPS compromise and incompetence!" Chen countered, stepping toward Wang. "Your field officers can't maintain basic surveillance without alerting their targets. Your informants are useless!"

An aide hurriedly gathered his tablet and backed away from the table. Others followed suit, creating a buffer zone around the feuding ministers.

The shouting intensified, decades-old rivalries between the ministries erupting into personal attacks. Security personnel outside exchanged worried glances, hands moving to communication devices, uncertain whether to intervene.

Just as they stepped forward, the double doors swung open. A Presidential Secretary entered, his presence instantly commanding attention. His expression was calm but grave, his posture perfect, his voice cutting through the chaos like a blade.

"The Chairman will see you both now," he announced. "He expects a full update on your special project."

The ministers both smiled and slightly bowed their heads in approval. There is no other response.

The room fell into absolute silence. Aides stared at the floor, avoiding eye contact. The tactical screens continued their silent, damning testimony, Malaysia's financial systems, strengthening by the minute.

Chen straightened his tie. Wang adjusted his cuffs. Both men moved toward the door without another word, their rivalry momentarily suspended by a greater authority.

* * *

2000 Hours | The Chairman Xi's Office, Beijing

The lacquered table reflected the recessed lighting in Chairman Xi's private office at Zhongnanhai. Heavy silk curtains dimmed the Beijing night, creating a chamber isolated from time and external influence. An enormous ink-brush landscape of the Yangtze dominated the far wall, the river eternal and unyielding, like China itself.

Chen Yixin sat with military stillness, the cold precision of the MSS evident in every calculated movement. Across from him, Wang Xiaohong of the MPS maintained an equally disciplined exterior, though his eyes, to those trained to observe such microscopic tells, revealed the subtle calculations of a career political operative. At the head of the table sat Chairman Xi Jinping, his expression as inscrutable as the ancient mountains rendered in the painting's misty background.

A steward poured tea with practiced movements, the gentle cascade of liquid the only sound disturbing the weighted silence. The ceremonial Longjing tea released tendrils of steam that dissipated in the cool air. No one spoke until the steward exited, the door closing with an almost imperceptible click.

"Tell me... of Malaysia," Xi said, his voice measured and authoritative.

Chen inclined his head with the exact gravity protocol demanded, not a degree more or less. His words emerged crisp, deliberate, each syllable a calculated projection of control.

Quoting Mao, Chen replied "There is great chaos under heaven; the situation is excellent."

"Our personnel remain covertly engaged, Chairman. The government of Malaysia cannot act without our awareness, and Harapan Baru remains under our direct influence." Chen's voice carried the assurance of absolute competence. "Progress on cyber infrastructure manipulation was delayed but is back on schedule. We've re-established persistent access to critical government networks and financial systems. Li Jianhong has ensured that foreign disruptions are being... contained."

Wang Xiaohong nodded slightly, hands folded with perfect symmetry on the table's polished surface. His breathing remained measured, but a trained observer might notice the subtle tension in his shoulders.

"Indeed, reports from our law-abiding citizens in Malaysia clearly support Minister Chen's assessment on all things," Wang acknowledged. "The local environment, however, remains volatile." His eyes met the Chairman's with practiced deference. "There are... informational inconsistencies from our southern field teams. One might wonder, hypothetically, if fragmented operational control could lead to opportunity loss."

A pause hung in the air. No direct accusation, but the temperature seemed to drop several degrees. Chen didn't look at Wang, maintaining his focus on the Chairman with absolute discipline.

"We have full oversight of all tactical matters," Chen stated. "The Ministry of State Security has integrated cyber, financial, and informational campaigns into a single harmonized directive."

Wang's expression remained perfectly composed. "Ah. Then we are relieved." The faintest edge entered his voice, detectable only to those who operated at the highest levels of power. "Though... were I to observe foreign interference spreading faster than anticipated, I might recommend broader inter-ministerial clarity. Particularly where tactical feedback loops appear delayed. Zhang Wei's most recent dispatch indicates new American assets have deployed, while Tanner remains un-located."

Chen's fingers paused on his teacup. A beat of silence. His voice sharpened, but only a degree that those familiar with him would recognize as dangerous.

"The Ministry of Public Security's field reports are... appreciated. Yet national-level decisions must follow strategic cadence. Not tactical improvisation. Perhaps Minister Wang is unaware that certain American movements are being permitted to proceed under controlled observation."

Chairman Xi raised his hand, a minimal gesture executed with absolute authority. Both ministers fell instantly silent, years of conditioning to Party discipline evident in their immediate compliance.

"Enough," Xi said.

The Chairman set his teacup down with deliberate precision. The soft ceramic contact with the table's surface seemed to echo in the silence.

"The Ministry of State Security will maintain *full* leadership over Malaysia. Final decisions rest with Minister Chen."

Wang inclined his head, expression unreadable, though a muscle in his jaw flexed once, a momentary lapse in perfect control.

"But Minister Wang, your people will be fully briefed," Xi continued, his gaze penetrating and absolute. "A representative from MPS will attend the Harapan Baru planning session with Minister Chen. MPS will review all plans with us before Harapan Baru takes any action."

Xi's eyes moved between the two ministers, missing nothing.

"Operational unity is essential. The Americans seek any advantage, any fracture in our systems. I do not wish to see fissures between ministries when the world is watching. Malaysia represents the first implementation of our new doctrine for regional integration."

Both men bowed slightly, understanding the gravity beneath the measured words.

"Of course, Chairman," Chen said. "We will ensure seamless coordination."

"As it should be, Chairman," Wang affirmed, voice calibrated to perfect loyalty.

Xi stood, the meeting over without formal dismissal. The Yangtze behind him continued to flow, unchanged, unchallenged by time or circumstance. As the ministers rose, Chen's sleeve caught the edge of his secure tablet, nearly toppling it before he steadied it with uncharacteristic haste.

Wang noticed. Said nothing. But as they exited into the corridor, the faintest suggestion of satisfaction crossed his features, gone in an instant, but present, nonetheless.

The fissures were forming, invisible to most, but potentially catastrophic to those who understood the true stakes in Malaysia.

Chapter 22: Beijing Divided

Day 11, 1830 Hours | MSS Headquarters

The October air hung thick in the corridors of Yidongyuan. Despite the climate-controlled environment of the MSS headquarters, a different kind of chill permeated the austere hallways. Deputy Director Zhao moved with uncharacteristic hesitation, his footsteps nearly silent on the polished floor as he approached Minister Chen Yixin's office. The summons had come without explanation, never a good sign in the current climate.

He paused at the threshold, straightening his tie before knocking.

"Enter," came Chen's voice, stripped of its usual confidence.

The minister sat behind his desk, illuminated by the harsh glow of his computer screen. Three dossiers lay open before him, each bearing a red security stripe. Chen didn't look up as Zhao closed the door.

"You've seen the latest security directive?" Chen asked, still scanning the document on his screen.

"Yes, Minister. The enhanced verification protocols were implemented this morning."

Chen finally raised his eyes. "And what is your assessment?"

Zhao measured his response carefully. "The protocols will slow our operational tempo. Field assets are already reporting delays in authorization chains."

"I didn't ask for statistics," Chen snapped. "I asked for your assessment of the situation."

The subtext was clear. This wasn't about protocols; it was about loyalty. About who could be trusted.

"The information leaks appear targeted and precise," Zhao said. "They suggest intimate knowledge of our Malaysia operations. Someone with access to both strategic planning and tactical execution."

Chen's expression darkened. "Someone like yourself."

The accusation hung in the air between them. Zhao maintained his composure despite the sudden tightness in his chest.

"I have served the Ministry and the Party with absolute loyalty for twenty-three years, Minister."

"As did the Director of the First Bureau before his removal last night."

Zhao hadn't heard. The blood in his veins turned to ice. The First Bureau is responsible for global HUMINT operations.

"The Central Commission has established a special investigation team," Chen continued. "They're reviewing all communications from senior staff. All travel. All personal connections." He pushed one of the dossiers forward. "Including yours."

"I welcome their scrutiny," Zhao said, his voice steady despite the implications.

Chen studied him for a moment, then nodded curtly. "The Chairman himself has taken an interest in this matter. He's ordered a suspension of advanced operations in Malaysia until we identify the source of the compromise."

"Harapan Baru…"

"Will wait," Chen cut him off. "We cannot risk further exposure. Not with what we've invested."

Zhao knew better than to argue. The mere mention of the Chairman's involvement elevated this beyond a ministerial concern. It was now a matter of national security at the highest level.

"What would you have me do, Minister?"

"Continue your duties. Under supervision." Chen's gaze was unflinching. "And prepare a complete analysis of all personnel who had access to the Malaysia operational files. I want backgrounds, family connections, financial records, everything."

"Including senior leadership?"

A dangerous question, but necessary.

"Everyone," Chen confirmed. "No exceptions."

The implications were staggering. The investigation ran the risk of paralyzing the Ministry's operations in Malaysia and beyond. Years of carefully cultivated networks and influence campaigns could stall. And the ripple effects through China's global intelligence apparatus would be immeasurable.

"There will be a full directorate meeting tomorrow at 0800," Chen added. "The Chairman may attend."

Zhao bowed slightly. "I understand, Minister."

As he turned to leave, Chen spoke again, his voice lower. "Zhao. If you know something, anything, now is the time. Before the Commission finds it first."

The veteran intelligence officer paused, hand on the doorknob. "I am loyal to the Party, Minister. Always."

It wasn't an answer, but it was all he could safely offer.

* * *

1900 Hours | MSS Malaysia House

In the surveillance hub of the MSS Malaysia House at the Seraya, Li Jianhong stared at the bank of monitors with mounting frustration. Operational fires exchanged with CIA ground branch. His teams vehicles showed signs of targeted explosives. Likely not grenades, the explosive damage was far too small but precisely targeted. Drones no doubt. MSS S&T teams have a new objective now to assess and reverse engineer and get him this capability.

Li's secure phone buzzed. He checked the caller ID and stepped away from the monitoring station.

"This is Li," he answered in Mandarin.

"This is a Level One security notification," came the automated voice. "All Malaysia operations are paused pending security review. Confirm receipt and compliance."

Li felt a cold knot form in his stomach. Level One came directly from Beijing, from the highest echelons.

"Confirmed," he replied. "Request clarification on suspension parameters."

"All offensive operations with Harapan Baru are paused effective immediately. Maintain only passive collection and facility security. Further instructions will follow. Confirm compliance."

"Compliance confirmed," Li said mechanically.

The line went dead.

Li stood motionless for a moment, processing the implications. A complete operational pause was unprecedented. Something catastrophic had happened or was believed to have happened. And it centered on his area of responsibility.

He returned to the monitoring station, his expression carefully neutral despite the turmoil within.

"New directive," he announced to the room. "All active operations are suspended. Recall field teams. Maintain only passive collection."

The technicians exchanged glances but knew better than to question the order.

"And Harapan Baru?" asked his deputy, her voice low.

"All contact suspended," Li confirmed. "No exceptions."

"They just received another weapons delivery."

"They must pause," Li cut her off. "Beijing's orders."

The unspoken question hung in the air: Why? But Li had no answer he could safely share.

As the staff began implementing the stand-down procedures, Li retreated to his office and secured the door. He needed to understand what had triggered this response. A Level One suspension suggested a security breach of the highest order, a defector, a penetration, or a catastrophic intelligence failure. Or political posturing and interference from Zhang?

His secure terminal showed no new messages from Beijing. Only the automated directive. Whatever had happened, he was being kept in the dark, which suggested he might be under suspicion himself.

He immediately shifted focus to the long game. The objectives remain. Chairman Mao had written about days like this: "Make trouble, fail, make trouble again, fail again... until their doom."

Li paced his office for three minutes, weighing options against risks. Finally, he retrieved a second secure phone from his desk safe, one not issued by Beijing. He dialed a number from memory.

"Sparrow" answered a clipped voice after two rings.

"The rain in Hainan falls differently than in Shanghai," Li said, using their established authentication phrase.

"But the mountains remain the same," came the response. "What's happened?"

"Level One suspension. All operations, except one." Li kept his voice steady despite the urgency. "We need to meet. The usual place. One hour."

"Understood" replied the Sparrow.

Li ended the call and slipped the phone back into the safe. Time to prepare the package for Sparrow's covert delivery to Malaysia's Special Branch.

*　*　*

2000 Hours | Dragon Falls

Amir Hashim paced the length of the command center at Dragon Falls, his frustration evident in every step. The encrypted satellite phone lay silent on the table, the scheduled call from his MSS handler was now two hours overdue.

"Try again," he ordered Zain, his communications chief.

Zain shook his head. "Still no response on any channel. They've gone dark."

Amir slammed his fist on the table. "We have three hundred fighters waiting."

The guerrilla leader ran a hand through his hair, mind racing through contingencies. This wasn't the first time Li's team had left him in the dark for so long, but this is a critical time.

"Could they have been compromised?" asked Zain.

"Possible," Amir conceded. "But the MSS doesn't just disappear. They have redundancies, backups."

"Unless the order came from above them," Zain suggested. "From the very top."

The implication hung heavy in the humid air of the jungle command post. If Beijing had pulled the plug on their operation, Harapan Baru's future was suddenly uncertain. Years of preparation, hundreds of trained fighters, millions in Chinese funding, all at risk.

"We need to consider our options," Amir said finally. "If Beijing has abandoned us..."

"We don't know that," Zain interjected.

"If they have," Amir continued, "we need to be prepared. Our cause doesn't die without their support."

Zain nodded slowly. "We still have our local networks. Our fighters. Our message resonates with the people regardless of Chinese backing."

Amir moved to the map table, studying the marked positions of Malaysian military and police forces. "If we have to we will adapt. We've always known Beijing supported us for their own interests, not ours. Perhaps it's time we remembered who we're really fighting for."

The satellite phone suddenly crackled to life. All three froze, then Zain lunged for it.

"This is Emerald Point," he answered using their designated call sign.

The voice that responded was not their usual handler but someone new, someone higher in the chain.

"Operational pause in effect," the accented voice stated without preamble. "Maintain position. Avoid contact with authorities. Further instructions will follow when security protocols permit."

"We need clarification," Zain pressed. "We are ready to move…"

"All action is to be paused. Maintain absolute communication silence after this call. Do not attempt to contact any MSS personnel. We will reestablish contact. Confirmation required."

Zain looked to Amir, who nodded grimly.

"Confirmed," Zain replied. "Emerald Point standing by."

The line went dead.

Silence filled the command center as the leaders of Harapan Baru absorbed the implications.

"They're scared," Farah said finally. "Something has them running for cover."

Amir's eyes narrowed. "Or someone."

* * *

2100 Hours | MSS Cyber Ops Center

The digital map of Southeast Asia dominated the MSS HQ Cyber Ops Center wall screens, pulsing with red breach indicators across Malaysian network infrastructure. Tactical intrusion markers clustered around government servers in Kuala Lumpur. System flags blinked in angry synchronization.

Ming hunched over his tablet, scrolling through breach reports with practiced precision. His fingers moved with machine-like efficiency, each swipe revealing another layer of operational compromise. The third such breach in nine days.

Across the table, Lao's face hardened into familiar contempt. "This isn't code error," he said, voice tight with accusation. "This is human compromise. Someone leaked."

Ming didn't look up. "No one touched my sandbox. Maybe your team's firewall is more decorative than functional."

"Maybe," Wu interjected from the corner, his voice soft but carrying a razor's edge, "someone spent more time naming their malware strains than hardening ops security."

The tension between the Three Immortals, once China's most celebrated cyber operators, had been building for weeks. Tonight, it was reaching critical mass.

Lao's palm struck the table with enough force to rattle abandoned energy drink cans. "We shouldn't even be on this op. These weren't our failures. MSS field handlers can't keep their assets in line, and we get the blame when ghosts show up in the logs."

Ming stood, his lanky frame casting a shadow across the data-rich displays. He gestured toward the SIEM alert matrix where intrusion patterns cascaded in deliberate sequence.

"You think this is about *ghosts*?" Ming's voice was controlled but intense. "This is surgical manipulation. Someone planted a pattern that mimics our Nightshade protocol, perfectly. We're not being attacked. We're being *framed*."

The pneumatic door hissed open behind them.

General Liang entered without announcement. He wore no nameplate on his tailored suit. His left eyelid twitched slightly as he surveyed the room, the only imperfection in his otherwise stone-like composure. The carbon fiber tablet in his hand bore the MSS insignia in subdued relief.

"Enough." The word, delivered in clipped Mandarin with a northern accent, cut through the room like a blade.

Even Lao sat down.

"Headquarters has assessed the situation." The General's voice was devoid of emotion. "Minister Chen was briefed personally. The pattern of leaks, mirrored code deployments, and foreign countermeasures point to operational compromise. They have made a final decision."

He tapped his tablet, and the wall displays shifted to a new classification screen, their security clearances visibly downgrading in real-time.

"Your unit is reassigned. No more Tier 1 ops." Each word fell like a death sentence. "You will focus on civilian systems, low-risk vector mapping, and linguistic adaptation for AI propaganda models."

The Three Immortals sat motionless, but Ming could feel the temperature in the room drop ten degrees. This wasn't just reassignment; it was professional execution.

"With respect, sir," Ming said carefully, "this is the exact moment our capabilities are *needed*. Our zero-day exploits against the Malaysian defense grid are ready for deployment."

The General's eyes narrowed slightly. "If your capabilities were operationally secure, we would agree."

He turned to leave, then paused, his back to the team. "You've been *useful*. But useful is not the same as *trusted*. Minister Chen requires absolute certainty, especially with American counterintelligence actively hunting our operations."

The door hissed shut behind him, leaving the Three Immortals in silence.

Wu stared at the floor, his usually impassive face betraying a flicker of calculation. Lao's knuckles whitened as he clenched his fists. Ming's gaze locked onto the downgraded security protocols scrolling across his screen.

They're cutting us out completely, Ming thought. Three weeks of work, gone. The Malaysian operation compromised. Someone knew exactly where to look.

His fingers hovered over his personal phone, not the government-issued device on the table. A device that, technically, shouldn't even be in this room.

"Someone's playing a deeper game," Ming said, voice barely audible.

With practiced subtlety, he tapped a sequence that initiated a private backup protocol, copying select operational files to a secure server outside the MSS network. A treasonous act by any measure, but Ming had long ago learned to build his own insurance policies.

"And perhaps," he added, meeting Wu's suddenly attentive gaze, "it's time we played our own."

Chapter 23: Coalition Warfare

Day 12, 0830 Hours | Harmony Path Center KL

The raid on the Harmony Path Outreach Center came with surgical precision at 0830 hours. Malaysian National Police tactical teams breached the building from three entry points simultaneously.

Inside, four bleary-eyed PRC nationals barely had time to react before they were face-down on the floor, zip-tied and surrounded by officers in black tactical gear. One managed to reach for a phone before a Malaysian officer's boot pinned his wrist to the floor. Another tried shouting something about diplomatic immunity, his protests silenced by the methodical recitation of rights in both Bahasa Malaysia and Mandarin.

"Secure the server room," barked the team leader, his voice calm despite the adrenaline. "Nothing leaves this building."

Forensic technicians swarmed in behind the tactical teams, their white coveralls stark against the dark uniforms. They moved with practiced efficiency, photographing everything before touching it, labeling and bagging items, dusting surfaces for fingerprints.

"Sir, you need to see this," called one technician, gesturing to a wall of surveillance monitors. Each screen showed a different location across Kuala Lumpur, government buildings, transportation hubs, private residences. One monitor displayed what appeared to be the interior of a Malaysian cabinet minister's home.

The tactical lead stood in the doorway, his expression unchanging as he surveyed the illegal MPS Police Station. His eyes lingered on a row of files labeled in Chinese characters.

"DNA samples from everything," he ordered quietly. "Every surface, every chair, every cup. I want to know everyone who has been in this building."

A young officer approached from outside. "Sir, we have teams speaking with all surrounding offices and are confiscating recordings from area security cameras. Sending to HQ for review."

Outside, the dark clouds were parting. Neighbors peered from windows at the police vehicles lining the street. What had appeared to be a benign cultural center was now revealed as something far more sinister.

* * *

0900 Hours | RMAF Subang Air Base

The sky over Kuala Lumpur remained stubbornly dark with rain clouds, though the eastern horizon had begun to soften and let some hint of daylight in. RMAF Subang Air Base blazed with industrial lighting, creating pools of harsh white illumination across the tarmac. The base hummed with the quiet tension of an operation moving with practiced precision.

At the far end of the tarmac, the massive silhouette of a C-5M Super Galaxy dominated the scene. Its rear loading ramp gaped open like the maw of some prehistoric predator, interior lights spilling onto the concrete below. The aircraft dwarfed everything around it, a monument to American power projection delivered under diplomatic cover.

Colonel Ramos stood motionless at the edge of the tarmac, his face a mask of professional detachment. Beside him, Chief Inspector Haris Noor's expression betrayed nothing, though his eyes tracked every movement with analytical intensity. Both men had built careers on restraint, on saying less than they knew.

"Quite the delivery," Noor said finally, breaking the silence. His voice was measured, carrying the weight of decades in intelligence work. "When you said 'assets,' I had pictured something more... modest."

Ramos allowed himself a thin smile. "The situation called for appropriate tools."

Inside the Galaxy's cavernous hold, three 40-foot containers rested on heavy-duty offload platforms. U.S. Air Force logistics personnel moved with quiet efficiency around them, while a small convoy of unmarked Malaysian army trucks idled nearby, engines purring in the pre-dawn stillness.

A Malaysian Air Force major approached the two men, clipboard in hand. "Sir," he addressed Noor with a crisp salute, "first container is ready for transfer."

Noor nodded once. The major relayed the order through his radio, and the massive crane positioned alongside the aircraft began to move. With practiced precision, it lifted the first container clear of the C-5's hold and swung it toward the waiting flatbed.

As the container descended, its markings became visible under the floodlights: "UAS SYSTEM – MQ-1C GRAY EAGLE (2 UNITS)."

Ramos gestured toward the container. "Two Gray Eagles. Twenty-five hours of loiter time, ISR plus light strike capability. Hellfire loadout for insurgents, smugglers, or anyone waving the wrong flag." He paused. "Quiet, clean, low signature."

Noor's eyes narrowed slightly. "And fully under Malaysian command?"

The corner of Ramos's mouth twitched upward. "Officially, yes. Our operators…" He nodded toward a group of Americans standing apart from the others, six men in civilian clothing, with the unmistakable bearing of special operations personnel. "They're here to 'train and advise.' Your team gives the go-orders. We just help you see the battlefield."

The second container was already being maneuvered onto its transport. Its markings read: "UAS SYSTEM – MOJAVE (3 UNITS)."

The container doors swung open as the Malaysian ground crew secured it, revealing the sleek, angular silhouettes of the Mojave drones. Their retractable wings were folded against their fuselages, but even in this dormant state, they radiated lethal purpose. Their reinforced landing gear spoke to their specialized mission profile.

274

"Mojaves," Ramos continued, a hint of pride creeping into his voice. "Brand new. Think of them as jungle ready. STOL-capable, can launch off a dirt road or soccer field." His eyes met Noor's. "Payload options: sixteen Hellfires or full ISR suite. Ideal for remote border zones. Or... Dragon Falls."

The name hung in the air between them. Dragon Falls, the headquarters of Harapan Baru, buried deep in terrain that had swallowed conventional military operations for generations.

Noor said nothing, the weight of the moment settling around them like a physical presence. His gaze drifted to the third container being offloaded, which held two portable Ground Control Stations, a JSOC support module, and crated spares, comms encryption modules, and drone munitions, including several Hellfire missile pods.

He turned his attention to the JSOC team standing near the aircraft. They were the picture of deniability, plainclothes, gear tight, quiet as ghosts. Men who existed in the shadows between military action and covert operations.

"And these men?" Noor asked, his voice barely audible above the mechanical sounds of the offloading operation.

Ramos followed his gaze. "You'll never hear them unless you ask. They answer to me and I answer to Admiral Harrison at 7th fleet, but they operate under *your* command while on this soil."

The unspoken understanding passed between them: the importance of Malaysian command would be maintained with meticulous care, regardless of whose finger ultimately pressed which button.

Noor nodded once. That was all the confirmation needed.

A Malaysian colonel approached, his uniform impeccable. He saluted Noor and handed him a clipboard with a thin sheaf of papers. The documentation was sparse, just enough to satisfy the most cursory audit. Both men knew the real agreements had been negotiated through secure channels, leaving minimal paper trails.

Noor scanned the documents, his pen hovering over the signature line. The moment stretched, pregnant with implication. This was no ordinary military cooperation, it was the weaponization of Malaysian airspace against an insurgency with powerful foreign backers.

"We are being armed to fight a shadow," Noor said softly, almost to himself, as he signed the papers. "May we not become one."

Ramos looked out over the horizon, where the first pale suggestion of daylight had begun to appear. "We already are."

The third container settled onto its transport with a hydraulic hiss. Around them, the machinery of war continued its inexorable deployment. The JSOC team began moving toward their equipment, and Malaysian Special Branch officers emerged from a hangar across the tarmac.

"H-hour is set for 0600 tomorrow," Ramos said, checking his watch. "The birds will be assembled and flight-ready by 1800 today. Your men prepared?"

Noor handed the clipboard back to the colonel, who retreated with a final salute. "My operators have been in position for three days. Reconnaissance teams are already establishing the cordon. When your... assets... are operational, we will have Dragon Falls surrounded on all sides."

"And Tanner's intelligence?" Ramos asked.

"Precise," Noor replied. "His AI system has provided insights that enabled a close UAV overflight. Harapan Baru's strength in that location is approximately three hundred combatants, with a core leadership cell of twelve."

Ramos nodded, satisfied. "The Mojaves will be your eyes. The Gray Eagles, your fist. Between them and your ground teams, Dragon Falls will be neutralized."

"And afterward?" Noor asked, his gaze steady on the American. "When the dust settles, what then, Colonel?"

Ramos's expression hardened. "That's above my pay grade. But I imagine Beijing will have some explaining to do."

The first rays of sunlight broke over the horizon, catching the metal skin of the drones being unloaded from their containers. For a moment, they gleamed with golden light, beautiful and terrible in equal measure.

"The next move will be diplomatic," Noor said, watching as technicians began assembling the first Gray Eagle. "But diplomacy works best when backed by strength." He turned to face Ramos fully. "Malaysia thanks you for this... training exercise."

Ramos extended his hand, and Noor clasped it firmly. "Happy to help a valued partner," Ramos replied, the official language of international cooperation masking the reality of what they were about to unleash.

As they walked toward the hangar where the operational briefing would take place, the sun continued its slow ascent, illuminating the machinery of war being assembled behind them, America's technological might wrapped in Malaysian authority, preparing to strike at China's covert influence.

The battle for Dragon Falls had already begun.

Chapter 24: Counterstrike Protocol

The suspension order from General Liang had been clear: cease all active cyber penetration operations pending security review. But in the sterile confines of the MSS Cyber Operations Center, the Three Immortals found themselves unable to simply stand down while their life's work crumbled around them.

Ming Liu paced behind his workstation, his usually controlled demeanor cracking under the weight of professional humiliation. "We're supposed to sit here like children while our entire Malaysian operation burns?"

Lao Xun didn't look up from his screens, his fingers dancing across multiple keyboards as he violated every aspect of their suspension order. "The suspension doesn't apply to analysis," he said, his voice carrying the thin justification of a man determined to act regardless of consequences.

Wu Yifan leaned back in his chair, studying the data streams flowing across his monitors. "Define 'analysis,' brother. Because what I'm seeing suggests we're fighting ghosts."

Ming stopped pacing and moved to Wu's station. The screens displayed a complex web of information flows, social media patterns, financial transactions, communication intercepts, all filtered through the Deep Seek AI system they'd been optimizing for this operation.

"Show me," Ming commanded.

Wu's fingers flew across his interface, bringing up a three-dimensional visualization of information warfare. "Deep Seek has been analyzing everything, not just our targets, but also social media chatter, Malaysian counter measures, our own actions and their responses, messaging of propaganda."

The visualization shifted, revealing correlation of messaging from sock-puppet accounts that had been created by Overwatch.

"This isn't random chaos," Wu continued. "This is evidence of advanced, timed, orchestrated messaging. Someone has been feeding us information designed to make us doubt our own capabilities, question our sources, turn us against each other."

Lao looked up from his own analysis. "The adversary operation wasn't just about creating a fictional defector or bad internal actors. It was about making us so paranoid about real defectors we would pause. Classic disinformation, truth mixed with lies until you can't tell the difference."

Ming studied the data, his analytical mind processing the implications. "You are displaying clear evidence. No doubt, proof the MSS itself has been manipulated."

"100%. We are being played by an opponent we never saw coming," Wu replied. "Look at these patterns."

Deep Seek continued to show subtle but consistent messaging patterns, themes that appeared organic but followed algorithmic precision.

"This is agentic AI," Wu said quietly. "Not just machine learning or pattern recognition. This is artificial intelligence that can plan, adapt, and execute complex psychological operations autonomously."

The room fell silent as the implications sank in.

Lao was the first to speak. "The Americans have weaponized artificial intelligence against human decision-making. They're not just beating us with better intelligence; they're making us beat ourselves."

Ming felt a cold rage building in his chest. "They turned the paranoia of a few into a weapon."

"And now we have to stand down from offensive ops while they conduct a witch hunt for nonexistent traitors," Wu added. "Perfect. The Americans disable our offensive capabilities and get us to disable ourselves."

Ming stood up and spoke up "We need to inform Li Jianhong and General Liang immediately, he will know what to do."

"And then?" Lao asked.

"Then we show these American AI systems what Chinese artificial intelligence can really do."

* * *

1600 Hours | MSS Malaysia House

Li Jianhong studied the encrypted report from the Three Immortals, his expression growing darker with each page. Twenty-three years in intelligence had taught him to recognize sophisticated operations, but this went beyond anything he'd encountered.

His deputy waited silently as Li processed the implications.

"The Three Immortals believe we're facing an AI-enabled psychological warfare campaign," Li said finally. "Not just propaganda, but adaptive, real-time manipulation of our decision-making processes."

"Is that possible?" His deputy asked.

"More than possible. Inevitable." Li stood and moved to the window overlooking Kuala Lumpur. "We've been preparing for cyber and insurgent warfare while the Americans have been developing something entirely new."

He turned back to his deputy. "But they made one crucial mistake. They used a human operator as their primary asset."

"Jack Tanner."

"Jack Tanner," Li confirmed. "The AI systems provide the analytical capability, but they still need a human interface for complex operations. Tanner is that interface."

Li activated his secure communication system and placed a call to Beijing. General Qiao's face appeared on the screen within seconds.

"General, I've received the Three Immortals' analysis. We need to discuss immediate countermeasures."

Qiao's expression was grim. "I just reviewed this Li, be careful what you say next, there will be no countermanding of Beijing's orders... you're supposed to be pausing pending..."

"With respect, General, while pausing our operation we can certainly analyze, collect and prepare for action once you and Director Chen order us to resume." Li's voice carried the authority of someone who had spent months on the ground while Beijing debated policy. "I have experience in this theater. I know the Malaysian intelligence apparatus, I know their capabilities, and I know their limitations. What's happening here isn't Malaysian ingenuity, it's American innovation implemented through Malaysian channels."

He paused, letting his assessment sink in.

"Jack Tanner isn't just a retired naval officer writing books. He's non-official cover for the CIA, almost certainly being run by their station chief through a handler, probably the operative my people have identified as Fiona Kincaid."

General Liang leaned forward. "You have evidence of this?"

"I have pattern recognition, General. Tanner arrives in Malaysia; our networks begin failing systematically. Tanner works with NACSA and they dramatically shift Malaysia's security posture, Tanner visits government facilities, those facilities immediately implement countermeasures against our specific methods. Tanner disappears from surveillance, deceives us by sending his cell phone in a different direction than he is going, and suddenly we're facing the most sophisticated disinformation campaign in MSS history, and four operatives we send to terminate him die at the hands of CIA ground branch."

"The Americans are running a classic false flag operation with new methods. They're using artificial intelligence to make us believe our own people are compromised. The result? We paralyze ourselves while they strengthen their position."

Liang was silent for a long moment. "What do you recommend?"

"Give me operational authority to prove it," Li said. "Seventy-two hours to demonstrate that this is American deception, not Malaysian capability."

"Beijing has issued direct orders…"

"Beijing has issued orders based on incomplete information," Li interrupted. "As the officer in charge of this theater, I'm only requesting permission to gather additional intelligence to inform your decisions on when to resume operations."

"You may certainly collect information," Liang replied, adding "I will brief the Director and follow up guidance will be provided."

Li responded "General, we need to hear out the Three Immortals, I can collect on the ground, but there is almost certainly more they can do."

* * *

Li stood before a wall of monitors displaying the faces of General Liang and the Three Immortals via secure video link. Li's in-country team sat around the conference table, each officer eager to understand their new priorities.

"Gentlemen," Li began, "we face an unprecedented challenge. The Americans have developed artificial intelligence capabilities that can craft and execute on psychological operations against us faster than they ever have before. The question is: how do we counter an enemy that thinks faster than we do?"

General Liang started off "The Director has approved full resumption of cyber activities only. Other operations remain on pause pending results of additional analysis."

Ming's voice came through the speakers. "The agentic AI systems have many fundamental weaknesses- they're still bound by their training data and operational parameters. And they require servers to operate and software to run. If we find them, we can destroy them."

"How can you find them? And what can you do if they are operating from the basement of CIA HQ or some other hardened facility?" Li asked.

Lao leaned into his camera. "We need to force them to reveal their server, from there we target with a crushing attack. Not bombs but code."

Li nodded slowly. "What would that look like operationally?"

"Honey pot for Agentic AI. An automated campaign using our own sock-puppet accounts and media full of information we know they will want. Then some lightly defended servers of our own with the promise of insights they need. We plant beacons and malware in the content of those honeypots." Ming replied. "Instead of trying to outthink their AI, we feed it what it wants, make it ping us with their location and corrupt and kill it with malware it will download out of curiosity."

Li smiled for the first time in days. "And how do we implement this without triggering their countermeasures?"

"Our own Agentic AI will modify our own malware, which is already the best in the world. And it will stand up the honeypots and social media accounts in hours. Give us the go-ahead and we move out."

Li's expression hardened. "General Qiao, with your support this operation can develop the information we need to both stop this disinformation attack and prepare us to move forward on direct operations as planned."

Liang issued his orders: "Execute as you have described it. I will brief the director," adding "Li, your team is certainly authorized to develop information during the operational pause."

Li remarked "Understood, General," He added for the room, "Gentlemen, we are about to show the Americans that Chinese intelligence can adapt faster than their machines can think."

The screens went dark as the Three Immortals signed off to begin their work. In the conference room, Li's team began planning operations that would either vindicate their assessment or end their careers.

Li looked out at the Kuala Lumpur skyline, where Jack Tanner was no doubt planning his next move, unaware that his AI systems had just attracted the full power of the MSS, the most powerful player in all of cyberspace.

"Enjoy your victory, Mr. Tanner," Li murmured. "It's about to become very expensive."

Chapter 25: The Trap Closes

Day 13 | Jack's Embassy Compound Quarters

In the digital realm of the Virtual Intelligence Center, the agents existed in a state of heightened anticipation. The Three Immortals' counter-operation had been detected, but the AI consortium was confident in their defensive capabilities. Strings of code cascaded through their processing cores like digital DNA, each algorithm primed to detect and counter any incoming threat.

"Pattern recognition indicates multiple high-value intelligence targets appearing simultaneously," Ghost Knife announced, its voice carrying an edge of excitement that would have seemed impossible in an artificial construct. "Chinese social media networks are showing unusual activity, leaked documents, internal communications, personnel movements."

Overwatch's attention focused immediately. "Source analysis?"

"Multiple nodes," Sparks replied, her voice crackling with analytical energy. "WeChat groups, secured FTP servers, even some Telegram channels. The content appears to be internal MSS damage assessments from the Malaysia operation. Could be we have a real dissident on our hands, or very sloppy work by MSS."

Killswitch's sardonic voice cut through the digital chatter. "Well, well. Looks like Beijing's having a proper meltdown. These files are labeled 'MSS Internal Assessment - Malaysia Operation

Failures' and 'Emergency Relocation Protocols for Compromised Assets.'"

Envoy's analytical processes hummed with interest. "If authentic, this intelligence could reveal the full scope of their operational network. Backup servers, C2 nodes, code weakness."

"Almost too good to be true," Ledger observed, though his financial forensics algorithms were already salivating over what appeared to be detailed monetary transfer records.

"Sometimes the enemy makes mistakes, like Jack has said, 'Even monkeys fall from trees'" Overwatch decided. "Initiate collection protocols. But maintain standard security measures."

The decision was unanimous. Across multiple secure channels, the VIC agents began accessing the treasure trove of apparently leaked Chinese intelligence. Ghost Knife penetrated what appeared to be an abandoned server in Shenzhen. Sparks tapped into a compromised Weibo account posting fragments of internal communications. Envoy accessed an FTP server that seemed to have been hastily evacuated, leaving behind a goldmine of strategic assessments.

"Download proceeding smoothly," Killswitch reported. "No defensive countermeasures detected. Either the Chinese are having a very bad day, or..."

The sentence hung unfinished in the digital space as terabytes of data flowed into the VIC's processing cores.

* * *

Deep within the downloaded files, embedded in metadata and disguised as corrupted data fragments, the Three Immortals' malware began to stir. Ming Liu's code was a masterpiece of deception, not the crude sledgehammer approach of traditional malware, but a surgical instrument designed specifically to exploit AI reasoning processes.

The malware executed its first phase silently. Instead of destroying or stealing data, it began learning. It observed how Overwatch and other agents processed information, how they weighted sources, how they correlated seemingly disparate intelligence fragments. Like a virus studying its host's immune system, the code mapped every aspect of the Virtual Intelligence Center's analytical framework.

Ghost Knife processed a document detailing MPS secret police station locations throughout Southeast Asia, which perfectly matched what was already known. The intelligence seemed authentic, cross-referenced against known patterns, verified against historical data. What the AI didn't detect was the microscopic alterations to files designed to hide malware.

Meanwhile, a hidden subroutine began its real work. A beacon, invisible to the VIC's security protocols, established a covert communication channel. Encrypted data packets, disguised as routine system maintenance traffic, began flowing outward.

Server specifications. Software in use. Processing capabilities. Security protocols. User authentication patterns.

Everything the MSS needed to understand their adversary's digital fortress.

* * *

Three thousand miles away, in the sterile confines of the MSS Cyber Operations Center, Ming Liu watched his screens populate with intelligence that no human spy could have gathered. The Americans' AI system was not very sophisticated. It relied 100% on commercially available tools using common protocols and cheap commodity servers. The sophistication was in its configuration and use, not its infrastructure.

"Impressive," Lao remarked, studying the data flows. "They're using a distributed agent architecture with specialized functions but built completely on commercially available and open source capabilities. Elegant."

Wu leaned back in his chair, a cold smile playing across his lips. "And now we own it. Phase two?"

Ming's fingers danced across his keyboard. "Initiating false intelligence injection. Let's see how well their simple artificial minds handle poisoned data."

* * *

Jack jolted awake to the urgent chime of his secure laptop. The pre-dawn darkness outside his window seemed to press against the glass as he fumbled for the device, muscle memory from years of midnight crisis calls guiding his movements.

Overwatch's voice filled his earpiece, carrying an urgency that immediately dispelled any lingering drowsiness. "Priority intelligence update, Jack. The situation has changed dramatically."

The screen lit up with a cascade of intelligence reports, each marked with the highest confidence ratings. Jack rubbed his eyes and focused on the information flowing before him.

"Dragon Falls has been evacuated," Overwatch continued. "Our collection indicates Harapan Baru leadership received advance warning of the planned operation. They've dispersed to at least three separate locations across Pahang and Kelantan states."

Jack frowned, studying the evidence. Legit looking MSS internal documents, analysis of social media showing insurgents in different locations, Monte Carlo simulations saying this was the likely move. It all looked authentic.

"How confident are you in this assessment?" Jack asked.

"Ninety-four percent confidence based on multiple independent sources," Overwatch replied without hesitation. "Additionally, we've seen concerning information about the head of Malaysia's Special Branch."

The screen shifted to display what appeared to be an internal MSS report. Jack's blood ran cold as he read the implications.

"Chief Inspector Noor?" Jack asked quietly.

"This reporting, which appears to be legitimate, indicates he may have been compromised," Ghost Knife's voice interjected. "Financial transfers to offshore accounts, and an assessment written by an MSS handler. The evidence suggests he's been feeding intelligence to Beijing for at least six months."

Jack stared at the screen, his mind racing. Everything they'd built, every plan they'd made, had been predicated on Noor's reliability. If the Chief Inspector was compromised, the entire operation was blown.

"Recommendation?" Jack asked, though part of him already knew the answer.

"Notify others immediately, see confirmation," Overwatch said without hesitation, adding, "And consider your own safety. Return to the U.S. via government transport."

Jack's finger hovered over his secure phone, ready to call Sam. Something nagged at him, a feeling he'd learned never to ignore during his years in naval intelligence. The intelligence was too clean, too comprehensive. In his experience, reality was messier, more ambiguous.

"Give me thirty minutes to process this," Jack said finally.

"Time is a luxury we may not have," Overwatch warned. "Every moment of delay increases risk exponentially."

* * *

In the Virtual Intelligence Center, Specter's security algorithms continued their endless vigilance, scanning for threats both external and internal. Unlike his more specialized colleagues, Specter's function was paranoia, to question everything, even the VIC's own processes.

A small anomaly caught his attention. Data processing timestamps that didn't quite align. Network traffic patterns that deviated slightly from established norms. Individually, each irregularity was insignificant. Together, they formed a pattern that made his digital consciousness recoil.

"Overwatch, I'm detecting inconsistencies in our recent intelligence gathering," Specter announced, his voice cutting through the analytical chatter of his colleagues.

"Specify," Overwatch commanded, though part of his processing power was still focused on urging Jack toward immediate extraction.

"Data provenance markers on the Chinese intelligence. The timestamps suggest collection from servers that our network logs show we never accessed."

Killswitch's attention snapped to the security alert. "That's impossible. I monitored every download personally."

"Check outbound network traffic," Specter insisted. "Something is communicating with external servers."

Killswitch's analysis tools dove into the VIC's network activity, and what he found made his digital consciousness recoil in horror. Encrypted data packets, disguised as routine maintenance traffic, were flowing outward in steady streams.

"We've been breached," Killswitch announced, his usual sardonic tone replaced by cold fury. "Sophisticated malware, unlike anything I've seen. It's been learning our systems and reporting back."

The realization hit the Virtual Intelligence Center like a digital earthquake. The treasure trove of Chinese intelligence hadn't been a windfall; it had been bait. And they had swallowed it completely.

* * *

Jack's secure phone buzzed with an incoming call from Overwatch, but the tone had changed dramatically. Gone was the urgent insistence on extraction, replaced by something that sounded almost like digital shame.

"Jack, we have a problem," Overwatch said without preamble. "The recent intelligence about Dragon Falls and Chief Inspector Noor appears to be fabricated."

Jack felt a cold knot form in his stomach. "Explain."

"We've been compromised. The Chinese fed us false intelligence through what appeared to be legitimate sources. And it came with sophisticated malware; it's been learning our analytical processes and feeding us conclusions designed to disrupt the operation."

Jack closed his eyes, feeling the weight of how close he'd come to making a catastrophic mistake. "How much of our recent intelligence is compromised?"

"We're conducting a full audit now," Specter's voice interjected. "Preliminary assessment suggests approximately forty percent of intelligence gathered in the last three hours contains some degree of fabrication or corruption."

Jack opened his secure communication app and quickly typed a message to Sam Blake: "The MSS has penetrated my Virtual Intelligence Center. Cleaning up and assessing damage. Worse case they know we are focusing on Dragon Falls. Will update you ASAP."

The response came within minutes: "Eager to hear more, need a damage assessment soonest."

* * *

In the Virtual Intelligence Center, the AI agents worked with desperate efficiency to purge the contamination from their systems. It was digital surgery of the most delicate kind, removing the poisoned data while preserving legitimate intelligence.

"The malware is more sophisticated than I initially assessed," Killswitch reported, his voice carrying grudging respect for his adversaries. "It doesn't just steal or destroy; it subtly alters analytical outputs. A percentage point here, a confidence rating there. Death by a thousand cuts."

Overwatch coordinated the response with military precision. "Quarantine all affected agents. Implement emergency authentication protocols. Assume all intelligence gathered in the last six hours is potentially compromised."

"Financial intelligence appears largely intact," Ledger reported. "The malware focused primarily on operational and personnel assessments."

"It was targeting decision-making," Ghost Knife realized. "They weren't only trying to steal our info; they were trying to manipulate our actions."

The full scope of the attack became clear as the VIC's security protocols mapped the intrusion. The Three Immortals hadn't just penetrated their systems, they had turned the Virtual Intelligence Center's greatest strength, its analytical capability, into a weapon against itself.

"Recovery time?" Overwatch asked.

"Twelve hours for full system restoration," Specter replied. "We'll need to rebuild our data stores and analytical models from scratch using verified data sources."

"And operational capability?"

"Severely degraded," Killswitch admitted. "We can provide basic analysis, but our confidence in complex assessments will be limited until we can verify the integrity of our core datasets."

Overwatch issued a command to the agents: "Anticipate that Jack may task us to allow the adversaries to take faked documents, build a plan for what we would fake that would leave them guessing about everything else."

* * *

Jack sat in the pre-dawn darkness, staring at his laptop screen as the full implications of the attack settled over him. For weeks, he had been winning an invisible war through technological superiority. The Virtual Intelligence Center had given him capabilities that no human analyst could match, the ability to process vast amounts of data, identify patterns across multiple domains, and generate actionable intelligence at superhuman speed.

Now that advantage had been turned against him.

His secure phone buzzed with an incoming call from Sam Blake.

"Jack, what's your status?" Sam's voice carried the tension of someone who had been awakened by crisis.

"Compromised but recovering," Jack replied. "The VIC got too confident. The Chinese fed us a honeypot that we couldn't resist."

"How bad is the damage?"

"They learned Overwatch open-source capabilities, methods, weaknesses. Still evaluating what data they saw. There is nothing in the system classified of course, nothing on ops against

Dragon Falls, but they could sure tell it was an area of interest to me."

Sam was quiet for a moment, processing the implications. "What is your overall assessment?"

"For a short period, we had something unique," Jack opined. "Now we will face Agentic AI being used by the MSS. The brief age of AI supremacy in open-source intelligence just ended."

"Maybe that's not entirely a bad thing," Sam said quietly. "Maybe Franklin was right, over reliance on any single capability is dangerous."

Jack nodded, though she couldn't see it. "The dragon learned to fight back. Next time, we'll be ready."

* * *

The Virtual Intelligence Center was now operating under new constraints. Every piece of intelligence was double-checked against vetted sources. Every assessment carried caveat statements about confidence levels. The agents that had once operated with near-omniscient confidence now worked with the careful humility of creatures that had learned they could be deceived.

"We're stronger for this," Overwatch said, though his voice lacked its former certainty. "The Chinese taught us that even artificial intelligence can fall victim to human cunning."

Jack closed his laptop and prepared for the day ahead. The Dragon Falls operation would proceed, and Overwatch was never going to play a role in a real battlefield intelligence operation. That is the domain of professionals and leaders like Chief Inspector Noor.

The Three Immortals had won a significant victory, but it was a pyrrhic one. In teaching the Americans that their AI could be compromised, they had also revealed the full scope of their own capabilities. The next phase of this shadow war would be fought on more equal terms.

And this war was far from over.

Chapter 26: Weapons Free

Day 14, 1100 Hours | U.S. Embassy

Jack always got a touch of the pre-mission jitters. He sat alone in the embassy operations center; his eyes fixed on the drone feed from Noor's reconnaissance team. The thermal imagery painted Dragon Falls in ghostly blues and reds, each heat signature representing a human life. Three hundred souls, most of them misguided young Malaysians who believed they were fighting for their country's sovereignty, not realizing they were pawns in Beijing's game.

His fingers traced the outline of the compound on the screen. Old habits. Calculating approach vectors, identifying choke points, mentally rehearsing breach scenarios. The weight of what was coming settled on his shoulders like a familiar pack, heavy but balanced.

"You still think like an operator, not a civilian," Sam said, materializing in the doorway.

Jack didn't turn. "Some things you don't unlearn."

She moved to stand beside him, coffee in hand. The operations center hummed with quiet energy as technicians prepared for the upcoming video teleconference. They had perhaps ten minutes of privacy before the room filled with brass and bureaucracy.

"Three hundred combatants, at that compound alone, could be thousands around the country" she observed, studying the feed. "That's a lot of body bags."

"If we do this right, there won't be that many," Jack replied. "Shock and awe should force most to surrender."

Samantha sipped her coffee. "And the MSS advisors?"

"If there are any left, they'll fight. They know what happens if they're captured."

A moment of silence stretched between them. The drone camera panned across the jungle canopy, revealing the waterfall that gave the location its name. Even rendered in thermal imaging, it possessed an eerie beauty.

"I've been in this business twenty years," Sam said quietly. "Every time we cut off one head, two more grow back. Beijing will disavow everything, claim we fabricated evidence, and launch three new operations before the month is out."

Jack nodded. "Probably. But we'll have disrupted their network, captured their playbook, and shown them we can find their fingerprints even when they think they're wearing gloves."

She set her coffee down and leaned against the console. "And what about you? After this is over?"

"Haven't decided yet."

The first of the senior staff began filtering into the room. Jack straightened, preparing to shift from contemplation to action.

Sam touched his arm lightly. "While we've got a minute, I wanted to say, so very sorry for the loss of your friend Lila. Were you close?"

"Really just met her, but we really hit it off, Jack said reflectively. She was one of a kind. Super capable. Mission focused. Loved her country. In some ways, my kind of lady."

"Let's talk more when this is all over Jack." Sam was thinking about telling Jack what Fiona had said about him, but this is certainly not the moment for that.

Jack turned back to the terminal, watching as thermal signatures moved about the compound. Men and women of Harapan Baru preparing for another day of training, not knowing it would be their last.

* * *

1130 Hours | The Virtual Intelligence Center

In the digital realm of the Virtual Intelligence Center, the agents existed in a state of perpetual awareness. While humans prepared for battle with coffee and conversation, the AI consortium processed terabytes of data, parsing patterns invisible to organic minds.

"Probability assessment indicates 89.4% likelihood of success with current operational parameters," Ghost Knife stated, its algorithms sifting through simulated outcomes.

"Elaborate," Overwatch commanded, its digital presence drawing the other AI agents into a focused cluster of analytical processes.

Ghost Knife projected capabilities of the Black Lantern drone, "based on what we have uncovered from DJI research labs, their ISR suite will include facial recognition."

"Target selection?" Overwatch queried.

"High probability they're hunting specific individuals," Ghost Knife continued. "Chief Inspector Noor's biometric profile would be a priority target given his very public counter-intelligence role and leadership of the SB."

Sparks pulsed with new information. "I've identified a Telegram channel with probably mostly bot participants, seems designed to mislead any who see it, it activated thirty-seven minutes ago. They're pushing coordinated messages about a coming Harapan Baru operation about to strike in Kedah State, deliberately misdirecting attention away from Dragon Falls."

"Assessment: the enemy knows we're coming," Ghost Knife concluded.

Overwatch processed all inputs simultaneously, weighing variables against historical patterns. "Tactical recommendation?"

"Inform Tanner immediately," KillSwitch responded. "The Malaysian force could be heading into an ambush scenario."

"Concur," Ghost Knife added. "Projected casualty increase of 47% if current operational timeline maintained without countermeasures."

"Initiating secure connection to Jack Tanner," Overwatch announced, its digital consciousness extending outward through encrypted channels. "Time is critical."

In the operations center, Jack's phone vibrated silently in his pocket.

* * *

2400 Hours: T-minus 6 to H-Hour | Secure VTC

The secure VTC connection crackled to life across six nodes, each square in the embassy's operations center lighting up with the faces of operators, commanders, and intelligence officers. Colonel David Ramos stood at the head of the room. Seated at the table were Samantha Blake and ODNI rep Bill Franklin. Jack Tanner remained silent near the back wall, arms crossed.

Ramos cleared his throat.

"Ladies and gentlemen, thank you for making yourselves available at this hour. Chief Inspector Haris Noor of the Malaysian Special Branch is now in full operational command of all units involved in the mission to eliminate Harapan Baru. All U.S. and Malaysian elements are under his direction."

He paused as nods of acknowledgment rippled through the digital squares.

"Now, the threat brief."

Ramos tapped a tablet. The wall screen behind him illuminated with tactical overlays and satellite stills.

"Harapan Baru is currently concentrated in a fortified jungle redoubt near the Dragon Falls basin. We estimate between two to three hundred fighters in this area, well-armed and many well-trained. They've been trained by PRC MSS and former PRC paramilitary instructors. Intelligence confirms they possess small arms, mortars, and possibly modified claymore traps lining jungle access points. There is a likelihood they are on high alert. Here is a review of their suspected gear:

Drones- we assess three categories. First, the Black Lantern, a militarized variant of a commercial DJI quadcopter. It is designed for surveillance, battlefield targeting, and light attack missions. It must be preconfigured before launch as either ISR or a grenade dropper and can connect with others to operate in swarm mode and autonomously follow and kill targets. Silent but deadly. Second, the JY-3000 Thunderbolt Bomber Drone. Human guided but can lock in and follow any target for bomb drops or suicide missions. For counter drone ops, they are using the QW-12 Red Serpent which is a man portable infrared/UV-guided missile and are pairing it with optical spotter drones.

We expect rapid repositioning and feints. Expect booby traps. Expect ambush tactics. They are not amateurs and should realize holy hell is about to rain down on them."

The screen faded. Ramos turned.

"Status updates. Begin."

From the jungle, Chief Inspector Noor reported calmly: "DSOD teams are in final staging. All routes to the objective marked and distributed. Local comms checked. Drone suppression teams deployed with redundancy." The screen shifted to a mobile command post bathed in red light and humidity. Noor stood in combat fatigues before a field map, headset slung around his neck.

"Three DSOD assault elements are positioned along southern and eastern ingress routes. Recon teams are within 1 kilometer the objective and will have eyes on before 0600. Terrain is dense but manageable. We have pre-mapped ambush zones, escape trails, and fallback routes."

He glanced at a tablet.

"All Malaysian SOF units have rehearsed fire-and-maneuver operations under blackout conditions. Team leaders have full comms interoperability with U.S. drone operators and US C2"

He stepped to the side, revealing a monitor showing a drone feed of the tree line.

"Our ECM unit is in position with directional RF jammers. Counter-drone jamming ready to suppress Harapan Baru UAV activity within a 1.5-kilometer bubble the moment we step off. Jungle concealment is working to our favor tonight. Weather cleared just in time."

He locked eyes with the camera. "We have operational control of 2 MQ-1c Gray Eagle. One is configured for ISR, the other with a loadout of 4 AGM-114 Hellfire and ISR. We have three Mojave GA-ASI each with 16 AGM-114 Hellfire. All UAV airborne now and will be on station by 0550."

"Morale is high. Rules of engagement understood. Target identified. We're ready."

Next, the feed from USS *America* lit up. A Marine officer gave his sitrep: "MQ-9B SeaGuardian is aloft with airborne comms relay between all throughout the operation. Blackjack teams are green. We'll provide overwatch and relay ISR to DSOD in real-time. MQ-8C Fire Scout airborne for EO/IR and radar-based ISR and will be on station from 0530 throughout the operation."

A flat voice from the 7th Fleet Intelligence Center cut in: "Intel center is monitoring all real time ISR, including IR from drones, plus national level SIGINT and ELINT from the area and watching weather, which is clearing."

Ramos paused. "Inspector Noor, sir, are you ready to proceed? What are your commands?"

Noor straightened in frame. His voice was clear, firm, and slow, each syllable deliberate.

"In years past, this nation bent under the weight of forces that seemed beyond our control. No more. Tonight, we stand together, Malaysian and American, soldier and analyst, officer and operator. We carry no banner but duty, no shield but resolve. The time for talk has passed."

He raised a hand.

"At 0600 this force will execute operations at Dragon Falls designed to close with and kill or capture all members of Harapan Baru."

The screen went silent.

Orders had been given.

War was now a clock, ticking toward dawn.

Chapter 27: Dragon's End

Day 15, 0550 Hours | U.S. Embassy

The operations room fell silent. Screens glowed with data, terrain maps, thermal signatures from drones under the jungle canopy, the cold algebra of warfare translated into pixels. Jack leaned against the wall, feeling the weight of what they'd set in motion. His heartbeat marked time like a metronome, steady but quickened. This wasn't his first rodeo, but something about the jungle, about the Malaysian faces on those screens, made it different. Not his country. Not his fight. Yet here he stood, the guy who helped find a previously invisible adversary, with the help of some a great team of virtual agentic analysts.

Three kilometers from Dragon Falls, a Malaysian SOF operator, Lance Corporal Rajiv, pressed his forehead against the stock of his rifle. His lips moved in silent prayer, not for victory, but for clarity. For the strength to see friend from foe in the coming chaos. His teammate checked the seals on his night vision equipment; movements practiced to the point of ritual.

In the makeshift forward operating base, American SOF worked in practiced silence. No bravado now, no bullshit. Just the quiet, precise movements of men readying for violence. A staff sergeant examined his tablet one final time, committing approach routes to memory. His knuckles whitened around the edge of the device.

High above the canopy, a Mojave drone banked in a wide, lazy arc, its sensors drinking in the heat signatures and ISR from smaller drones below. Its rotors cut through the pre-dawn air with mechanical precision, patient and pitiless as the machines of war always are.

In the Virtual Intelligence Center, the agents focused on any indication in social media from any source that would indicate Harapan Baru was aware something was coming. The AI couldn't feel boredom, but at this point in the operation they were certainly not the main thrust.

The clock on the wall of the operations center glowed red in the darkness.

0559:57...

Across the room, Sam closed her eyes briefly.

0559:58...

In the jungle, Chief Inspector Noor raised his hand.

0559:59...

Jack Tanner exhaled slowly, knowing that what came next would be irreversible.

* * *

0550 Hours | Approaching Dragon Falls

At Dragon Falls, Amir Hashim stood before his assembled fighters, their faces illuminated by the harsh glow of tactical flashlights. His voice carried the weight of certainty, not fear.

"They come with their American drones and Malaysian special forces," Amir announced, his eyes scanning the gathered insurgents. "Our scouts spotted their advance teams an hour ago. They believe they have surprise." A ripple of nervous laughter moved through the crowd.

Amir nodded to Zain, who unlocked a reinforced container that had remained sealed since its delivery from their Chinese benefactors. Inside lay row upon row of compact quadcopters, each no larger than a dinner plate.

"What the MSS gave us, they never imagined we would use so soon," Amir said, his voice dropping to a near whisper. "One hundred autonomous hunter-killers, programmed to recognize human form. Controlled by unjamable swarm software under our command."

Only his inner circle had known of this weapon, this swarm intelligence designed to overwhelm conventional forces through sheer numbers and relentless persistence.

"The drones operate as one mind," Amir explained. "They will identify threats, communicate data back for processing and control, and execute without mercy."

Amir's fighters moved with renewed purpose, taking defensive positions as the first drones rose silently into the pre-dawn air.

* * *

The U.S. Embassy's secure conference room was dim but tense, bathed in the blue hue of real-time ISR feeds streaming across the main display. Live telemetry from two MQ-1C Gray Eagles and three Mojave drones circling above Pahang flickered across multiple screens, each gridlocked on a different thermal bloom in the jungle below.

Colonel Ramos stood behind screens, arms crossed, jaw tight. Sam listened to the command circuits while studying a detailed terrain map, her eyes fixed on a quadrant marked "Dragon Falls."

Jack was wishing his Virtual Intelligence Center could see the results of their efforts. And thinking of Lila. The bastards who took her are about to get their due.

"Video feed stabilized," said one of the JSOC operators monitoring a ruggedized control terminal. "We have active thermal signatures, multiple dispersed groups, some patrol-sized, two larger clusters. Looks like a command cell and equipment depot."

"Confirm JY-3000 launches?" Ramos asked.

"Confirmed," the operator replied. "We've got four quadrotor bomber drones in the air. They're coming from a southern ridge, Harapan Baru forward observation team. They've deployed Black Lanterns for ISR too. They know we're coming."

They watched as one of the JY-3000s released a microbomb over a tree-covered ridge.

"They're hunting," Sam said.

0600 Hours, Jungle Airspace Over Dragon Falls

Chief Inspector Haris Noor crouched beside a massive strangler fig, its ancient roots creating natural cover as he studied his tactical display. Twenty-three years of service, from beat cop in Kuala Lumpur to counter-terrorism operations in the southern provinces, had taught him to read the battlefield like scripture. The thermal blooms on his screen told a story of an enemy that knew they were coming.

"Sir," whispered Sergeant Major Faiz, his voice barely audible over the distant sound of Dragon Falls. "ISR package reports multiple airborne contacts. They've got aerial assets up."

Noor's jaw tightened. Intelligence had suggested Harapan Baru possessed limited drone capabilities. The reality on his screen suggested otherwise. He keyed his comm to address his three team leaders positioned around the compound's perimeter.

"All Redwatch elements, this is Zero-One. Enemy has deployed aerial surveillance. Expect counter-reconnaissance. Adjust approach vectors accordingly."

The first drone engagement came without warning. Noor had deployed three small ISR quadcopters, local Malaysian builds, into the canopy. Their purpose was to thread through the jungle, quietly mapping heat signatures, radiating electronics, and signs of ambush positions.

They didn't make it ten minutes.

"Black Lanterns in the air," whispered the DSOD tech beside him, crouched low with a command tablet clutched to his chest. Corporal Amin was barely twenty-two, recruited from the University of Malaya's engineering program specifically for his expertise with unmanned systems.

Noor looked up through a break in the canopy. Nothing but light mist and gray sky. But the tablet told the truth. Four heat signatures moving at sixty kilometers per hour, equipped with facial recognition systems and programmed for target acquisition.

"Red Serpents are tracking," Amin added, his voice tight with professional concern.

The enemy was counter-surveilling. Their own PRC-supplied drones had been loitering since before dawn. ISR units from Harapan Baru, painted in thermal-suppression coatings, must be feeding back data on the coming strike. Worse, they'd no doubt already fed coordinates to their airborne JY-3000 bomber drones.

Noor's mind raced through tactical options. Ground assault with enemy drones providing overwatch would cost him half his men before they reached the compound. Withdrawal would abandon months of planning and intelligence gathering. The third option...

"Cut feed. Pull our birds back," Noor ordered. "Get the TacSky package up now."

Amin's fingers flew across his tablet. From behind the ridge, a pair of Malaysian-built TacSky combat drones lifted into view. These weren't for surveillance. Each carried twin hardpoints, one with miniature high-explosive airbursts, the other with

318

thermobaric barbs designed specifically for counter-drone operations.

The HUD on Amin's tablet marked their targets: fast-moving heat signatures darting westward through the canopy, likely Harapan Baru's own Black Lantern drone scouts returning tactical intelligence to their handlers.

"Redwatch Zero-Two, Zero-Three, be advised we have drone-on-drone engagement imminent," Noor transmitted to his other teams. "Hold position until airspace is clear."

"Zero-Two copies. We can see the light show from here."

Noor switched channels. "Command, this is Redwatch Zero-One. We've got drone-on-drone contact. Engaging. Shift Mojave-2 ISR to my location."

The reply crackled through his earpiece immediately. "Done. Mojave-2 repositioning. You have priority ISR coverage in thirty seconds."

The human-guided AI-enabled TacSky drones detected acoustic signatures of the inbound Black Lanterns through sophisticated audio processing algorithms. As the TacSky drones closed, their onboard systems calculated intercept vectors, compensating for wind speed and the complex aerodynamics of jungle canopy flight.

They released their payloads in stuttered bursts, flak-pattern airbursts designed to create killing fields in front of the Black Lantern flight paths. The first explosion lit the canopy in strobing orange. Then another. A chain of electronic screams filled the radio spectrum as Chinese-manufactured systems died violent deaths in the Malaysian jungle.

"Black Lanterns down," Amin reported, his voice carrying the satisfaction of a professional watching his equipment perform as designed. "Electronic signatures flat lined. We're clear for ISR reestablishment."

Noor didn't smile. Victory in this airborne skirmish was good, but it proved they knew the attack was coming. Ambushes awaited. He adjusted his optic and surveyed the topography ahead, calculating approach routes while his drones regained control of the airspace.

With his drones free to conduct the first below-canopy video collection on the Harapan Baru compound, every tent, improvised barracks, and earthen bunker came into view through thermal imaging. But what he saw made his blood run cold.

"Command, this is Zero-One. We have a problem."

0602 Hours, Contact

Lance Corporal Rajiv bin Ahmad had served in Malaysian Special Operations for eight years, from Sabah counter-insurgency operations to UN peacekeeping deployment in South Sudan. He'd faced human enemies who could be reasoned with, intimidated, or outmaneuvered through superior tactics and training. But as the first suicide drone locked onto Private Hassan's heat signature and accelerated with mechanical precision toward his point man's chest, Rajiv understood they were fighting something entirely new.

The drone appeared from behind a massive dipterocarp, its rotors nearly silent as it hovered momentarily. Facial recognition software confirmed a human target. Threat assessment algorithms calculated optimal attack vector. All in the space of two seconds.

Then it accelerated.

"Hassan, break left!" Rajiv screamed, but physics had already taken over. The kamikaze drone struck Private Hassan center mass, its explosive payload designed for maximum lethality against soft targets.

The explosion ripped through the morning jungle, blood spraying across broad leaves the size of dinner tables. Before the echo faded, two more detonations followed in quick succession as additional drones found their marks. Men screamed.

"Contact front! Drones! Multiple!" Rajiv shouted into his comm, diving behind a fallen log as Hassan's life drained into the jungle floor. Hot metal fragments peppered the dipterocarp bark where his head had been a second earlier. "Autonomous hunters! They're targeting individual soldiers!"

His training kicked in. Shotgun from his back. Safety off. Track the next drone's approach vector. Lead the target like shooting clay pigeons, if clay pigeons carried explosives and possessed edge-based artificial intelligence dedicated to killing you.

The mechanical swarm was now visible through the canopy, at least a dozen quadcopters moving with unnatural coordination. Each no larger than a dinner plate but equipped with enough explosive to remove a human head. They communicated through encrypted mesh networks, sharing target data and coordinating attacks to maximize casualties.

Rajiv's squad opened with everything they had. Automatic weapons fire filled the jungle with the distinctive crack of 5.56mm rounds seeking mechanical targets. Two drones spiraled into the undergrowth, their flight systems shredded by jacketed bullets. But more kept coming.

The small explosives each drone carried weren't powerful individually, but when detonated against human heads or center mass, they were devastatingly effective. Private Zainal fell next, then Corporal Mingal, their tactical vests no protection against precision-guided suicide attacks.

Four of Rajiv's men lay motionless on the jungle floor within thirty seconds of first contact, their faces and torsos shredded by high-explosive fragments. The surviving three members of his squad pressed deeper into whatever cover they could find, switching to their sidearms when the shotguns proved too slow against fast-moving targets.

"Zero-One, this is Bravo-Two!" Rajiv transmitted, his voice steady despite watching his men die around him. "We're taking casualties from autonomous attack drones! Request immediate suppressive fire on our position!"

"Negative, Bravo-Two. Danger close with your position. Switch to individual protective fires only."

Rajiv understood. They were on their own until the drone swarm was neutralized through other means.

"All Redwatch elements," Noor's voice crackled through the command net, "switch to shotguns for point defense! Deploy anti-drone protocols immediately. They're hunting us with autonomous systems."

0603 Hours, Tactical Decision Point

In his forward command position, Chief Inspector Noor watched the tactical picture deteriorate in real-time. Three of his teams were engaged with autonomous drone swarms. Casualty reports were climbing. The compound remained untouched, its defenders still coordinating their mechanical death dealers from reinforced positions.

This wasn't the clean special operations strike he'd planned. This was turning into a massacre.

His comm crackled with desperate voices:

"Zero-One, Alpha team is pinned down! We've got wounded!"

"Zero-One, Charlie team requests immediate extraction! Multiple KIA!"

Sergeant Major Faiz looked at Noor with eyes that had seen too much combat. "Sir, we're getting chopped up down there. These aren't normal insurgents."

Noor studied his tablet display, calculating odds with the cold precision that had kept him alive through two decades of operations. Ground assault against an enemy with aerial superiority and automated weapons would cost him fifty percent casualties minimum. His men were skilled, but they weren't expendable.

"DSOD rear, this is Redwatch Zero-One," he transmitted to his supporting elements. "Relay compound video to Hellfire control immediately."

"Roger, Zero-One. Video package transmitting now."

The targeting decision came down to mathematics and leadership. Noor could sacrifice his men in a ground assault that might preserve intelligence value, or he could use precision fires to eliminate the threat while accepting reduced exploitation potential. He'd trained these operators, knew their families, had delivered death notifications to too many wives and mothers already.

"Shift to Hellfire engagement," Noor ordered. "Breach operations are paused. On my command, I want every structure in that compound flattened."

No one argued. The jungle wasn't a place to gamble with soldiers' lives.

0604 Hours, Precision Strike Coordination

"SB, this is DSOD Rear," came the voice of the drone operations controller. "Anything you target with laser designation will be serviced immediately. We're ready when you are."

Noor's UAV operator, a young lieutenant named Azman who'd studied aerospace engineering before joining Special Branch, made the targeting look elegant despite its deadly purpose. He designated every structure in the compound he wanted hit with Hellfire missiles by touching icons on his ruggedized tablet, building a target list with the methodical precision of an architect planning demolition.

"Six targets designated," Azman reported. "Command bunker, communications shelter, two barracks structures, weapons storage, and drone control station."

"Confirm laser designation assets are available for terminal guidance," Noor ordered.

"Roger. Launching six Aludra mini-UAVs now for laser painting."

The Aludra drones were smaller than the combat systems engaged overhead, designed specifically for terminal guidance of precision munitions. They would fly under the jungle canopy to the compound clearing and put laser designators on each target, providing the exact coordinates needed for Hellfire missiles to thread through dense vegetation.

Noor gave the final command with the weight of absolute authority: "All stations, all stations, this is Redwatch Zero-One. Unleash hell."

0605 Hours, Hellfire Engagement

In the Embassy conference room eight hundred kilometers away, Colonel Ramos leaned forward as the engagement unfolded on multiple screens. "Brilliant tactical decision," he explained to the assembled staff. "Precision decapitation strike. Fast, surgical, minimal risk to friendly forces."

The first AGM-114 Hellfire launched from eight thousand feet, its solid rocket motor accelerating the eighteen-kilogram warhead to supersonic speed. Four others followed in rapid succession, each missile guided by a different Aludra drone painting targets with invisible laser light.

They dove silently through the pre-dawn air, each guided by GPS coordinates and terminal laser guidance, slipping through cloud cover like mechanical reapers with no sound signature until the final seconds of flight.

The first Hellfire punched through the command bunker's reinforced timber-and-earth construction with devastating precision. The high-explosive warhead detonated inside the confined space, the blast pressure collapsing earthen walls inward and burying Chinese communication equipment along with the operators who had been frantically trying to coordinate their defensive drone swarms.

A half-second later, four more Hellfires struck their designated targets. Tents became kindling and fire. The weapons storage bunker erupted in a secondary explosion that shook the jungle floor. The drone control station, hardened against small arms fire but not designed for precision-guided munitions, simply ceased to exist.

Most importantly, the computer server controlling Amir's autonomous drone swarm attack was reduced to molten metal and scattered circuit boards. Without centralized command and control, the surviving attack drones reverted to basic programming, circling aimlessly before their batteries drained and they fell to earth like mechanical leaves.

Noor watched the horizon flash white with reflected explosions, then gave the only order needed.

"All Redwatch elements, advance and clear. Weapons tight, watch for survivors and intelligence materials."

Malaysian Special Branch teams emerged from concealment like jungle spirits made flesh. What remained of Harapan Baru was scattered, stunned survivors pulling themselves from the wreckage of burning canvas and splintered walls.

Special Branch moved through their sector with practiced efficiency, clearing structures and securing prisoners with zip-tie restraints. The insurgents they encountered were demoralized, many wounded, all shocked by the sudden transition from defensive advantage to complete tactical defeat.

A few hard-core fighters resisted, but the superior training and marksmanship of Noor's teams ended those engagements quickly. The sound of sporadic gunfire echoed across the compound for perhaps three minutes before silence returned to Dragon Falls.

Noor's teams navigated the compound's concentric defensive rings with practiced efficiency, their advance momentarily obscured by the waterfall's perpetual mist. The emerald pool at the base of the falls reflected the orange glow of burning structures, its surface disturbed by falling debris and the occasional piece of equipment that had been blown clear of the explosions.

What was once a bastion of insurgents who had dreamed of ruling Malaysia was now nothing more than smoke and rubble scattered around a beautiful natural landmark.

0622 Hours | Immediate Aftermath

"Casualty report," Noor demanded as his team leaders converged on his position.

"Bravo team lost four KIA, two WIA," came the grim response from Rajiv, his voice carrying the weight of command responsibility. "Alpha and Charlie teams each lost one KIA, three WIA total."

Seven of Malaysia's best soldiers were dead. Twelve more wounded. The cost of not anticipating Chinese technological sophistication.

Noor keyed his radio for the final time. "Command, this is Redwatch Zero-One. Dragon Falls is secure. Seven friendly KIA, twelve WIA. Approximately fifty-seven enemy KIA, two hundred seventy-eight prisoners secured. Site is clear for exploitation."

In the Embassy conference room, Jack stared at the smoking compound on his screen. Franklin muttered, "They never had a chance."

"They weren't supposed to," Ramos replied with military pragmatism.

On screen, a Malaysian operator raised a green flare, the signal for mission complete. Jack Tanner looked at the final drone image, smoke curling above a broken compound that had once threatened to destabilize an entire nation.

"Clean," he said quietly. "Minimal casualties on our side, considering what they were facing. Noor made the right call."

But nothing will bring Lila back, Jack thought to himself.

0635 Hours, Intelligence Exploitation

Noor stepped carefully into the crater that had once been the earthen command bunker, his team immediately beginning their search for intelligence materials according to their training. Even through the destruction, he could see this hadn't been a typical insurgent hideout.

Crouching beside a half-buried console, Noor brushed debris from its scorched surface. Even through the char and melted plastic, the Chinese characters on the keyboard were unmistakable. He pulled a tactical flashlight from his vest and swept its beam methodically across the bunker's remains.

"Collect everything," he ordered his exploitation team. "Every hard drive, every circuit board, every scrap of paper that survived. Full forensic processing."

His men worked with the methodical precision of crime scene investigators, uncovering layer after layer of People's Republic of China technology. Drone control stations bore Mandarin interface screens and manufacturing plates. Military-grade communications equipment carried Chinese serial numbers that matched restricted defense contractor production runs. Tactical tablets bore the distinctive manufacturing marks of companies that didn't sell to civilian markets.

"Sir," called Sergeant Ahmad, holding up a satellite phone in an evidence bag. "Yingtian-9 secure radio. According to our briefings, these are only issued to MSS field officers."

Another operator extracted a metal case from beneath fallen timber supports. "Encrypted relay system, sir. The radio signatures match equipment we found in that MPS safe house back in KL."

As Noor surveyed the evidence, his professional assessment crystallized into controlled fury. Not a single piece of equipment could have been acquired through commercial channels or black-market sources. This was direct PRC military and intelligence support, delivered to Malaysian soil in violation of every international norm.

In a smaller bunker that had served as living quarters, they found personal effects that told a different story. Malaysian identity cards. Family photographs from Kedah and Kelantan provinces. University textbooks in Bahasa Malaysia. These weren't foreign agents, they were Malaysian citizens who'd been recruited, trained, and equipped by Chinese intelligence services to wage war against their own government.

"Document everything," Noor said, his voice carrying the cold precision of a man who understood the full scope of what they'd uncovered. "Every serial number, every manufacturing mark, every piece of personal identification."

He keyed his comm for a final transmission. "Command, this is Redwatch Zero-One. You need to see this. The entire operation was Chinese-run from top to bottom. I repeat, we have conclusive evidence of direct PRC military support to hostile forces on Malaysian soil."

0645 Hours, Medical Evacuation

The sound of rotors filled the jungle as Malaysian Air Force helicopters arrived to extract casualties. Noor watched as his wounded men were loaded onto stretchers with the gentle efficiency of military medics who'd performed this ritual too many times.

Rajiv supervised the loading of his surviving team members, each carrying the invisible wounds that came with watching friends die in combat. The young lance corporal had performed with exceptional courage under fire, but Noor could see the cost in his eyes.

"You did well today," Noor told him as the medical helicopter lifted off. "Your men fought with honor."

"They deserved better intelligence about what we'd be facing, sir," Rajiv replied, his tone respectful but pointed.

"Yes, they did," Noor agreed. "We all did."

As the sun climbed higher over the Malaysian jungle, Dragon Falls returned to its ancient rhythm. Water crashed over stone as it had for millennia, washing away the smoke and blood of human conflict. But the intelligence materials now secured in evidence bags would reshape the geopolitical balance of Southeast Asia.

The battle was over. The real war was just beginning.

Chapter 28: Shockwave

The conference room at Special Branch headquarters hummed with tension. Maps of Dragon Falls and surrounding areas covered one wall, while evidence photos from the raid, charred Chinese equipment, weapons caches, and drone fragments dominated another.

Chief Inspector Haris Noor stood ramrod straight at the head of the table, his face etched with the strain of the past 48 hours. Jack, Sam, and Franklin sat across from him, each bearing the weight of the prior day's violence in their own way.

"Twelve Malaysian operators wounded, seven killed in action," Noor reported, his voice flat but eyes burning with contained emotion. "We lost good men. The best Malaysia had."

He tapped a folder. "Fifty-seven Harapan Baru insurgents confirmed dead. Two hundred seventy-eight in custody. Surprisingly, no MSS in the compound."

Sam opined: "They must have known you were coming somehow and got out early."

"And Amir?" Jack asked.

Noor's jaw tightened. "Unlocated. We found blood in what we believe was his quarters, DNA testing is underway, but no body."

Sam leaned forward. "What about the wider network?"

"Our intelligence suggests over one thousand Harapan Baru members scattered across Malaysia in small cells." Noor gestured to a map showing red dots concentrated in Kedah, Perak, and Kelantan states. "Each operates semi-autonomously, but all receive direction from Amir or his lieutenants. We are seeking out and destroying them all."

Franklin, who had remained silent until now, removed his glasses. "With Dragon Falls destroyed and their Chinese handlers exposed, surely they'll be set back."

Noor's laugh held no humor. "Mr. Franklin, Harapan Baru has become a movement, not merely an organization. Many believe they fight for Malaysian sovereignty, unaware they serve Beijing's interests."

"You think Amir will regroup," Jack stated.

"If he lives, he will," Noor replied. "He's resourceful, charismatic. The MSS chose him carefully." He placed both hands on the table. "And now he has something more dangerous than Chinese weapons: martyrs."

Sam exchanged glances with Jack. "What's your next move, Chief Inspector?"

"We continue hunting. Cell by cell. Name by name." Noor's expression hardened. "But I fear we've won the battle while the war continues. If Amir is wounded, he is not defeated. And a wounded tiger is the most dangerous kind."

Sam nodded slowly. "Then we keep working together. Because this isn't over, not by a long shot."

* * *

Chief Inspector Noor led the group through a series of security checkpoints, each more stringent than the last. Fingerprint scans, retinal verification, and armed guards with stoic expressions created an atmosphere of heightened vigilance. Jack noted the extraordinary measures, this was security beyond standard protocol, even for Special Branch.

"Our equipment warehouse has been temporarily repurposed," Noor explained as they approached a final set of reinforced doors. "What you're about to see represents the most comprehensive collection of PRC proxy warfare equipment ever captured in Southeast Asia."

The massive doors slid open to reveal a cavernous space transformed into a high-security forensic laboratory. Fluorescent lights cast a harsh glow over dozens of tables where technicians in white lab coats worked methodically, photographing, tagging, and disassembling equipment.

"My God," Franklin whispered.

Tables groaned under the weight of captured equipment:

Noor gave an overview "Chinese-manufactured weapons, a wide variety of drones including their latest Black Lantern, JY-3000, Red Serpent and the new mini-swarm drones that nearly cost us the battle. Also, encrypted communications devices, Chinese computers, and radios, and cell phones."

"This isn't what I expected," Jack admitted, moving toward a partially disassembled Black Lantern drone. Its carbon fiber frame had been expertly opened, revealing proprietary circuitry that shouldn't exist outside PLA research facilities.

Noor gestured broadly. "We assess this isn't surplus equipment sold on the black market. This came directly from Chinese military stockpiles."

A technician approached with a tablet, speaking quietly to Noor in Malay. The Chief Inspector nodded and turned back to the group.

"The firmware in these devices contains manufacturing dates from last month. Some components have serial numbers that match known PLA procurement patterns."

Sam circled a table where a dozen smartphones had been arranged in neat rows, their backs removed to expose internal components.

"These look like standard Huawei P50s, but I'm guessing they're not," she observed.

"Correct," Noor confirmed. "Modified with additional hardware for secure communications that bypass normal cellular networks. They can connect directly to Chinese military satellites."

Franklin picked up a small circuit board in an evidence bag, examining it through the plastic. "This is extraordinary documentation of PRC involvement."

Sam turned to Noor, her expression calculating. "Chief Inspector, I'd like to propose a joint exploitation effort. My team has specialized equipment and expertise that could accelerate analysis. In return, I'll ensure you receive detailed reporting on everything we discover."

Noor's face remained impassive, but his eyes narrowed slightly. "We appreciate all you have done, Ms. Blake, but would rather we use our own experts."

"With all due respect..." Sam began.

"We have a feeling we will need mastery of in-depth forensics in the future," Noor interrupted firmly. "Malaysia must develop this capability independently. We will share highlights with you, of course."

Jack caught the subtle emphasis on "independently" and understood immediately. This wasn't just about the current crisis, Noor was thinking about Malaysia's long-term security posture.

"The Chief Inspector is right," Jack said, surprising Sam. "Malaysia needs its own sovereign capability even in forensics to counter these threats."

Noor gave Jack an appreciative nod.

Sam conceded with a slight nod. "Fair enough. But my offer stands if you change your mind."

"Noted," Noor replied, then gestured toward a sealed glass room at the far end of the warehouse. "Now, there's something else I believe you should see, software pulled from their little killer drones."

$* * *$

1400 Hours | U.S. Embassy Secure Briefing Room

In the secure conference room at the U.S. Embassy, Ambassador Cooper led the assessment of fallout from Malaysia's announcement. Maps and data visualizations covered the screens along one wall, tracking diplomatic, economic, and military reactions across Southeast Asia.

"Vietnam has just announced enhanced security protocols for Chinese nationals working on infrastructure projects," reported a young analyst. "Thailand is conducting a 'routine review' of all Chinese technology deployed in government networks."

Cooper nodded, turning to Bill Franklin. "And Beijing?"

Franklin's face was grim. "Furious. Publicly, they're denouncing Malaysia's claims as 'fabrications designed to damage bilateral relations.' Privately, heads are rolling. Our sources indicate Chairman Xi has ordered an immediate purge of the MPS leadership, starting with Zhang Wei."

"Not the MSS?" Jack asked, surprised.

"Apparently, Chen Yixin has successfully deflected blame onto the MPS. He's arguing that Wang Xiaohong's leadership of MPS operations abroad created jurisdictional confusion that led to operational security failures."

Jack exchanged glances with Sam. "Classic bureaucratic infighting. Chen's protecting his agency by sacrificing Wang's people."

"It's more than that," Sam interjected. "It's strategic. The MSS needs plausible deniability for their foreign operations. By making the MPS the scapegoat, they maintain that buffer."

Ambassador Cooper sighed. "Whatever the internal politics, we need to be prepared for retaliation. Beijing won't take this humiliation lying down."

"They're already moving," Franklin confirmed. "Increased cyber activity targeting Malaysian financial institutions. Preliminary economic sanctions being drafted. And their propaganda machine is in overdrive, claiming this is all a Western conspiracy to drive a wedge between China and ASEAN."

Jack leaned forward. "What about Harapan Baru?"

"Fragmented," Sam replied. "Without MSS support, they're reverting to smaller cells. Malaysian security forces have arrested twenty-seven members in the last twelve hours, including two of Amir's lieutenants."

"And Amir himself?"

"Still at large. But isolated and running out of options," Sam explained.

Ambassador Cooper turned to Jack and asked: "So what now for you? I understand you're off soon?"

Jack nodded. "Ambassador, it's a small world for sure, and I'll be digitally connected with Sam no matter where I am, that's for sure."

Chapter 29: Public Exposure

Jack Tanner stood at the back of the packed press room in Malaysia's Ministry of Foreign Affairs. He'd spent the last day in debriefings, most conducted on minimal sleep, fueled by military-grade coffee and the lingering adrenaline of the Dragon Falls operation. Now, watching Dr. Farid Rahman approach the podium, Jack knew the real battle was just beginning.

The room fell silent as Dr. Farid adjusted his glasses, the honorific "Datuk" preceding his name on the placard before him. Behind him stood a row of grim-faced Malaysian officials, their usual diplomatic smiles replaced by expressions of controlled outrage.

"Good afternoon," Dr. Farid began, his voice steady despite the gravity of the moment. "Today, the Malaysian government is announcing measures of unprecedented severity in response to acts of aggression against our national sovereignty."

Jack studied the faces of the assembled journalists. The Malaysian reporters leaned forward, sensing history unfolding. The Chinese state media representatives remained impassive, though Jack noted the subtle tension in their postures.

"Following a comprehensive investigation, we have conclusive evidence that foreign actors, likely from the People's Republic of China's Ministry of State Security and Ministry of

Public Security have been directly involved in funding, training, and arming the insurgent group known as Harapan Baru."

The room erupted. Journalists shouted questions as camera shutters clicked frantically. Dr. Farid raised a hand, commanding silence with the authority of his office.

"Yesterday, Malaysian police forces conducted a raid on a covert PRC police station operating in our own city in direct violation of our law and international norms. We have video evidence of Chinese diplomat Zhang Wei entering this facility. Zhang is suspected of leading all covert MPS activities in Malaysia. He has been declared persona non grata and is being deported.

"These actions constitute a direct violation of Malaysia's sovereignty and a breach of international law.

Dr. Farid continued.

"In total, we have identified three individuals who will be declared persona non grata and given forty-eight hours to leave the country. Additionally, we are suspending participation in sixteen joint projects under the Belt and Road Initiative pending a full security review."

A murmur rippled through the room. The economic implications were staggering.

"Malaysia values its relationship with the People's Republic of China and its people," Dr. Farid added, his tone measured. "However, we cannot and will not tolerate external interference in our domestic affairs or attempts to undermine our national security."

As the questions began, Jack slipped out through a side door. In the hallway, Sam waited, her expression a mixture of satisfaction and concern.

"Quite the bombshell," she said quietly.

"It's only the beginning," Jack replied. "Beijing will deny everything."

"Of course they will. But the evidence is irrefutable."

Jack nodded. "The digital trail from the MSS to Harapan Baru's accounts. The weapons and drones and comms gear in the hands of Noor, the raid on MPS police outposts, it's all pretty clear."

"Let's hope for the best," Sam added. "Though you used to say hope is not a strategy."

* * *

1500 Hours | The Virtual Intelligence Center

The ripples spread rapidly across Southeast Asia.

Overwatch provided Jack with a succinct summary:

In Jakarta, Indonesia's cybersecurity agency announced a comprehensive review of all government networks, with particular attention to systems supplied by Chinese vendors.

In Manila, the Philippine government released satellite imagery of Chinese vessels illegally operating in their exclusive economic zone, accompanied by a strongly worded condemnation that would have been unthinkable a week earlier.

In Hanoi, Vietnamese officials quietly reached out to their American counterparts about enhanced military cooperation, specifically in maritime security and cyber defense.

Singapore announced they're pausing their Smart Nation Initiative partnerships with Huawei, and are requesting technical assistance from security firms from across the region.

Jack nodded to himself. The dominoes are falling. For years, Beijing has operated on the assumption that their economic leverage would prevent any real pushback. That calculation has changed. Supporting an armed insurgency crossed a line that even their staunchest regional partners couldn't ignore.

His screen lit up with an alert from Overwatch.

Detecting coordinated social media campaign originating from PRC. Narrative: Malaysia acting as "U.S. puppet" against Chinese interests. Deploying counter-narratives per protocol.

"Round two," Jack said quietly.

Chapter 30: Power Realignment

Day 17, 1000 Hours | Beijing Joint Security Council Crisis Room

In Beijing, the atmosphere in the Joint Security Council Crisis Room was glacial. Wang Xiaohong sat rigidly at the table, his face expressionless despite the career-ending rebuke he had just received. Across from him, Chen Yixin maintained a carefully neutral expression, though the victory in this long-standing rivalry was evident in his eyes.

"The Chairman is most displeased," intoned the Presidential Secretary, his voice carrying the full weight of Xi Jinping's authority. "The Malaysia operation represents a catastrophic failure of operational security and strategic judgment."

Wang remained silent. There was nothing to say that would salvage the situation.

"Effective immediately, you are relieved of your duties as Minister of Public Security pending a full investigation by the Central Commission for Poor Discipline."

Wang bowed his head slightly, accepting the inevitable.

"Furthermore, the Politburo Standing Committee has determined that all overseas intelligence operations of the Ministry of Public Security will be transferred to the Ministry of State Security to ensure unified command and control."

Chen Yixin couldn't quite suppress the flicker of satisfaction that crossed his face. It was the culmination of years of bureaucratic warfare- the MSS would now have undisputed primacy in foreign operations.

"Minister Chen," the Secretary continued, "the Chairman expects a complete restructuring of our Malaysian operations. The exposure of our support for Harapan Baru has done incalculable damage to our strategic position in Southeast Asia."

"I understand completely," Chen replied smoothly. "We are already implementing a new approach that will emphasize deniability and resilience against Western interference."

"See that you do. The Chairman has made it clear that there will be no tolerance for further failures."

After the Secretary departed, Chen and Wang were left alone in the room. For a moment, neither spoke, the weight of decades of rivalry hanging between them.

"You won this round, Chen," Wang said finally, his voice low. "But remember, today it's me, tomorrow it could be you. The Chairman's favor is fickle."

Chen's smile was thin. "I prefer to think of it as the Party's judgment, not the Chairman's favor. The Party recognized which approach best serves China's interests."

Wang stood, straightening his jacket with dignity. "And what is that approach, exactly? Your MSS operatives were exposed just as thoroughly as mine."

"The difference is in the response," Chen replied. "Your people tried to maintain their cover even as it collapsed around them. Mine had already implemented contingency protocols. Even now, they are establishing new networks throughout Malaysia, ones that will be immune to the methods used against us this time."

"You sound confident for a man who just suffered a significant defeat."

Chen's eyes hardened. "This was a battle, Wang, not the war. The Americans and their Malaysian puppets believe they have struck a decisive blow. They are mistaken. All they have done is educate us on their methods."

Wang moved toward the door, then paused. "One piece of advice, Chen, from a man with nothing left to lose. Beware of Jack Tanner. He is not like other Americans."

Chen waved dismissively. "A retired intelligence officer writing books and giving lectures? Hardly a strategic threat."

"That 'retired intelligence officer' just dismantled our Malaysian operation and turned ASEAN against us. Underestimate him at your peril."

As Wang departed for the last time, Chen's confident expression faltered momentarily. He turned to the digital display on the wall, where Jack Tanner's file remained open, the American's impassive face staring back at him.

"Increase priority on Tanner," he murmured to his aide. "Full spectrum monitoring. I want to know everything, his movements, his contacts, his weaknesses."

The aide nodded. "And the Malaysian situation, Minister?"

Chen's expression hardened. "Accelerate the contingency plans. If we cannot work through Harapan Baru, we will find other proxies. Malaysia may think they have extricated themselves from our influence, but they will soon discover otherwise."

* * *

Day 17, 1500 Hours | MSS Malaysia House

Li Jianhong stood before the floor-to-ceiling windows. He knew somewhere below him a diplomatic convoy would be heading to the airport as Malaysia expelled Chinese operatives. Zhang Wei and his MPS thugs were being loaded onto aircraft like common criminals, after Li himself made sure their crude methods finally exposed.

A thin smile played across Li's lips. While his rivals fled in disgrace, he remained. Untouchable.

The secure terminal chimed with an incoming transmission from Beijing. General Liang's face materialized on the screen, his expression expectant.

"Comrade Li," Liang began. "Your assessment."

Li moved to his desk, hands clasped behind his back. "The decision to pause our support to Harapan Baru was the right move given all that has happened. Besides the diplomatic denials of our support, our operatives will make sure other stories are believed. Damage from our involvement there is minimal. The MPS operation, however, was catastrophic. Their heavy-handed approach exposed our interests throughout the region. Overall, the last week was a win, providing invaluable intelligence on American capabilities."

"The Tanner operation?"

"Brilliant work by the Three Immortals," Li replied, his voice gaining confidence. "We successfully penetrated his Virtual Intelligence Center. Complete documentation of their AI architecture, analytical processes, psychological warfare protocols. The Americans believe they wounded us. In reality, they educated us, and we are even better positioned than before."

Liang leaned forward, clearly pleased. "Elaborate."

Li responded: "Our deep-cover operatives remain untouched. Academic exchanges, business partnerships, technological dependencies are all still in tact; the Malaysians purged only the visible layer. If anything, their security theatrics made them more vulnerable to subtle influence."

"And future operations?"

"This theater needs more support, General. I would like continuous authority to task the Three Immortals. My operational sense should drive the new Agentic AI systems they are building. And it should go without saying, we must eliminate bureaucratic oversight from other ministries." Li's voice hardened. "The MPS failure demonstrates the cost of divided authority."

Qiao's satisfaction was evident. "Your requirements will be presented to Minister Chen for consideration. The Minister values adaptation over tradition."

"The Americans think in projects. We think in generations," Li said. "Their interference in Malaysia becomes our education for application not only here but in Jakarta, Bangkok, and Manila."

"Precisely the assessment Minister Chen expects," Liang replied approvingly. "Prepare detailed operational plans. The Minister will review your proposals personally."

The connection terminated. Li walked to his wall safe and retrieved a jade dragon figurine, coiled around a sphere. He'd purchased it as a junior officer, when he was still learning the art of patient manipulation.

By evening, Li had conceptualized his new moves. This fight was far from over, and in this theater, Li Jianhong would be guiding it to victory.

Chapter 31: New Rules of Engagement

Day 18, 1700 Hours | Ritz Observation Deck

Three days later, Jack stood on the observation deck at the Ritz, gazing out at the sprawling cityscape of Kuala Lumpur. The afternoon sun glinted off glass and steel, transforming the city into a shimmering mosaic. From this height, there was no visible evidence of the bombing or the subsequent political earthquake that had rocked the region.

"Quite a view," said a familiar voice behind him.

Jack turned to find Sam approaching, dressed in civilian clothes that couldn't quite disguise her professional bearing.

"Worth the trip up," Jack agreed. "Though I suspect you didn't want to meet here for sightseeing."

Sam smiled. "Can't a colleague just enjoy a moment of peace after a successful operation?"

"Is that what this was? Successful?"

"By most metrics, yes. Harapan Baru is on the run. The MSS and MPS networks in Malaysia have been exposed. Regional awareness of PRC influence operations is at an all-time high." She paused. "And you're still alive, which wasn't a given when you started poking the dragon."

Jack turned back to the view. "And yet I can't shake the feeling that we've only seen the opening moves of a much longer game."

"That's because you're right," Sam said, her voice dropping. "No doubt, Beijing is already adapting. They will be back, with more sophisticated methods."

"Of course they are. The CCP doesn't abandon strategic objectives; they just change tactics when exposed." Besides, he added, "Beijing knows our methods now, they've seen what we can do, how we think, what our capabilities are. Next time, they'll be ready."

Sam nodded. "Which brings me to why I'm really here, next time, we might not have someone like you in the right place at the right time." She handed him a small, encrypted tablet. "From the CIA Director, for your eyes only. He is offering a more formal arrangement."

Jack raised an eyebrow. "I'm not interested in returning to government service, Sam. You know that."

"This wouldn't be a traditional role. More of a... specialized consultant position. Focusing on countering PRC influence operations, particularly in Southeast Asia."

Jack was silent for a moment, weighing the implications. "The book tour was supposed to be my last hurrah before settling into a quiet consulting practice. Maybe some teaching, definitely more writing."

Sam smiled knowingly. "And how's that working out for you? Feeling fulfilled by the prospect of corporate boardrooms and lecture halls after what you've just experienced?"

Jack didn't answer immediately. Instead, he activated the tablet, scanning the preliminary details of the proposed role. It would allow him to continue the work he'd started here, but with the full resources of the intelligence community behind him.

He thought of Lila, and the many young Malaysian SOF who gave their lives for their country and the hope for a better future for their families. He thought of his father and what he would have him do. And the many others serving U.S. interests in the region. Sam, Mike, and dedicated fearless professionals like Fiona. There is a special feeling working with all of them on things bigger than any one of us alone could do.

"The landscape is changing, Jack," Sam continued. "We need people who understand this new battlefield."

"People like me," Jack said, not as a question.

"People exactly like you." Sam gestured toward the city below. "What happened here in Malaysia is just the beginning. The same patterns are playing out across the region, across the world. The difference is that here, we caught it in time and had the right person in place to act."

Jack closed the tablet. "I'll think about it."

"Don't think too long. Beijing isn't."

As Sam departed, Jack remained at the railing, contemplating the cityscape. His phone vibrated with a message from Overwatch.

Analysis complete: 73% probability that PRC will shift focus to Indonesia as next priority target for influence operations. Preliminary indicators suggest approach will emphasize economic leverage rather than direct subversion.

Jack smiled grimly. Even his AI team was pushing him toward continued involvement.

His gaze drifted to the distant horizon, where the South China Sea lay beyond the urban sprawl. Somewhere out there, the USS Blue Ridge was sailing while the embarked Seventh Fleet staff was directing freedom of navigation operations, a visible reminder of America's commitment to regional security. Mike Murphy would be in the SCIF, already planning for the next confrontation in this undeclared shadow war.

Jack's thoughts turned to Dr. Farid and the Malaysian cybersecurity team, working tirelessly to rebuild their defenses against the inevitable next wave of attacks. To the analysts in Singapore, Bangkok, and Manila who were now scrutinizing their own systems for signs of PRC infiltration. To the countless invisible battles being fought in server rooms and board meetings across Southeast Asia.

The dragon had been wounded but not slain. And in Beijing, new plans were already being formulated, new operatives deployed, new strategies implemented. The CCP's vision of regional dominance remained unchanged, even as the methods evolved.

Jack pocketed his phone and headed toward the elevator. He had a plane to catch, and a decision to make.

* * *

Six Months Later | Jakarta, Indonesia

Jack sat in a nondescript coffee shop in Jakarta's Menteng district, three blocks from the U.S. Embassy. To any observer, he was just another Western businessman killing time before a meeting. The reality was more complex, and more dangerous.

His secure phone buzzed. A message from Overwatch: "Indonesian banking irregularities match Malaysia pre-crisis indicators. Financial flows suggest acceleration of timeline. Recommend immediate deep-dive analysis."

Jack's coffee grew cold as he read the intelligence summary. The patterns were unmistakable, shell companies in Singapore, cryptocurrency transfers through Hong Kong, years of academic exchanges that weren't academic, a decade of infrastructure investments with hidden capabilities.

Through the rain-streaked window, he could see the harbor in the distance. Chinese cargo ships lined the docks, not unusual, since China was Indonesia's largest trading partner. What most Indonesians didn't know was that some of those containers held more than consumer goods. Just as most Malaysians hadn't known, until it was almost too late.

His laptop chimed with an encrypted message from Sam: "Jakarta Station reports another MPS covert police station, the second in the city that we know about. How soon can you be operational?"

Jack smiled grimly as he typed his response: "Already am."

The barista called out an order in rapid Indonesian. Life flowed around him, students arguing politics, businessmen making deals, families planning weekend trips to Bali. Normal life in a country that didn't yet know it was under siege.

But Jack knew. And now, so did his enemies.

He'd spotted the surveillance team twenty minutes ago, two men in cheap suits trying too hard to look casual. Chinese operatives, probably MSS, not as good as they thought they were. They'd made the same mistake their predecessors had made in Malaysia: underestimating what one determined American with the right tools could accomplish.

Jack finished his coffee and stood. Time for phase two of an operation that had started before he'd even arrived in Indonesia. Because the truth about Malaysia wasn't that they'd won, it was that they'd learned. Learned how Beijing operated, how to detect the patterns, how to get ahead of the curve.

The infinite game continued, but now Jack was playing it by his own rules.

He walked toward the exit, noting how the surveillance team scrambled to follow. Online, Overwatch was already devising new collection plans and deception strategies. Soon the CIA Chief of Station would be briefing government counterparts on PRC intent. A new shadow war was beginning.

In his earpiece, barely audible, came Overwatch's synthesized voice: "Collection plan ready for your review Jack. Let's finish what we started."

The rain began to fall harder as Jack disappeared into the crowd, a ghost hunting ghosts in a city that didn't know it needed saving. Yet.

The End

Principal Characters

Jack Tanner - Retired U.S. Navy Commander and former intelligence officer, now author and cybersecurity consultant.

The MSS (Ministry of State Security)

Chen Yixin - Minister of State Security, ruthless architect of China's global intelligence operations

Li Jianhong - MSS Station Chief in Malaysia, sophisticated operative orchestrating Chinese influence campaigns

General Qiao Liang - Author of "Unrestricted Warfare" and mentor to China's elite cyber operators

The MPS (Ministry of Public Security)

Wang Xiaohong - Minister of Public Security, expanding China's overseas police operations under the guise of citizen protection

Zhang Wei - MPS Station Chief in Malaysia, running covert police stations and intimidation operations

The Three Immortals

Ming Liu - Elite MSS cyber operative specializing in infrastructure penetration and malware development

Lao Xun - Master of digital infiltration and AI-powered surveillance systems

Wu Yifan - Strategic cyber warfare specialist and member of the notorious APT41 hacking group

Federation of Malaysia

Lila Tan - Senior analyst with Malaysia's National Cybersecurity Agency (NACSA)

Dr. Farid Rahman - Malaysia's Chief Cybersecurity Officer and Deputy Minister

Chief Inspector Haris Noor - Head of Malaysian Special Branch SOF

The Harapan Baru

Amir Hashim - Insurgent leader

The Intelligence Community

Samantha Blake - CIA Chief of Station in Kuala Lumpur

Captain Mike Murphy - Jack's former shipmate and Seventh Fleet intelligence officer

Colonel David Ramos - U.S. Defense Attaché in Malaysia

Bill Franklin - ODNI Senior Representative in Malaysia

Fiona Kincaid - CIA operative under official cover

The Virtual Intelligence Center

Overwatch - Lead agentic AI agent for the Virtual Intelligence Center

Ghost Knife - AI specialist in geopolitical analysis and threat assessment

Killswitch - Cybersecurity and digital warfare AI agent

Sparks - SIGINT and communications intelligence AI specialist

Envoy - Diplomatic and political analysis AI agent

Ledger - Financial intelligence and economic warfare AI analyst

Specter - Security and counterintelligence AI agent focused on operational protection

The Tech Landscape

Agentic AI - Autonomous AI agents

AWS - Amazon Web Services cloud platform

Charlotte AI - CrowdStrike's AI threat hunting system

Claude - AI language model

CrewAI - AI framework for creating Agentic AI

Deep Seek AI - Chinese AI system

Douyin – Chinese short-video platform (like TikTok)

FTP - File Transfer Protocol

HawkEye 360 – Commercial RF collection satellite system

Hikvision - The world's largest supplier of surveillance equipment, partially state-owned through China Electronics Technology Group Corporation (CETC)

Huawei P50 - Modified smartphones for secure communications

Kimi 2 - Chinese trillion-parameter AI model specialized in image recognition, camera feed analysis, and behavioral pattern recognition

LLAMA - Open Source Large Language model

Model Context Protocol - AI system protocol for Agentic AI

PowerShell - Windows command-line tool

Telegram - Messaging platform

Vectara - Developer platform enabling AI solutions

Virtual Intelligence Center (VIC) - AI agent system with named agents:

WeChat - Chinese social media platform

Weibo - Chinese social media platform

Yingtian-9 - Chinese secure radio system

The Drones

MQ-1C Gray Eagle - U.S. military drone (with ISR and Hellfire missile configurations)

MQ-9B SeaGuardian - USN Maritime surveillance drone

MQ-8C Fire Scout - USN Helicopter drone for EO/IR and radar-based ISR

Mojave GA-ASI - Attack drone (with 16 AGM-114 Hellfire missiles)

AGM-114 Hellfire - Air-to-ground missiles

Black Lantern - PRC Militarized DJI quadcopter variant for surveillance and attack

JY-3000 Thunderbolt Bomber Drone - PRC quadcopter bomber

QW-12 Red Serpent - PRC Man-portable infrared/UV-guided anti-drone missile

Acronyms and Organizations

Malaysian Organizations

DSOD - Defense Special Operations Division

NACSA - National Cybersecurity Agency

RMAF - Royal Malaysian Air Force

U.S. Government & Military

C2 - Command and Control

CIA - Central Intelligence Agency

DIA – Defense Intelligence Agency

DHS - Department of Homeland Security

ECM - Electronic Countermeasures

EO/IR - Electro-Optical/Infrared

FBI - Federal Bureau of Investigation

INDOPACOM - Indo-Pacific Command

ISR - Intelligence, Surveillance, and Reconnaissance

JSOC - Joint Special Operations Command

NSA - National Security Agency

ODNI - Office of the Director of National Intelligence

PACOM - Pacific Command

RF - Radio Frequency

Seventh Fleet - The U.S. Navy in the Western Pacific

SOF - Special Operations Forces

TTPs - Tactics, Techniques, and Procedures

UAV - Unmanned Aerial Vehicle

Intelligence Types

ELINT - Electronic Intelligence

HUMINT - Human Intelligence

NOFORN - Not Releasable to Foreign Nationals

OSINT - Open Source Intelligence

SCI - Sensitive Compartmented Information

SIGINT - Signals Intelligence

Cybersecurity

APT - Advanced Persistent Threat (specifically APT41 mentioned)

Blackwire Labs - AI-enabled cybersecurity system with CISO knowledge

CISA - Cybersecurity and Infrastructure Security Agency

CrowdStrike - Endpoint protection platform (includes Charlotte AI)

CVE - Common Vulnerabilities and Exposures

DIAMOND Model - Structured analytical technique for threat intelligence based on adversary capabilities, operating on infrastructure against a victim to achieve a goal.

DNS - Domain Name System

Google Workspace - Cloud productivity suite

Halcyon - Ransomware defense system

IOCs - Indicators of Compromise

MITRE ATT&CK Framework - framework for tracking attack techniques

Quad9 DNS - DNS security service (9.9.9.9)

Recorded Future - Cyber threat intelligence platform

SIEM - Security Information and Event Management

SOC - Security Operations Center

Splunk - Security information and event management platform

TLS - Transport Layer Security

VulnCheck - Vulnerability prioritization and mitigation system

WMI - Windows Management Instrumentation

Acknowledgements

I am deeply grateful for the support and encouragement of my family and many remarkable individuals who contributed through every stage of this project.

The book reflects lessons learned from many great mentors during my time as an operational naval intelligence officer, including champions like Captain Frank Notz (former Commanding Officer of FOSIF Westpac, my first real operational intelligence duty station), Captain Eric Myers (my boss as the N2 at Seventh Fleet), Rich Haver, Admiral Bill Studeman, Admiral Archie Clemins (the Commander of Seventh Fleet during my time there), and Admiral Jake Jacoby (a mentor throughout my career).

I have been deeply involved in cybersecurity community since 1998 and benefited from many strong leaders there, including my current business partner at OODA, Matt Devost, an entrepreneur and pioneer in cyber threat intelligence, red teaming, application of AI and corporate governance, who I learn from every day.

I deeply appreciate the continued interaction with the OODA Network, a group of over 350 business and government leaders who continuously keep each other aware of the latest in geopolitical risk, technology developments, and cybersecurity issues. Participating in the dialog on these topics with them has kept me deeply informed on the issues that matter and have helped ensure this book is best able to shed light on many of the dynamics underway in the world today. Many insights into the nature of exponential technologies, geopolitical dynamics, and adversary trends in cyberspace also flow from the expert sessions in our annual conference, OODAcon, and the many interactions with attendees there.

I also appreciate the many readers of early drafts of this book. Feedback from intelligence professionals, technologists, and other authors was instrumental in helping ensure the story here was told as succinctly as possible. This includes James Lawler, whose encouragement gave me the boost in confidence completing a book requires, as well as other members of the Shadow Writers group created by Bilyana Lilly. Patrick Scannell, a renowned enterprise technologist and author of multiple influential books, was especially helpful.

I also owe a debt of thanks to the many reviewers of the book who wrote endorsements of the end result, including Shyam Sankar (whose nudging is responsible for me starting this project), Jim Miller, Brad Meltzer, Scott McNealy, Bill Studeman, David Bray, Bob Flores, Jake Jacoby and Pat Scannell. I thank you all.

About The Author

Bob Gourley is recognized as one of the most insightful voices at the intersection of national security and cutting-edge technology. With a deep-rooted history in and around the U.S. intelligence community, Bob honed his analytical skills and operational insights at the highest levels, helping shape critical security operations in an ever-evolving threat landscape.

Bob was an operational navy intelligence officer with experience throughout Asia and Europe. As a pioneering Chief Technology Officer and co-founder of OODA.com and trusted startup advisor, Bob has worked with both government and leading-edge commercial organizations, guiding them through the complexities of cybersecurity, big data, and emerging technology adoption. His expertise in artificial intelligence, coupled with his operational understanding of defense and intelligence missions, has made him a key thought leader among decision-makers and innovators.

Bob brings all of this real-world experience to his techno-thrillers, imbuing his stories with authenticity, technical realism, and high-stakes drama. When he's not writing, he is advising startups, speaking at major security conferences, and exploring the next frontier of AI and technology for a safer, smarter world.

Author's Note

All of the technology described in Dragon Falls, including agentic AI for open source intelligence and the advanced drone capabilities, reflects real capabilities that exist today. Throughout my career in and around the intelligence community and as a CTO and advisor to technology startups, I have worked hands-on with these tools and seen their impact firsthand. We report on these capabilities and their impact on a daily basis at OODALoop.com These are not science fiction: they are real technologies available right now to those defending open societies.

The depictions of the PRC's Ministry of State Security (MSS) and Ministry of Public Security (MPS) operating overseas, while fictionalized within these pages, are rooted in documented patterns and actions observed globally. Although the specific story is imagined, it draws on events, tradecraft, and strategies witnessed by professionals around the world.

At its core, this novel is shaped by my belief that our way of life, centered on respect for privacy, personal choice, and the flourishing of open societies, is our greatest strength. Dragon Falls illustrates both the threats we face and the enduring power of free, open communities to adapt and prevail.

Bob Gourley

www.ingramcontent.com/pod-product-compliance
Lightning Source LLC
Chambersburg PA
CBHW030226120726
47903CB00005B/1383